SUMMER LOVE:
Stories of Lesbian Holiday Romance

SUMMER LOVE:
Stories of Lesbian Holiday Romance

Edited by Harper Bliss and
Caroline Manchoulas

CONTENTS

INTRODUCTION

We fell in love summer. Just two people meeting by chance on a hot summer night, and recognising *that* feeling. Many summers have passed since that one in 2000 when I first laid eyes on Caroline, now my wife, co-editor, co-publisher and co-founder of Ladylit. These days, we live in Hong Kong where, come May, summer suddenly hits you like a brick, and all you want is to find somewhere to cool off. But back then, at the turn of the millennium in Ghent, Belgium, it was an ordinary Western European summer, with long hazy nights, occasional rain beating down on the city streets, and those first butterflies awakening in our bellies.

Thus, the idea to put together a lesbian summer romance anthology for our first collaboration as editors, was an easy one. It takes us back to staying up late while lingering outside with one last drink, to finding each other, to the sweet hesitation when we said goodbye outside my front door for the first time, and to not knowing what the future would bring, but having a premonition anyway because, sometimes, you just know.

While selecting stories for this book, we wanted to capture the essence of summer *and* the essence of romantic love. Now that *Summer Love: Stories of Lesbian Holiday Romance* is a finished anthology, we couldn't be more pleased. The tales that follow are expertly constructed by their authors, evoking the atmosphere of sun-soaked beaches, of crashing waves and blue pool water, and of the sort of nostalgia that only summer can conjure up.

There are summer festivals, poolside love-making, old friends reconnecting and 'Latebians'. The settings will take you from the beaches of Australia, over the soggy meadows of Britain, to volcanos on Lanzarote. We hope you enjoy this collection of lesbian romance stories. It was an honour and a joy for us to put it together.

Harper Bliss,
Hong Kong

STEPPING OUT
CHEYENNE BLUE

"It's the air here." The teacher's enthusiasm is contagious. Her skinny body seems to burst with the desire to share her passion. "We have less pollution. Our soil may be poor, but with care, we can grow some of the most flavorsome food in the world."

Irene dumps herbs into the mortar and starts grinding. It was a good idea, this women's cookery course, here in the Victorian high country. Six women, all enthusiastic amateurs like herself—moneyed, like herself, she adds with wry honesty—here to learn, to improve their skills and cooking creativity, with the added bonus of a holiday in the Australian bush. Miriam Stockard, a retired restaurateur, runs the course at her property on the edge of the Great Dividing Range.

Irene has come alone. This is just one of her filler-times, as she likes to call them, a way of occupying herself in a most convivial way. It's too easy to be alone in Los Angeles. And she's a "women only" course junkie; maybe, just maybe, she'll meet someone special.

There's nobody promising at Wannaroo though. Nobody, except Miriam herself.

Irene watches surreptitiously out of lowered eyes as Miriam circles the room. The morning light touches her wild hair, burnishing the silver streaks, mingling them with the gold to some fantastic new alloy. Miriam wears a faded t-shirt, baggy shorts, and Swedish massage sandals on her bare feet—unconventional garb for a chef. The light catches the sun-bleached hairs that overlay her tanned forearms like the pelt of a large cat. Her hair spills out of the fuzzy ponytail that barely contains it, as she leans over Lucy's bowl to taste her seasonings with a finger. Miriam must be over forty, Irene muses, but her wiry frame, tanned nut-brown by the Aussie sun, quick way of speaking, and unconventional approach make her appear younger.

Sometimes, she imagines Miriam is watching her too, swift glances out of the corner of her eye, but she puts it down to wishful thinking. Miriam is probably checking she isn't using too much salt.

The class works quietly for an hour. Outside, the liquid notes of a magpie overlay the buzz of cicadas, providing a musical backdrop for Miriam's muted voice as she encourages and draws out each woman in turn. The course encourages a creative approach. No slavish following of recipes here, no automated adding of a pinch of nutmeg and a sprig of parsley; here they invent, mix, blend, experiment, embellish. Melding flavors that challenge the imagination, often supplementing them with the bush tucker that they gather outside. Lilly pilly and tamarillo custard. Yabby ravioli with lime and shiitake mushrooms. There are no limits, Miriam explains, no preconceptions. They are here to expand their horizons, challenge their creativity, become artists.

And Irene watches Miriam, and challenges her own creativity by imagining what she would do to her if they were naked under the lazy fan in the high-ceilinged bedroom with the verandah that opens to the world.

The women break for morning coffee each day around eleven. Miriam's daughter, Janey, carries in freshly-baked scones and dishes of Miriam's home-made jams. There's a running competition to guess the ingredients. Irene takes it seriously, savoring the flavor, trying not to be fooled by the color.

Quandong? She wonders idly, spreading some on a wholemeal scone. Maybe loquat—the hard yellow fruit from the old spreading tree in the backyard. She smiles at Janey, who steadies the plate with a twelve-year-old's concentration. "A dollar if you'll give me a clue," she whispers in mock-seriousness.

Janey's hazel eyes open wide. "I can't do that," she replies. "Mum would kill me."

* * *

The evening is molten and saturated by an abrupt thunderstorm that starts as if someone has opened sluice gates. Irene sits quietly under the covered verandah, and listens to the rain lash the corrugated iron roof. The air is so liquid that she cleaves through it, and her sweat shines on her skin.

She's alone. The other women departed earlier for a folk night in Beechworth—an evening of red wine and song. Normally, Irene would go too—the unforced spontaneity of instant companions is partly why she came—but she is behind on her diary. It lies untouched on her knees, its brocade cover damp from the air.

The creak of the fly screen alerts her to another's presence. It's Miriam, a steaming mug in one hand. She opens the fly screens so that the air can move more freely, and props her bare feet on the rail. In profile, her face is serene as she stares out into the night.

Irene doesn't want to interfere; she senses Miriam is after solitude. After all, she's a vital presence to the smooth running of the course, encouraging the diverse group of women to mix, throw away their inhibitions and enjoy themselves. She probably welcomes a rare evening alone. But Irene's pen rolls off the diary and drops to the floor with a clatter.

Miriam jerks, then calls out, "I didn't know anyone was there. You must think me rude, ignoring you like that."

Her face is smiling and open, so Irene picks up her diary and her glass of local Tokay and joins her. "I wanted to catch up with my writing," she raises the diary, and lets it fall back on her bare legs, "but it's more pleasant to simply watch the rain."

Miriam nods, and her face relaxes. "I love storms like these. When you can smell the earth, and the bush. It's when I love my home the best."

"Do you ever not love it?"

"Sometimes. Last summer, there was a bushfire burning out of control in the foothills. It came down the ridge, and Janey and I had to evacuate. They got it under control, eventually, but when we came back we didn't know what we'd find. We were lucky, the house was untouched." She sips the steaming tea. "Then I hated this place. And in winter, when the air is so chill and crisp, and your breath freezes in your lungs, I'm not too keen. But I wouldn't leave it for anything."

"Have you been here long?"

"Nearly twenty years. Janey was born in your bedroom."

Irene thinks of the echoes of pain that must still linger in a corner of the room. She wonders who was there at the birth with Miriam. "Where does Janey go to school?" she asks instead.

"Beechworth. She gets the school bus from the end of the road. But now, it's the holidays and she's trying to earn enough to buy herself a pony. She bakes the morning scones, cleans up in the kitchen, and also works on a neighbor's property, helping with the livestock."

"She's a good kid."

"The best." There's a silence, broken only by the battering rain and a persistent mosquito. "What's it like where you live?"

A thread of genuine interest colors her voice, so Irene tells her about Santa Monica, and the insanity of

L.A. life.

"You live alone?"

"Yes. For the last four years since my partner and I split. It was amicable," she hastens to add. "Monica moved to the East Coast to take a promotion."

Miriam nods, a sharp gesture, as if she expected nothing less. "Why are you here?"

Irene swirls the Tokay in her glass. "I'd never been to Australia." She sips, waiting to see if Miriam will notice the unspoken addendum.

"There must be cooking classes in L.A.?"

"Too many."

"Big city got too small?"

"Guess you could say that. I wanted different. To meet new people."

"Yes. Ours is a small world at times."

Irene notices her phrasing, but the evasive dance continues.

"Where are you going after here?" Miriam scuttles over one of the clean glasses on the table, and pours herself some of Irene's Tokay.

"Sydney for a week. Guess everyone should see the Opera House and the Harbour Bridge, right?"

Miriam's hesitation creeps into the room. A pause, too long to be careless, too studied not to be meant. And then she says, "Or you could stay here."

At first, Irene thinks it's a question. The Aussie accent tilts up at the end of the word, like a ski jump. She opens her mouth to say that she's already seen the sights in this parched land of drooping gums and cackling birdlife, but then, in the other woman's face, she sees that no, it isn't a question. It's a statement of something offered, something known. She waits, studying Miriam's face. It's all there, a quiet knowledge, maybe a touch of wistfulness.

"How long?" she asks instead. "You've probably

got my room booked for your next course."

"There's a week in between," says Miriam.

It's one of those times, Irene thinks, when you instantly know all there is to know about what's important. You can sift seamlessly through the layers of politeness, and the mouthing of words to the meaning behind them. Miriam isn't simply offering her bed & breakfast as an alternative to a Sydney hotel.

"What about Janey?"

"Janey's cool. She knows. There's no hiding around here."

"No." There isn't with Miriam. No facades, no games, no pretense. "That's what I like about you Aussies. Your directness."

Miriam laughs, relaxes. Offer down on the table and accepted. "It's our curse too. No polite place to hide when it goes wrong."

Their eyes meet, cling across the table. Emboldened, Irene reaches out a hand, covers Miriam's where it lies on the scarred wooden surface. She grips hard, and Miriam turns hers around, so they are clenched palm to palm. Irene studies the contrast: soft white city hand to narrow, sun-browned paw.

A clatter outside announces the return of the rest of the group. Reflexively, Irene jerks, her hand twitching before withdrawal. It's not that she minds, but she thinks that Miriam might. After all, she's the leader, the tutor. But Miriam's hand bites down hard and so she lets it lie.

The rest of the women sweep in with a cacophony of good-natured comments. They throw themselves down on the overstuffed battered couches around the verandah and demand some of the Tokay. If anyone notices Irene and Miriam's clasped hands, it goes unremarked.

* * *

The group disbands in an exchange of email addresses,

and a flurry of future plans. Elsie's going to Melbourne to visit her sister, Lucy to Sydney and her inner suburbs terrace. Alynna is also going to Melbourne to catch the plane to New Zealand, the others scatter like grass seeds in the wind.

Lucy asks if Irene wants to ride with her to Sydney.

"No," says Irene, simply. "I'm staying here another while."

"No worries then." Lucy leans in, pecks her on the cheek, tosses the car keys from hand to hand. "Look me up when you do make it to Sydney."

"I will."

Cars chug off in clouds of dust. Irene watches the dust settle again, her hands gripping the verandah rail. She turns to find Miriam watching her. Irene's tongue-tied. The moment of knowledge when she decided to stay seems hazy; had the Tokay dulled her senses, made a simple offer into something else? Maybe Miriam only wanted an extra week's board and lodging. But then Miriam crosses the worn boards to her side, rests a hand on Irene's hip in an intimate gesture.

"I'm glad you stayed," she says. "I'm looking forward to getting to know you better."

Out of the corner of her eye, Irene sees the fuzzy down on Miriam's cheek. A wisp of hair curls around her ear, silver in the low sunlight, and there, on her own hip, is a small hand radiating heat and possession. Irene covers it with her own, and leans just enough that she can feel the warmth of Miriam's body against her side. It's like orbiting the sun. She's taller than Miriam, who leans her head down on her shoulder. They rest in this pose for long minutes.

It's a peaceful evening, now that the other women have gone. Miriam reheats leftovers, and they eat it with a simple salad in the wide, modern kitchen. Janey chatters about a horse she's caring for—the owner wants her to ride it in a showing class. If she notices Miriam and Irene's closeness, she holds her silence. After dinner, the three of them take a walk outside, where the ground is hard and unyielding and the gum trees droop. The night sounds of the bush surround them.

Irene takes Miriam's hand again, threading her fingers through, and they walk through the tinder-dry grass, clasped hands swinging.

* * *

The next day they kiss. An almost-accidental kiss, one that Irene carefully planned. She turns from the kitchen bench, rests a hand on Miriam's shoulder, leans in to hear what she is saying, and her lips find Miriam's in a nuzzling, questing way. As kisses go, it's short, but the spark arcs between them, strung fine and glowing in the humid air. The sweetness of it steals Irene's breath away, and she rests her forehead against Miriam's, so that their breath mingles between them.

The day after, Irene knows she's falling. Fast, hard, and helpless for a woman she barely knows. Immediately the problems tumble in her mind: the distance—an Australian and an American—the culture, immigration requirements, Janey. If it comes to it, she should be the one to relocate. Miriam has a house, a daughter, a business, and Irene has so very little that is fixed and immutable. But it's too soon to think like that. She knows the logic of restraint, even as the promise of *them* tumbles through her mind.

By the middle of their week, Irene knows she wants to stay. More than a week, more than a month. She wants to wake beside Miriam, turn to her and kiss her sleep-slack lips. She wants to drop Janey off at the school bus and feel a parent's pride as she wins a ribbon on her horse. The thought of merging into Miriam's life is compelling. She wants to be a part of this place, this family, this community, even of this laconic country.

The day before Irene leaves, they make love. It is a silent glide to Miriam's bedroom. There are no words spoken, no offer, no acceptance. They simply rise together, from the battered couch on the verandah, hold hands and walk upstairs. Miriam doesn't pause in front of Irene's door, as she has for the last few nights for their kiss. Instead, she leads her past to her own room. It's a cool sanctuary of sea-green, and the bed is wide and firm. Theirs is an unhurried loving, punctuated by the rhythmic whop of the ceiling fan, stirring air over their bodies.

When it's over, they lie side by side on their backs, their fingertips touching. When Irene dares to look across to Miriam, she finds Miriam already staring at her with a curling half-smile.

Miriam touches Irene's face, brushing her fingertips over her lips. "I love you," she says.

Irene's breath hitches, and for a moment she can't reply.

"Too soon?" The curling smile is still in place, but there's a fixed quality to it that wasn't there a moment before. "Blame my Aussie directness again. I—"

But Irene smiles, rolls, stopping her words with a kiss. "Not too soon," she says.

The day that Irene leaves, they start making plans. Irene will return to L.A., sublet her apartment, organize her finances, her mail, contact the Australian embassy about a visa, cancel subscriptions, notify her friends, sell her car... The list overflows her head, building a wall between them, brick by brick. What seemed so easy, so obvious, is now already a trial. The hurried conversation, held in the front of Miriam's battered old Holden as she drives Irene to Tullamarine airport, seems strained. But if they don't say it now, Irene knows it will go unaddressed. So she pushes her worries aside and concentrates only on Miriam and how much she loves her.

* * *

Irene waits at the boarding gate at LAX. Any minute now, they will start boarding her flight to Melbourne, Australia, and she will wait until they call her row number. Then she will stand, fold her copy of the *Los Angeles Times*, leave it on the seat for someone to find, open her passport to the page with her photograph, and join the line to board the plane.

And then there will be no going back.

Her boarding card is damp from the sweat of her hand. She checks her waist belt for the umpteenth time: passport, some of the bright, brash Australian currency, a few gray American dollars, rolled and secured with a rubber band, the key to her apartment in Santa Monica, and the last email that Miriam sent her. She resists the temptation to unfold it and read it once more, even though the words are already imprinted in her brain.

"Come," says the final sentence. "Just catch a plane. Janey and I are longing to see you again."

The desk attendant taps the tannoy and announces boarding for passengers needing assistance, those with small children, and those passengers traveling first and business class.

Irene stands, takes out her passport, and moves closer to the desk for the general boarding call.

Even as she shuffles along the aisle, she's thinking how much she'll miss L.A. The palm trees, the boardwalk, the vibrant street life, the myriad restaurants, the long hazy marine days. But her long scribbled lists of pros and cons are weighed and balanced and set aside.

Does everyone feel this way, she wonders, as she fastens her seatbelt and stows her magazine in the pocket in front of her. Does everyone feel they're stepping out into the stars without a space suit? She can always change her mind, and return; this she knows. She clings to the thought to help make the leaving easier.

But fifteen hours later, as the plane bumps onto the runway at Tullamarine, as she clears customs and immigration and wheels her trolley out into the arrivals hall, as she sees Miriam's dear face, and Janey's smiling one, her heart is singing.

MOTHER TONGUE
CAMILLE DUVALL

Where I was born in Italy, when the waves hit the pebbles on the shore you hear a cracking, snapping sound, like the sharp flap of a swan's wings about to take flight. The breeze is a beautiful contradiction; it pretends to be your friend, bringing refreshing relief from the sun's hot glare. Then, when you feel your skin tightening you realise the sun and wind are in league; your skin prickles and crisps and you wish you had sought the shade's cool protection.

It's not warm like that here, not Italian warm. I live in Belfast, the capital city of Northern Ireland. My father moved my mother and me here in 1985, a few months before my eighteenth birthday. That was almost thirty years ago and even though I don't possess my family's olive-toned skin—I look like a Celt with my auburn hair and pale complexion—I still miss the heat. In Ireland, we have pale imitations of sunkissed summers, the temperature barely rising above sixty-four degrees Fahrenheit. Except for that one summer a year after we settled in Belfast, when the heatwave stretched for weeks on end so that even the locals declared their city a tropical paradise. It was certainly good for business.

The elaborate writing on our café window proclaims 'Finest Italian Ice Cream'. Our recipe is a closely guarded family secret. Cafe Bianchi is a Belfast landmark, situated on a leafy tree-lined avenue in the south of the city near the University Quarter. What we sell never goes out of fashion; we've been feeding the locals, students and tourists for three decades. There's always a queue for our pizza and if you're lucky, you might be able to grab a table—there's only four of them—and have a sit-down meal. Red leather seats, Formica table tops and pictures of Italian sunsets and Roman ruins clutter the walls. Mama once had a notion to give the café a make-over but Papa wouldn't hear of it. He was right; the place has an authenticity that comes only with the passing of time. Some of the newer cafés have tried to create instant charm, with signs for 5¢ colas and Corvettes. We've earned our reputation, our faded Formica table tops aren't fake.

Last night I dreamt in Italian again. What a strange yet welcome occurrence after all these years. I felt lightheaded yet serene as I went about my business this morning, the residue of the dream floating inside me, making me wistful and longing for the sea. I think it might be because I saw Susan on yesterday's news. She was standing in the ancient quad of Queen's University, shaking hands with another dignitary, having been made an honorary Doctor of Literature. She was radiantly regal in her academic's gown, beaming with pride. Her hair looked as dark and lustrous as it did thirty years ago; mine has long since lost its copper hues. Even if the reporter hadn't said her name, I would still have recognised the sideways tilt of the head that preceded her mischievous peel of laughter. What surprises me most this morning is the realisation that Ms. Susan Grace still makes my heart race.

At first, Susan had been just another customer who liked to hang out at Bianchi's, but then she began to frequent the café on a regular basis. She was from Swallow Bay, a small seaside town about thirty miles along the coast. When she addressed us in Italian one day, we discovered that she studied languages at Queen's, the country's most prestigious seat of learning. Perhaps it was this knowledge combined with her ink-black hair, dark eyes and olive skin that endeared her to my father. Papa warmed to her instantly, calling her Bella Susanna and kissing her hand in an over-the-top chivalrous fashion. Susan responded in kind, but she always did so in such a comical manner that it was impossible to take her seriously. It felt like a silly game, a merry dance that was acted out the moment she entered the café and concluded as she said her goodbyes. I also knew Mama didn't take her seriously. She used to frown and tut-tut but she did this with a twinkle in her eye. It was when I stole glances at Susan only to find her watching me, that I began to suspect her real motive for spending so much time with us.

"Rina is an unusual name. Is it short for anything?" We were seated at one of our tiny tables during a quiet spell. Papa was outside the shop, smoking and joking with the other business owners on our street. Mama was upstairs in bed with a migraine.

"Carina."

Susan's dark orbs gleamed at me. I blushed. She smiled.

"So, you're telling me that your full name is Carina, Italian for 'little darling'?"

I nodded and Susan tilted her head, assessing me. I blushed again. Out came her slow smile again.

"It's beautiful."

"Rina is b-b-better."

"No it is not. I'm going to call you Carina, *mi Carina.*"

I knew then for certain that when she called me her little darling I hadn't been imagining things, she did like me. Right now she was looking at me intently and I was held captive by her, mesmerised. But then the spell was broken when a customer entered and I had to take their order.

* * *

When we first moved to Belfast, Italian was my mother tongue, but within six months I could speak fluent English. Fluent in my head but not always when I spoke. For when I was nervous or under pressure my words trembled out in a stumbling gush. It didn't help that my father mocked my stutter in private "Ca-ca-carina B-b-bianchi. Don't speak with the customers Rina, the ice cream will have melted by the time you finish a sentence!" It is one of many things for which I will never forgive him. Nowadays, I can say my name with a flourish and take pride in what it means to others: Carina Bianchi, owner and Managing Director of Bianchi's, the United Kingdom's favourite ice cream.

Whenever Susan was around, I got to speak Italian. Susan said it was helping her studies and Papa was delighted the *estudiosa* had chosen us to help her. We conversed in Italian, whether it was to discuss football—she would have furiously contested debates with Papa about national teams—or to complain about the weather. For anyone listening to us, we must have sounded like a stereotypical Italian family with our boisterous, rapid-fire chat; the splendid rat-tat-tatting of mock-incredulity when something deliberately outrageous provoked debate. At first I watched these exchanges wishing I could join in, but I didn't have the nerve. I was easily tongue-tied and despite Susan's attempts to include me I would blush and shake my head no. I would smile and roll my eyes, enjoying the spectacle as this vibrant woman ran linguistic rings around my father. I was just happy to have her near. When Susan was in the café, the workload felt less like a captive burden, the heat from the huge pizza oven not so furnace-like. Papa would joke with customers, smile at Mama, and his monosyllabic interactions with me would take a back seat. But as time wore on, I started to contribute, encouraged by Susan—she was so persistent. Papa didn't appear to notice. In fact, it was probably the only time he didn't make some wisecrack about my stammer, because when I spoke Italian I did so fluently and unbroken.

I was smitten. How transparent I must have been, I felt so awkward and ungainly around Susan, around the lithe gracefulness of her. How could someone like me think I could ever be with someone like her? If I wasn't torturing myself wondering if she really did like me or if she was merely playing with me, then I was spending sleepless nights in my sweat-drenched bed imagining what making love with her would be like. My imagination was vivid but limited. I had never been kissed thanks to the watchful eye of an over-protective father. And so while my fantasies allowed me to indulge what it might be like to let my fingers caress her skin, to experience the sensation of her full lips on mine, or what it would feel like to take her breast in my mouth, I would have to stop short, unsure of what to do next. My fitful, fantasy-driven sleep would leave me exhausted and frustrated.

I had lived a sheltered life in Italy and in Belfast my existence was limited to the café; back then the boundaries of my world were small and tight and closed. Airless and graceless. Just a few hundred yards away was the university, where people from all over the world came to study. I knew Susan would allow me a glimpse into that world and one day lead me to its doors.

Mama was a kind, peaceful woman, but she suffered from depression, no doubt exacerbated by marriage to a domineering husband. She was often powerless to protect me from his cruel taunts; he simply ignored her. My stutter infuriated him and he used it to taunt me mercilessly. He would complain that I didn't have his business acumen or I lacked his natural flair with customers. I was consigned to the pizza oven, sweltering in silence at the café's coalface, while he played the gregarious Italian for our customers. I know now that there was nothing I could ever have done to please him. I was the only child to come from his loins and the daughter he never wanted.

When Susan suggested she take her Italian lessons up a notch, beginning with the two of us visiting the local art galleries and museums, my father didn't object. He probably didn't want her to think he was impolite and he had to agree with her that the world didn't revolve around politics and football. Spending time with Susan away from the café was bliss. We visited galleries and museums where she would regale me with the sordid details of the tortured artists' scandalous lives. She also introduced me to her world as a student, sneaking me into the university library where she studied and to her dorm where she lived with other female students. This place was a hive of activity and deafening noise, we never had any peace there so instead we would find little coffee houses that were off the beaten track. I had been oblivious to the existence of these places and it was gradually dawning on me that I needed to live a little.

"Let's speak in English." We were in a coffee house on the outskirts of the city. My eyebrows danced in surprise. Susan had been insistent that I never let her speak anything but Italian when we were together.

"Whatever you wish, Susan. I think, perhaps, you have tired of my mother tongue?" I was trying my best to be cavalier.

"I could never tire of it. Or you, mi Carina."

Mi Carina. It got me every time. I blushed—so much for my cavalier attitude. I watched Susan as her eyes followed the scarlet flush that spread from my face to my throat. Then her eyes met mine. She tilted her head and smiled mischievously.

"You are evil, Susan." I laughed.

"You are beautiful, Carina. Accept the compliment for once. Please?"

"Stop it."

"Why? I'm only stating the facts. You have the most exquisite green eyes and your beautiful red hair makes you look more Irish than me." She paused for a moment, drinking me in. "And that skin of yours, it's like porcelain. I can only imagine how smooth it is to the touch." She reached across the table and took my hand, but I pulled it away. She looked hurt. We sat in silence, Susan staring out of the window, me fiddling with my spoon as my brain raced frantically for something to say.

I took a sip of coffee and pulled a face. "This stuff is foul."

"I know. Isn't it criminal that we actually paid for this?" She smiled then and the atmosphere around our little bubble improved instantly.

"We have gallons of great tasting coffee back at the café," I offered, "free for the likes of us."

Susan's face clouded over. "Why do you let him treat you like dirt? I hate it."

This had become a familiar talking point. I was routinely quizzed about why my father got away with being so harsh with me. Susan didn't seem to understand that it was just his way. I had never known him to be any different.

"It's just the way it is. He's my father, I have to respect him."

"He's a bully who doesn't deserve your respect. He'll never earn mine."

"How come then you act like you think he's so great? You spend most of your time cracking jokes with him, talking nonsense about football. In fact, you spend more time at Bianchi's than you do in class."

"Because I put on a good act of letting him think he's Mister Wonderful. I can't stand the man. I'm sorry

Carina, I know he's your father but he's holding you back. You should be out in the world, doing something, anything, that pleases you." She ran her fingers through her hair. "And I spend time at the café because it means I get to see you. Even when I have to spend time in his company, I manage because I know you're near." She leaned forward in her seat. "I've said too much. I'm sorry."

"It's okay. I know you're right, but for now there's nothing I can do. Don't ever let Papa hear you talking like that. You don't want to anger him."

"Don't fear, I won't. And while we're on the subject of talking, have you noticed anything?"

I shook my head, puzzled. "No. What?"

"Mi Carina, your stammer is gone." Susan took my hand and this time I didn't pull away; I felt her strength and confidence surge through me like an electrical bolt.

* * *

The heatwave that had the city sweltering for weeks offered a welcome hiatus one Thursday afternoon when overcast skies threatened to bring summer to an abrupt end. It seemed to suit my mood. Susan had graduated several weeks earlier, coming top of her class. In two days she would be en route to America to join her family's annual vacation. She breezed into the café with her customary flamboyance and conducted her ritual with my father. But then she whispered to me in a quick, hushed voice too low for Papa to hear, "It's time I took you to Swallow Bay. Grab your shades and an umbrella, you'll probably need both." She turned then to address my father and told him she was taking me to meet her family. He wasn't to know that they had already left the country, but the surprised look on Papa's face was priceless, his eyebrows rising into his hairline at the thought of anyone wanting to introduce me to their family. He had no time to find reasons to keep me in the café that day. Susan and

I exited as quickly as we could, leaving a thunder-faced Papa in our wake.

We took the train from Botanic station for a journey that would take thirty-three minutes. What a strange thing to recall now, the digital departures board boasting its accuracy: thirty-three minutes. Susan sat next to me and held my hand. She arranged her jacket so as to conceal our interlocking fingers. I remember her soft, delicate hands; the calmness that enveloped me the moment I touched her smooth skin.

Susan took me to a small stretch of beach that only she knew about. It wasn't immediately visible and it required determination to make the fifteen minute hike across jutting rock before the little cove revealed itself. The journey was worth it. The pale white sand covered only a few meters before it met the clear blue water. We were surrounded by the jutting shoreline, protected from prying eyes. I knew I was venturing into unchartered waters.

Susan began at once to take off her clothes. I stood motionless. She realised I hadn't moved.

"What are you waiting for? Get a move on before it starts to rain!"

I was shocked into action. "Are you out of your mind? What will we do for swimwear?"

"You don't need it. Come on. Just imagine you're back in Puglia and you need to cool off." She ran then, naked, into the water. It's no lie that I was curious to see what her body looked like. I had already guessed from the clothes she wore and her contours that her build was slim and boyish. I wasn't shy about exposing my own nakedness, I knew I was well defined. I had inherited my mother's genes and never gained weight. I suppose it helped that I didn't succumb to the café's diet of pizza and ice cream, preferring instead the healthy rustic fare I had been raised on. I joined her in the water. Could it have been warm? I don't remember.

I tried not to stare at Susan's breasts. Her nipples poked out defiantly above the water. She caught me looking. "I know they're small," she grinned, "but they're perfectly formed. And you know what they say?"

"No, tell me, what do they say?"

"Anything more than a handful is a waste!"

We dried as much of ourselves with our clothes as we could and lay on the sand to let the weak sun do the rest. It was getting cold, but I didn't care. I had never had such unguarded access to her before, such space and time to linger over her. My gaze followed the length of her body, taking in her long, toned limbs and flat belly, the small breasts and graceful neck. When my eyes travelled to her face I found her looking at me intently. I looked away, but then gradually my eyes journeyed back to hers and there she was, gazing at me, smiling.

"You look happy, mi Carina."

"I am. I am exquisitely happy."

"Why?"

"I don't know why. It's probably spending time in the water. I miss it."

She sighed then. I searched her face. "What is it?"

"Give me something to work with here." Susan was being playful but I knew she found me exasperating.

"Okay. I'm happy because I'm with you."

"At last. A declaration!"

"Of sorts." I added. I couldn't help it.

"Of sorts? A compliment followed by a retraction of aforementioned compliment. Cheers, Carina."

"Don't be like that, Susan. Just as we're getting close, you're leaving. Anyway, I might even like men. Who knows?"

"Who are you trying to kid, mi Carina? You're into me and I'm into you. Fact. That's why we're here today, to do something about it. Then we can plan how to spring you from your Papa's prison. Let's get dressed, we're going to my house."

I had never been kissed before that day, had never been intimate with another human being. Many women have come and gone in my life but the experience of that afternoon has never been bettered. We barely spoke during the twenty-minute walk to Susan's house. Once inside, we went straight to her room. She asked me if I would like some water and I shook my head. She put her arms out and drew me into her and began to slowly undress me. At first I didn't know how to react, but the heat rising inside me took over and I followed Susan's lead, unbuttoning her shirt, unbuckling her belt. Soon we were tearing off each other's clothes, kissing, biting, and licking as we tumbled naked onto the bed.

Susan tenderly stroked my body. I responded, gently flicking her nipples as she caressed my breasts. I felt Susan's tongue begin its slow descent. When she nibbled and licked me I gasped with surprise; her probing tongue unleashed sensations I never knew existed until that moment. I was sure I would explode as Susan expertly drank in my juices, causing me to almost faint with desire as my nerve endings reached a crescendo. I exploded in orgasm, my back arching involuntarily as I came. Just when I got my breath back, when I thought I was spent, I felt Susan's fingers slip inside me, finding purchase in the hot wetness. Again my body responded, wave after convulsing wave of pleasure before the final release.

Susan held me in her arms as my heartbeat resumed its normal pace. Feeling bold, encouraged, I kissed Susan hungrily; I could taste my sweet juices on her lips, and the passion rose in us again. My efforts became more urgent as I mounted her. I wasn't sure what came next, but instinct told me that I was on the right track; it was as if we were meant to fit together, the wetness and friction melding as one. Our bodies rode together, the intensity of the motion driving me wild. Susan's breathing rasped. She groaned aloud as she begged me to take her. I was amazed by what was happening; this woman was in ecstasy beneath me. My confidence grew and I bit into Susan's neck as she juddered and screamed out her orgasm.

I will never forget the sweat-soaked sheets as I went down on Susan for the first time. My tongue probed as I plunged my fingers inside her, feeling the swell of her as her thighs began to tremble. She began to pant out my name "mi Carina, mi Carina" to the rhythm of my fingers, faster and faster. For a moment she was silent as her head snapped back on the pillow and I thought something was wrong, but then she emitted a howl as another orgasm revealed itself.

Later as we lay in each other's arms, I murmured a thank you. She laughed and sighed contentedly. "Believe me, it's me who should be thanking you. I just knew you were a natural."

* * *

When we got back to Belfast, Susan insisted on walking me to the café. It was late and the entrance to the apartment was via a secluded alleyway. She wanted to come in to talk to my parents about me joining her family vacation, but I wouldn't allow it. I was afraid they would see how everything had changed between Susan and me. She promised to come to the café the next day and then kissed me goodnight. The kiss was swift and chaste, we had to be careful, but our tight embrace betrayed our true intentions. We heard a foot scrape some loose stones. It was my father. I don't know how long he had been standing there, what he had heard or seen. Susan opened her mouth to speak but he was upon us in one motion, sweeping her aside and shoving open the apartment door. He threw me inside, a snarl of disgust on his lips. He manhandled Susan along the alley, and I heard her protest that if he didn't let her go she would call the police. That was July 1986. Susan and I have not seen or spoken to each other since that night.

That's how I've come to be in Swallow Bay today, led by memories almost thirty years old. I don't know if Susan's family still live here, it's just the place where everything finally came right before it unraveled again. For all I know, Susan flew in for her graduation and is on a plane on her way back home. It would be nice to think that she would have called into Café Bianchi. She might even be there right now. If she is, then she will find it just as she left it, the decor intact and now fashionably retro-chic. The young staff are not Italian but the produce is. If she asks about me, they will tell her that I no longer work in the café but manage the ice cream side of the business. I'm to be found, these days, in our city centre headquarters or in London, where I oversee the ever-expanding Bianchi brand. But she probably won't do any of this. Why would she? She has probably forgotten all about me. I wish I knew more about her. The dust jackets of every one of her novels offer the same maddeningly scant information: born in Swallow Bay, educated at the Queen's University of Belfast and resident of Puglia.

Puglia. That's the bit that breaks my heart, to know that Susan lives in the town where I was born and lived until I left for Ireland. I'd love to know why she chose there of all places. She doesn't have a Twitter account, a dedicated website or even a Facebook page. Perhaps I could write to her via her publisher, but what would I say? I would want to know why she disappeared from my life and what part my father played in this. I never knew what he said to her that night, what threats were made. She never came back to the café, or if she did then we were deliberately kept apart. I know now that I should have acted differently that night. I reacted with a misplaced, unnecessary guilt, and it revealed itself to my father just enough for him to use it to shame me into submission. Over the next days, weeks and months, he bombarded me with insults, my poor mother's depression meant she was powerless to challenge him. It was when he resorted to one of his old taunts that I finally found the key to my liberation.

"D-d-d-dyke. You're a bloody d-d-d-dyke!"

I slapped him. Once, hard. In the few moments that he was shocked into silence the scales were lifted from my eyes.

"Are you jealous, Papa? Jealous that she wanted me and not you? That's the last time you will ever goad me about who or what I am. And you will never, ever again make a mockery of how I speak."

I never spoke to my father again. He lived for another few years but by then I had been to university and earned my business degree. I inherited the café when Mama died and I began to transform the Bianchi name into a major ice cream brand.

* * *

I return to the city, to a beautiful summer's afternoon brimming with promise. I decide to pay Café Bianchi a visit. I stroll down the leafy tree-lined avenue, thinking of the times when Susan walked beside me. Her life-force had brought opportunity and light into my dull little world. Perhaps I *will* write to her publisher, what harm could it do? It would be good to meet her again, to sit and talk in my mother tongue; to acknowledge the wonderful changes she brought to my life. When I enter the café, the young waiter beams at me from behind the counter.

"Hi, Miss Bianchi."

"Hi, Steve. How's business today?"

"Splendid as always. Here, I have something for you."

I watch as he reaches behind him to lift an envelope

from the shelf. He turns and hands it to me. "I didn't know you had such famous friends."

I stare at him for a moment as his words sink in. I nod, barely able to speak. I take the envelope to one of the little tables and sit down.

Steve goes back to his duties. I turn the envelope over and over in my hands, the blankness on both sides declaring that its contents could be meant for anyone. I open it. Inside is a single sheet of paper. I recognise the flamboyant scrawl. It begins: *Mi Carina...*

DRIVE ME CRAZY
TAMSIN FLOWERS

I begged. I pleaded. I offered to clean his room for the rest of his summer break from uni. I said I'd bring him breakfast in bed every morning for a month. But finally, I think my brother gave in simply to shut me up.

"Okay, Melody. Yes, you can come..."

His voice was drowned out by my screaming as I danced in circles around the room.

"Glastonbury, here I come," I shrieked, leaping onto the sofa to play air guitar.

"But," he yelled over the noise, "there are a few ground rules."

"Yeah, whatever," I said.

"You can get a lift with us in the car, but you're not staying in our tent."

'Us' was him and his girlfriend, Katie. So I wouldn't want to share a tent with them anyway.

"You pay for your own ticket, you get your own food and, in fact, once we get there, I don't really want to see you again until it's time to go home."

That sounded fine to me. I was on a mission and the last thing I wanted was my kid brother getting wind of what I was hoping to get up to. Because it wasn't so much about the festival, though I knew it would be fun. It was more to do with a certain person who would be there. My all-time crush, Danny Marks, was playing one of the smaller stages with his band The Tomahawks. And now I was going to be in the audience!

Of course, I'd seen The Tomahawks live loads of times. Last year, they'd played three gigs at the students' union and I went to all three. I'd been a fan practically since the group formed and I was reaching the point where the guys in the band recognized me when they saw me in the front row or the mosh pit.

But Glastonbury! It offered a world of opportunities. A band like The Tomahawks would probably hang around for the whole of the festival. Last year, I'd seen plenty of the smaller acts hanging out in the bars—it was only the really big names that stayed secluded in the VIP sections backstage.

So my mission was simple. Go to Glastonbury, see The Tomahawks, seduce Danny. I wanted to move from number one fan to favored groupie. If I slept with the lead singer of the band, maybe the next time he sang their biggest hit, *Drive Me Crazy*, he'd be thinking of me. So, no, there was no danger that I was going to try and hang around with my brother Rick and his girlfriend, let alone spend three days with them in a two-person tent.

* * *

Of course, it was raining when we arrived. Actually, raining was an understatement for what was coming out of the sky over Glastonbury that afternoon. A steady procession of cars and camper vans were turning off the road and churning up the mud as they trundled slowly to the allocated parking areas.

But there was no need for me to wait in the queue. I grabbed my bag and my tiny tent and waved Rick and Katie goodbye.

"Phone me a couple of hours before you're leaving on Monday and I'll come and find you," I said as I slammed the car door.

Katie wound down her window.

"Have fun and don't do anything..."

"Yeah, I know," I said with a grin. There wasn't

much Katie wouldn't do, so that gave me pretty much free reign.

With my boots squelching in the mud, I headed for the campground that was closest to the stage The Tomahawks would be playing. They weren't on until the following night, but I was going to check out the area sooner. And this particular campground had the added advantage of being on a hill, practically essential if my tent wasn't going to be flooded within five minutes of putting it up.

Even so, the ground was a quagmire. I went up to the top of the field and hung my bag on a fence post. Time to attempt the tent. Notice that word: attempt. It had looked easy enough when the girl in the shop had showed me how to do it. Perhaps if I'd watched what she'd done rather than stared at the way her jeans hugged her tight, hard little butt, I might have stood a chance of doing it for myself. But her ass had been more interesting than the tent and now my erection technique was sadly lacking.

I pulled it out of its bag and waited for it to pop up, ready to be anchored to the ground with pegs. But instead, it just sort of flopped and folded itself in half. And then as I struggled to straighten it out, I sort of flopped and folded in half, landing on my bum in the mud and skidding down the slope.

"Fuck!"

"Need a hand?"

I could hear laughter in the girl's voice and I looked up with a scowl. She was tall with blond undercut hair and dressed in typical festival uniform: mud-spattered wellies, skinny jeans and a green parker that had evidently seen duty at more than one Glastonbury. I could see part of a tattoo on her neck, trailing ivy leaves twisting up into her hair.

"I'm fine," I snapped, struggling to my feet.

Her bee-stung lips parted with laughter.

"You are so obviously not fine. Do you have any idea what you're doing?"

"Okay, so be my guest."

Petulance is a specialty of mine. I stepped away from the mess that was supposed to be my tent. Two minutes later, the mystery girl had it sorted and was busy hammering pegs into the ground.

"Thanks," I said, joining in to secure the tent down.

"I'm Sadie," she said. "If we're going to be neighbors we might as well be friends."

"Sure," I said. "Melody. Though I don't expect to be around very much."

"Suit yourself," she replied. "Anyway, that's my tent, so come see me if you get bored. If I'm not around I'll be with my mates—that's their tent over there."

Bored? That was never going to happen. The hunt was on—as soon as I'd stashed my sleeping bag and spare clothes in my tent, I headed off to the heart of the action to start checking out the bars.

The rain blew away and the sun broke through by early evening. The festival started to heat up and there was a palpable sense of excitement in the air. Cars and people were still streaming in, sound systems were gearing into action and the queues for the loos were growing. I took a tour around the whole massive Glastonbury site, stopping here and there to grab a sandwich or a coffee, browsing the stalls that were setting up in the craft market—and, of course, all the time scanning the crowd for members of The Tomahawks.

Finally, as the sun dipped lower, I settled myself in the bar nearest to the stage where the band would be performing the following evening. I knew it was a long shot but just sitting on a low bench, nursing a cider and people watching, was in itself a cool end to the day.

Of course, there was no sign of The Tomahawks

and I didn't stay late. The festival would kick off properly the next afternoon and that was when my hunt for Danny would start in earnest. I finished my drink and headed back to my tent. The field was pretty quiet and Sadie's tent was dark and silent, though I could see lights and hear laughter coming from her friends' much larger tent. I unzipped my tent flap, kicked off my boots and crawled into my sleeping bag. I thought I might be too excited to sleep but in my dreams I was making love with Danny. Until suddenly he morphed into Sadie and I woke up with a start.

* * *

I pinched myself to make sure I wasn't dreaming. No, I was really awake. It was Friday afternoon and finally, finally, there he was, sitting on a bar stool not more than ten feet from where I was standing. I tried not to stare. I tried not to drool. But Danny Marks tended to have that effect on fans. From the top of his spiky black hair to the pointed toes of his battered Chelsea boots, he was a skinny dose of pure bad-boy sex.

"Hey, I know you, don't I?" he drawled in the gravelly voice I knew so well.

I glanced around to see who he was addressing, but there was no one else looking at him.

"Me?" I stammered. "Sure, I've been to loads of your gigs."

I stepped closer. Close enough to smell the patchouli.

"Yeah, always at the front, aren't you?"

I nodded, tongue-tied. This was my big chance and I couldn't think of anything to say. I took a sip of my drink and tried to look cool, letting one hip jut out and wriggling my shoulder so my t-shirt slipped down on one side. But then, to my horror, a small, sexy redhead in the tightest leather trousers I'd ever seen came and draped herself around his shoulder.

Danny's attention switched immediately and he turned his head up to give her a lingering kiss on the lips.

I cleared my throat and the two broke away from each other to look at me.

"Oh, this is Suze," said Danny apologetically. "My better half."

What? He had a wife?

"Suze, this is one of our mega-fans..." He glanced at me questioningly.

"Melody," I said.

I smiled at Suze even as the bottom dropped out of my world.

"Nice to meet you, Melody," she said. "Pretty name."

She even had a French accent. The bitch.

Then they were kissing again and I knew it was time for me to leave before I burst into tears or tried to scratch her eyes out.

Back in my tent, I was able to let it all go and, boy, did I. How could I have been so stupid? Had I really thought I could just walk up to Danny Marks and entice him into my sleeping bag? Why had it never crossed my mind that he'd be married or have a girlfriend or simply could have found someone else far more attractive than me?

My face was burning with humiliation and great big sobs were racking my body as I writhed on my sleeping bag. I was making so much noise that I didn't hear the tent zipper opening. But then I felt a hand softly touch my leg and I sat up with a jolt, wiping my forearm across my eyes.

"Hey, Melody, what's the matter?"

It was Sadie with a look of concern wrinkling her pretty elfin features.

I shook my head, more embarrassed than upset now.

"Nothing. I'm fine, honestly."

"No, you're not," she said with a soft smile. "And I don't think you should be alone."

She crawled into the tent and watched me as I found a tissue and blew my nose loudly. The noise seemed to reverberate in the tiny space and when she laughed, I suddenly found that I could manage a small smile despite my despair.

"Now, you can tell me all about it here or you can tell me outside at the top of the next field—there's an amazing sunset brewing and I don't want to miss it."

"I'm okay, honest," I said. "You go and see your sunset. I'll be all right here."

She took my hand and shook her head.

"No, you can't stay here on your own like this. Come on."

With that, she pulled me toward the tent flap and, for someone who prides herself on not letting anyone push her around, I was strangely compliant. I followed her outside and up towards the gate behind my tent. And when she helped me climb over into the next field, I had to admit that it felt good to be with someone after a couple of days all alone in that huge crowd.

"This way," she said, leading me across an expanse of long grass. "This is the best place—I came up here last night and it was beautiful."

On the far side of the field, we came to a fallen tree and Sadie hopped up onto the vast trunk and straddled it, using a protruding branch as a backrest.

"Here," she said, indicating the space in front of her, and I climbed up too.

I straddled it, facing her, and she laughed.

"Other way, silly, you've got your back to the sun."

Grasping my arms, she helped me spin round and as I did, I gasped. Spread out below us, the whole festival was bathed in the soft orange glow of the setting sun, a giant blood-red orb on the far horizon.

"Wow, Sadie!"

She pulled me back until I was leaning comfortably against her and then she linked her arms around my waist.

"It's great, isn't it?" Her voice was close to my ear. "Now, tell me why you were crying just now."

"God, it's too embarrassing," I said, letting my head relax back on her shoulder. She smelt faintly of oranges and a little musky, reminding me that I hadn't showered for more than a day.

A hand brushed hair back from my forehead.

"Tell me—it won't be any worse than anything I've done."

And with relief, it all flooded out of me. How I'd thought I was in love with Danny Marks, how I'd planned to find him and seduce him, and how humiliated I'd felt on being introduced to his wife.

"You see what an idiot I've been?" I said, fighting the urge to cry.

I wiped my eyes as tears blurred the fiery orange ball that was now slipping below the line of the horizon.

Sadie wrapped her arms around me more tightly.

"Poor girl," she whispered. "But I've done the same myself. I've spent two days obsessing about a girl I just met. I've followed her around the festival, hoping she would notice me, which of course she didn't, and now I've found out that she's in love with someone else. I'm just as big an idiot."

I twisted slightly and looked at her.

"But Sadie, if you're interested in this girl, what are you doing here with me?"

Sadie sat up straight and used her arms to pull me round to face her. In the soft golden light of dusk, she looked like a statue of burnished bronze. It was a vision that stole my breath with a gasp. Her dark eyes sought mine, glancing intently from one to the other. Then her face dropped, breaking the eye contact and at the same moment she placed her hands on my hips.

"I am with her," she said, so quietly I hardly heard the words.

What? I wanted to yelp, but Sadie looked like a frightened animal and I didn't want to startle her. Inside, my stomach flipped. It was so unexpected. I'd never really been interested in girls before and they hadn't been interested in me. But it seemed that this one was. And... I felt okay about it.

I put out a hand to Sadie's chin and tilted her face up so I could look into her eyes again. Yes, I definitely felt okay about it. She still looked scared, so I smiled to reassure her but I knew that if anything was going to happen, she'd have to lead the way. This was virgin territory for me and suddenly I was the one feeling nervous.

Time stood still and, as we searched each other's eyes, I think we both knew we were standing on the brink of something. She took my hand and I took the plunge. As our lips tentatively came together, I heard the familiar opening chords of *Drive Me Crazy* crashing out in the distance. The Tomahawks were on stage and I wasn't there. And it didn't matter one bit.

Sadie's lips were soft and pliant beneath mine and then they moved across my mouth and I felt her tongue very slowly tracing the outline of my lips. My breath caught in my throat—it felt different to being kissed by a man, in a good way. She sucked my lower lip into her mouth and when I felt her teeth on it, my insides turned to liquid.

I wrapped my arms around her and pressed my body against hers, feeling the jut of her nipples brushing against my t-shirt. But even as I reveled in the new sensation of being breast-to-breast with another woman, she pushed me back.

"Are you sure?" she said. "You really want to do this?"

I nodded. "I want to," I said.

"Have you been with a girl before?"

"No."

She sighed and at that moment I couldn't think of anything I wanted to do more than surrender myself to this beautiful girl high on the hillside above Glastonbury, to the sound of The Tomahawks playing in the background.

"Christ, Sadie. I mean it—I really want you."

I kissed her savagely, pushing her back against the branch she'd been leaning on before, and as she responded to me with a hungry mouth, I placed both my hands on her narrow waist. Our tongues came together as mine slid into her mouth and hers pushed into mine. She tasted so sweet; her teeth felt smooth as I explored and her hands latched into my hair to keep our contact as close as possible.

Breathing through my nose, I prolonged the kiss and as our tongues moved together, I felt my hips rising and falling in expectation.

"Can I take off your t-shirt?" I said, running my hands up her sides. "I want to see your tattoo."

In one fluid movement the t-shirt was up and over her head, to be discarded on the ground beside us. She wasn't wearing a bra and in the dying light I could just make out the thread of twisted ivy that stretched from her hairline at the back of her neck to undulate across her left clavicle, before dropping down to entwine her left breast. From there it twisted across her rib cage, twirling at the side of her waist, to swing across her belly and drop beneath the waistband of her jeans. It was so delicate and as I traced its path with my finger, I felt her shiver.

"You're cold?"

"No," she said, nibbling my earlobe and sending a shiver through me in return.

She slipped off the tree trunk and held out her hands to help me down. Then she dropped to her knees in the long grass.

"No one will see us behind here," she said, pulling me down.

I knelt in front of her, smiling.

"I want to undress you," she said. "Ever so slowly."

I was wearing a crumpled linen shirt with at least twenty tiny buttons running down the front. One by one, she undid them, and after undoing each one, she planted a soft kiss in the space that opened up. From the flat plain at the top of my chest, she worked her way slowly down my cleavage and then lower to my ribs and belly. I could hardly stay still as each soft kiss brushed my skin.

When all the buttons were undone, she pushed the blouse back over my shoulders so it slipped down my arms. Before I realized it, she darted behind me and tied the shirt in a knot around my arms, pulling them behind me as she did.

I gasped in surprise.

She ducked back around to the front, grinning widely.

"Now you're really mine," she said. "Stand up."

I willingly did as she said. The restraint on my arms made my heart beat faster and my breath came in ragged gulps.

"Will I need a safe word?"

"Maybe. Pick one," she said, as she ran a finger around the top rim of my jeans, making me squirm with ticklish pleasure.

"Crazy," I said without hesitation.

"You won't need it," she said. "I'll only torture you with pleasure. I'm not into pain."

Her hands went to the fastening of my trousers and flipped open the brass button. Then, as she slowly lowered the zip with one hand, she let her other hand slip down into the opening. I felt smooth, cool fingers on my belly and then sliding lower into the narrow strip of hair.

I groaned as they pushed down further, gently stroking the outer edges of my lips. With her free hand she yanked my trousers down to my knees and then quickly pulled my panties down. My legs turned to jelly. I felt so vulnerable and I'd never felt so turned on in my life. As she held me steady, she gently guided me to step out of my jeans and panties. Then she backed me up against the tree trunk and knelt in front of me.

"Spread your legs," she said. "I need to see you."

I planted my legs as far apart as I could manage and leaned back against the rough bark of the tree. She brought her face in close to the cleft between my legs and traced the shape of it with her finger.

"You're very beautiful, you know," she said.

I chewed on my bottom lip, waiting for what she would do next.

Leaving one hand cupped between my legs, she slid herself up my body until her mouth was able to alight on one of my breasts. A sharp nip with her teeth had my nipple standing to attention and I yelped as the pain radiated through me. But between my legs, I could feel heat growing and the soft pressure of her hand on my pussy dampened the pain with a dose of pleasure.

With her teeth still clamped tight on my breast, she stretched my nipple outwards. With her other hand she pulled and twisted on the opposite side, making me moan so loudly that I could no longer hear The Tomahawks playing far below us. I pressed against the tree trunk and felt the rough bark against my back, mirroring the sensations of pain and pleasure that were radiating through me from the front.

Without speaking, Sadie roughly flipped me around so I was lying bent forwards over the trunk. My hands were still bound in the linen shirt so I was unable to use them to protect my chest. My breasts rasped across the tree bark, bringing tears to my eyes. But Sadie's firm hands running down my back and sides quickly soothed me and my taut body relaxed into its new position. Sadie briefly untied my wrists, pulled my arms above my head and retied them there, so she had access to the full expanse of my back and shoulders.

She rubbed her body up against mine and her breath caressed the back of my neck.

"You're magnificent from every angle," she breathed into my ear.

I could feel the softness of her breasts against my scratched back like a salve and seconds later, her hands were smoothing the rounded swell of my buttocks. They slipped down to my inner thighs and pushed my legs apart, exposing my moist cunt to the cool night air. Then her lips crept down my spine in a flurry of kisses, never stopping, never pausing as my lower back gave way to the crevice of my ass. I grunted and my hips ground against the trunk as she kissed ever lower and I felt her breath on my rear.

Gentle fingers parted my labia and softly explored my depths, sending shock waves of pleasure up my body. With a moan her tongue slipped inside me. I splayed my legs further and pushed my hips out to let her go deeper. Whimpering as I experienced new and delightful sensations coursing through me, I clung onto the trunk.

Sadie's tongue darted in and out of me like a hummingbird at a tropical flower. Then she spun me round again and swooped in on my clit. I could feel that it was already standing proud and engorged but as her mouth closed on it, it swelled further, making my back arch and my hips flex. Two fingers pushed deep into my pussy as she sucked and nibbled relentlessly on my most tender spot. When a third finger, already slick with my juices, pushed its way, oh, so slowly, into my ass, I could hold it together no longer.

Even with my teeth gritted together, a low cry marked the climax that tore through me, tightening every muscle, flooding every nerve with waves of pleasure. Sadie's teeth pulled hard on my clit, her fingers pushing deeper inside me, while I fought for breath, writhing under her touch, uncaring that the rough bark was scratching my back.

As my orgasm finally subsided, Sadie lifted me tenderly from the fallen tree to lay me down on the grass beside it. She untied my hands and kissed me gently. I could taste my own salty juices on her mouth and it made me feel sexy all over again.

"Sadie..." I breathed softly against her lips.

She sat and pulled my head into her lap, stroking my hair and bending low to kiss me some more.

"Look, you're scratched all over, poor baby," she whispered.

"I'm fine," I said, rolling onto my front.

Sadie was still wearing her skinny jeans, but I needed to see where the ivy tattoo led. I pushed her back until she was leaning against the tree. Then, without even undoing them, I pulled her jeans down over her hips, her panties riding down with them. She wiggled and maneuvered to help me, grunting as the tight denim raked her skin.

Once they were over her hips, they slid off easily and, tossing them to one side, I repositioned myself between her legs. And what a sight awaited me. Instead of hair, the delicate tendrils of ivy twisted their way down and ever further down, disappearing between the soft, velvety lips that were pursed over the very part of her I most wanted to explore.

I followed the path of the ivy with the tip of my index finger. Sadie sighed and threw her head back, eyes closed. I gently parted her soft flesh and as I did I discovered a world of wetness. Her aroma bombarded my nostrils as I took a deep, appreciative breath. God, I'd had no idea I'd find another woman so sexy. I plunged my face into the vortex between her thighs, content to immerse myself in the very essence of her.

Sadie pushed her hips forward and tilted them up, allowing her pussy to open further beneath my mouth. Slowly, tentatively, I put out my tongue until it made contact with her wet skin. She tasted similar to the flavor of my own juices on her mouth. Sweet. Salty. Indescribably delicious, making me want more. I wanted to drink her up. I sucked hard, moving my mouth up and down the deep rift, until I found the nubby bud of her clit. I swirled around it with my tongue, pulling and sucking, until I felt her hips mirroring the action underneath me. Her hands were in my hair, holding me in position, but it was hardly necessary. I wasn't going anywhere.

I slipped my hands underneath her to knead her buttocks while I continued to work my mouth between her legs. She raised her hips with a low groan.

"Melody, are you sure you've never been with a woman?"

Her voice cracked and I knew she was close to coming. I slid one hand down between her buttocks and slid my fingers inside her, all four of them, pushing up hard. She was so wet and I felt her stretching to accommodate me. With a yelp and then a whimper, her orgasm broke and I felt her muscles clench tightly around me. I pushed back against them and she arched up on my hand.

Far away I heard the final chorus of a Tomahawks song, drowned out again as Sadie moaned above me. She pushed my head hard against her soft flesh and I loved it, lapping up her juices as I slowly withdrew my fingers. Then I quickly pushed them back in again, tipping her over the edge again. This time she screamed my name, driven by powerful spasms that drew me deeper into her.

She leaned forward so she could catch my breasts in both her hands and as she came, she grasped my nipples, squeezing them and twisting them, then pushed my face away and slid a hand between my legs until I, too, was wrought by another crashing climax.

Finally, we both rolled out flat on the grass, side by side, totally spent. The music had finished and I could hear the crowd roaring for an encore.

"Do you think they're shouting for us?" I said.

Sadie laughed.

"An encore? Yes, please, but I'll need a little time..."

"Take as much time as you want," I whispered, rolling onto my side so I could throw an arm around her.

"Did it make up for not getting your way with Danny?" she said with a naughty leer.

"Danny who?"

And then it started raining again. Raining was an understatement for what fell from the sky over Glastonbury that night. But could I have cared less?

Could I hell!

IN THE HONEY–SWEET SUNSHINE

KATYA HARRIS

"Put. That. Tablet. Down."

Guiltily, Astrid dropped her computer tablet into the bag beside her sun lounger. "I have no tablet. That was a complete figment of your imagination." Looking up at me with a frown of concern wrinkling the skin between her eyebrows, she said, "You really are over-stressed, baby."

I stared back down at her, and then threw the towel I had gone back into the villa for, at her face. "You're full of shit," I declared over Astrid's giggle. Folding myself onto the lounger next to hers, I glared at my girlfriend. "If I'm stressed, it's because of you."

Astrid's giggling stopped on a gasp. "I'm insulted."

"You're impossible."

"True." Astrid's grin was irrepressible. Her sunglasses hid her eyes, but I knew their blue-green color would be dancing with her amusement. "But you love me anyway."

Reaching over I pinched the taut flesh of her thigh. Yelping, she slapped my hand away. "Bitch!"

My hand darted toward her again, fingers closing in a sharp nip on her waist. It earned me another slap, but I was laughing too hard to feel the sting of it.

"You keep laughing like that, and your boobs are going to fall out of your bikini," Astrid warned me.

"Ha, as if you wouldn't love that," I accused.

"Pervert."

Peering over the tops of her sunglasses, she leered at my chest area. "With ta-tas like those, could you blame me?"

"And yet you were sitting here on our holiday *working*?"

Astrid pouted. "Oh baby, did I hurt your feelings?"

"Yes," I told her, and although we were teasing each other there was a note of truth in my voice. This was our first vacation together in forever, and we were in a tropical paradise. On our own stretch of private beach, we were staying in a private villa that looked out onto golden sand and water the color of aquamarines and Astrid's eyes. We even had our own pool in case we didn't want to brave the sea, and beside which we were currently lounging. The sun was shining, thick and golden, and a soft breeze was blowing, laden with the scents of the sea mingled with the honeyed sweetness of the flowers and plants that surrounded us. It was heaven, the most romantic place we had ever been together. Shouldn't the last thing on Astrid's mind be work?

Astrid slid off her sunglasses. Tossing them to the end of her lounger as she sat up, she swung her legs over the side and leaned toward me. The usually full curve of her lips was a little flat. "I was just checking to see whether Jerome had gotten that report, that's all."

"It's our vacation," I reminded her, "and you promised."

Astrid's eyebrows pulled together. "I did, didn't I?"

"I know it's hard for you." That was a complete understatement—Astrid defined the meaning of the word workaholic. "But we need this time together."

Her frown deepened. "Is there something I should know about, Lena?"

Shit. I bit my lip, wishing I hadn't said anything. The day suddenly didn't seem as beautiful, the sun a little dimmer than it had been only moments before, the air not as sweet.

"Lena?"

Astrid reached over and slid her hand into mine. Her palm was warm, the familiar touch of her fingers threading through mine reassuring. The tightness in my chest eased a little.

"I'm sorry," I whispered. "I shouldn't have said anything."

Astrid's hand tightened around mine. "No, I shouldn't have broken my promise. I don't need to check up on Jerome. He knows how to do his job." She sighed. "And I should have left my tablet at home. I didn't need to bring it with me."

I gripped her hand back, my thumb rubbing a soft circle over the delicate bones pressing against her soft skin. "It's okay," I whispered.

"No, it isn't." Astrid moved from her lounger to sit on the edge of mine. She was wearing a bikini even skimpier than mine, a tiny snow-white number that barely covered her slender body, and the curve of her butt pressed against the outside of my thigh. "I know this vacation is important to you, but I thought I could sneak in a little bit of work. That was wrong of me."

Sitting up, I brushed a kiss over Astrid's cheeks. "It's okay."

Cupping the side of my face with her free hand, Astrid looked at me. "You're too good to me."

I smiled. "No, I'm just a sucker for you in a string bikini." It was true. My eyes trailed over her body, her slender shape more naked than not. Even the scant coverage of her tiny bikini was no use at all. I could see the tips of her nipples pressing against the thin, clinging fabric, the shadow of her waxed cleft between her thighs.

Astrid's eyebrow quirked upward. The contrition on her face melted into a slow smile. "I do look good, don't

I?"

I rolled my eyes at her, clicking my tongue. "Vain."

Leaning into me, Astrid murmured, "Probably, but it's you who made me that way. The way you look at me, Lena. It makes me feel like a goddess."

My breath hitched, and then Astrid's lips were on mine. Her tongue slipped into my mouth and she tasted so sweet, like fruit juice and liquid sunshine. She tasted like the heaven surrounding us and I wanted to devour her, take a piece of this paradise into myself and make it a part of me forever. I moaned, kissing her back. The heat of the tropical sun beat down on us, but it was nothing compared to the blaze that rose up in me.

With a moan, I melted. The core of me turned liquid, warm honey slipping from between my thighs to wet my bikini bottoms. I squirmed a little in my seat, trying to ease the tickle of my aroused clit and get closer to her at the same time.

Astrid chuckled against my lips. "See? A goddess." Her hands curled around my waist, long fingernails scraping lightly over my skin. She did it on purpose, I knew, knowing that it would turn me on even more. She kissed me a little more, sipping the breaths from my lips as she teased me. "I love the way you respond to me. Even after all these years, it's like you still can't get enough of me."

"It's true," I whispered back. I clutched at her slim thighs, needing something to hold on to. Desire was making my head spin. "I always want you." It's what made her workaholic ways so hard to bear at times; I wanted her all to myself. "I'm greedy."

"You say that like it's a bad thing." Astrid's hands smoothed up my sides to bracket my ribcage. The edges of her thumbs whispered over the undersides of my tits. I was so sensitive there I trembled.

"Do you think I don't feel the same way about

you?" Astrid asked. Tilting her head to one side, she considered me. "Lena, I want you so much."

Insecurity fluttered inside me. "Really?" Sometimes I wondered. Astrid was the epitome of confidence and independence. Even though I knew she loved me, at times it felt that she didn't really need me.

Astrid's brow wrinkled, and then smoothed out. A wicked twinkle glittered in her blue-green eyes. "Really." She shifted even closer to me, leaning over me and forcing me to lean back on my elbows. "Maybe I need to show you."

I licked my lips. Sweat trickled down my back, drawing a ticklish line along my spine. "Show me what?"

Astrid smiled, a slow stretching of her full lips. Crawling over me, she straddled my hips. Hovering over me, she blocked out the sky, the sun. She became all I could see, my whole world. "Show you just how much I want you."

"Okay." The word was a breathy tremble. "Let's go inside."

The twinkle in Astrid's eyes became even brighter. My heartbeat stuttered. She looked devilish, my very favorite look on her. "Why would we do that?"

She wasn't suggesting what I thought she was suggesting, was she? Interest unfurled in my stomach, even as anxiety skittered under my skin. "Astrid, no. Someone could see."

Keeping her eyes locked on mine, she slowly shook her head. "This is our very own slice of beach, remember? No one will walk past and see. Even if someone did, fuck them. I need to see you naked in the sunshine." Sitting up on my thighs, she ran a coral-tipped finger along the inner edges of my bikini. My skin prickled beneath her light touch, my nipples tightening to aching points.

"So how about it, baby?" she asked in a husky voice.

"Why don't you show me these pretty breasts?"

I gulped. Sitting up, I reached behind me, and pulled the string across my back and then the one around my neck, the only things keeping my bikini top on. The scraps of fabric fell into my lap. Negligently, Astrid tossed it to the side. She was too busy paying attention to my exposed chest.

Leaning back on my elbows, I arched my back and displayed my breasts for her. The irises of her eyes were thin rings of brilliant color around her inky black pupils. Twin swipes of red painted themselves across her tanned cheeks. She wriggled a little against my thighs, and I could feel the dampness seeping through her bikini bottoms.

"Damn Lena, your tits are so gorgeous." Her thumb swept over my nipple. It pouted even more beneath her touch, begging for more attention. Covering them with her hands, she gave it to them. My breasts were larger than Astrid's. They over-filled her hands, ample flesh trying to spill free from her grasp. "Magnificent," Astrid murmured. Bending down, she drew one nipple into her mouth. Astrid licked and sucked at the tender morsel of flesh, her hand playing with its twin. I groaned, throwing my head back as ribbons of pleasure unfurled through my body all the way to my aching clit.

"More," I demanded and whimpered as Astrid's touch grew rougher, her teeth biting down and nibbling on first one nipple and then the other.

Astrid's breasts brushed against me, taut nipples raking over the trembling plane of my stomach.

"I want to touch you too," I complained.

"In a minute." Astrid's lips brushed against the tip of my nipple as she spoke, her breath gusting cool over the damp skin. "I want to enjoy you a little more first."

"You're going to drive me mad."

Astrid chuckled. "I hope so. I want to make you scream as you come."

My flush seared my face, but honey spilled from my overheated pussy.

"Lay back."

I eased myself down. Grabbing hold of my hands, Astrid made them cup my breasts. Her gaze intent, she adjusted me until my tits were mashed together. "Perfect," she announced a moment before she enveloped both nipples within the warm wetness of her mouth.

"Fuck," I moaned. I couldn't stop myself from fondling the curve of my tits as she sucked me. Sensation whipped through me, a rising storm, and I squirmed and wriggled beneath her.

"Astrid, please."

Lifting her head slightly, Astrid rolled her eyes to meet mine. "What, baby?" she asked. Her tongue snaked out and flicked over the reddened peaks of my nipples. "What do you want?"

"I want to come," I told her in between panting breaths. "I need it."

Sitting up, Astrid asked, "Do you?"

Her hands went to my hips, her fingers toying with the strings that fastened my bikini bottoms. I held my breath, releasing it on a whimper as she pulled the bows free. Tugging the bottoms away, she discarded them on the ground. She breathed a sigh as she looked at my exposed pussy. "Baby, you're so wet."

I was. I could feel the dampness of my arousal spread over the smooth petals of my sex. I parted my thighs, just a little because she was sitting on top of them, but it was enough to flash the slick inner flesh. It was enough to invite Astrid to touch.

She slipped a long finger into my slit, rubbing between the soft lips. The back of her finger grazed my clit, sending electric tingles sizzling through my body. I twitched, soft moans falling from my parted lips. Afraid that someone would hear, I folded my bottom lip into my mouth, biting down to stifle the involuntary noises. Bracing her hand by my head, Astrid leaned over and gently pulled it free with her own lips.

"Don't," she murmured. "I want to hear your noises."

Embarrassment burned in me, its fire adding to the lust blazing beneath my skin. Sweat slicked me, helping my hands move over the aching mounds of my tits. I hadn't realized I was still fondling myself, and I didn't think I could stop. A cool breeze blew across me, kissing my skin. I made a low, throaty noise, and Astrid grinned down at me with a flash of bright white teeth.

"If I'm naked, you should be too."

Astrid's grin widened, her eyebrows lifting. "Oh, should I?" Straightening, she lifted her arms and stretched. Next to my curvy figure, she was reed slim. Her body was athletic, taut sun-kissed skin covering toned muscle. Her breasts were small, but perfectly formed, firm and tipped with tight pink nipples I longed to see, to taste. If I was a landscape of hills and valleys, Astrid was a topography of sweeping, elegant planes. Why did I need to touch my flesh, when I could touch hers?

I reached for her, but Astrid pushed my hands away. "Nah-ah-ah," she admonished, a playful gleam in her eyes. "Not yet, greedy girl."

A couple of gentle tugs and her bikini top fluttered down to drape across my hips. The sun stroked her golden skin with loving rays, burnished it to a warm sheen that just begged to be touched, caressed. Her bronze-colored hair tumbled around her shoulders in a tousled mass of loose waves. She looked so beautiful, wild and sexy, she made my heart ache and clit throb. No wonder I was greedy.

Astrid cupped her breasts in her hands, feathering

her thumbs over the dusky pink nipples. "I love the way you look at me."

"Let me touch you and it will feel even better."

Astrid chuckled. "I'm sure it would." Her breath hitched, her body writhing slightly on my lap. She was turned on. Smoothing her hands down her stomach she slid one hand into her bikini bottoms and wedged the fingers of the other between my thighs.

We both groaned as she played us both at the same time. Lust hazed my thoughts, eroded my inhibitions like the tide washing sandcastles back into the sea. I didn't care that we were out in the open, that at any moment someone could accidentally wander into our private slice of heaven. All I knew was Astrid's touch, my desire for her and hers for me.

"Please." The word whispered past my lips, and Astrid smiled crookedly. She looked a little drunk. I suspected I looked the same way. Both of us drunk on lust and love and tropical sunshine.

"Okay," Astrid whispered.

She came down over me, her mouth claiming mine in a hungry kiss. Our bodies pressed together, our breasts rubbing against each other's with maddening friction. Legs tangling together, we tried desperately to get closer, to rub our aching pussies against each other. Every time my swollen clit brushed against the bikini bottoms Astrid still wore, I gasped. She did the same.

With a muttered curse, Astrid rolled to her feet. Through squinted eyes, because the sun was directly behind her, I watched breathlessly as she tore away her bikini bottoms. Her cunt was flushed and slick with her arousal. Reaching out, I touched the delicate folds, nudging them apart to get to the throbbing pearl of her clit. It thrummed against my fingers.

Voice tight, Astrid said, "See how much I want you."

I nodded, unable to get words past my constricted throat. I did see, and it made my heart sing more beautifully than the birds around us.

Spreading my thighs, I grabbed her hand and pulled her toward me. "I need you."

Bending at the waist, she kissed me. It was soft and sweet. "I need you too." And I knew she didn't just mean now, she didn't just mean sex. She meant me.

I tugged on her hand. "I want to taste you."

Astrid's eyes sparkled. "I was thinking the exact same thing."

This time she straddled my head. My heart leapt with excitement, and with eager hands, I pulled her hips down toward me. Impatient, I lifted my head to take a long lick of her glistening pussy. The taste of her was sea-salt and honey on my tongue, and I moaned as I took another taste, a sound that deepened when she buried her head between my spread legs and licked me in return.

Beneath the blazing sunshine, we pleasured each other with lips and tongues and nimble fingers. We trembled against one another, bodies writhing in restless energy. Astrid came first, her spine bowing, her head thrown back, gasping and crying her orgasm out to the cloudless blue sky as she ground her pussy onto my madly licking tongue. I followed only moments later, her plunging fingers sparking the onslaught of my pleasure. I dissolved into a puddle of liquid sunshine, a smile wreathing my face.

Sated and drowsy from pleasure, I was barely aware of Astrid moving to lie beside me, her head next to mine. Automatically, I turned onto my side and we put our arms around each other, although not too close as we were drenched in sweat and overheated from our exertions.

A muffled chime sounded. I stiffened. It was the email notification sound on Astrid's tablet.

Silent, I watched as Astrid sat up. Leaning over me, she reached out and snagged her bag, dragging it toward her. A little rummage and she pulled out her tablet.

I sighed and then gasped. Droplets of water hit my feet as the tablet splashed into the pool beside us.

"Astrid!"

Lying back down next to me, Astrid made a contented noise. "They can survive without me for two weeks." She smiled at me. "I have much better things to do with my time."

I put my arm around her waist, pulling her close as the sun smiled down on us both.

Heaven.

THIRD TIME LUCKY
A. L. BROOKS

As I pulled back into the slow lane after overtaking an old coach, I risked a glance across at my passenger. She was dozing, head tilted back against the headrest, mouth slightly open, hands folded neatly in her lap. I turned my eyes back to the road, inwardly shaking my head in disbelief. For the hundredth time since we'd agreed to this trip, I found myself wondering just how I'd got myself into this situation. And for the hundredth time, I told myself I had only myself to blame. Or rather, my mouth, which for one key moment, two weeks ago, had refused to have anything sensible to do with my brain.

It had been a slow day at work, and when my personal phone rang I welcomed the interruption. That is, until I heard my sister's voice on the line. Samantha, the most flighty, unreliable woman on the planet, and yet the person I had agreed could join me on my long-planned week in Cornwall. She had meant well, I knew. My heart was still in pieces after Trudy left me, the holiday had been booked and paid for while we were still a couple, and Samantha didn't want me to take the week on my own. I didn't either, if I'm honest—as much as I had always wanted to go, the idea of a week in wild Cornwall on my own, with a broken heart, was not conducive to recovery from said broken heart.

So, originally, the holiday was supposed to be a retreat for Trudy and me, a chance to reconnect after her busy schedule since Christmas. Trudy was an actress, not hugely famous, just working the circuit, doing anything and everything to get exposure. First the panto, then straight off to a small Southern England tour, then back for a local residency in a Noel Coward play. However, sometime in April, Trudy discovered Catherine, the house manager of the theatre where the Noel Coward was playing, and suddenly our two-year relationship was over. I had been captivated by Trudy since the minute I had met her, and I had fallen hard and quickly. When I look back now, with the magic of hindsight, I realise it was never as deep for her—she was always looking forward, looking beyond, dreaming the next dream. My mistake was thinking that was limited to her acting career. I'm amazed we lasted two years, actually.

Samantha, for all her usual incapacity to commit to a single thing for more than five minutes, surprised me with her sisterly concern and her willingness to take sobbing phone calls from me at all hours. She pulled me out of it, slowly but surely, and so, when I eventually remembered the holiday that was booked, she seemed the natural choice to go with me instead of Trudy. She had heartily agreed, and it was all settled. Until two weeks ago, and that phone call.

"Hi Jess, it's me." Her voice had that simpering, overly sweet tone that people use when they know you are not going to like what they are about to say.

"Why do I get the feeling this is not good news?" I decided to get straight to the point; it was usually best when dealing with Samantha. I heard her sharp exhale, and knew she was biting back a stinging retort.

"Well, okay, if you want to be like that about it. Yes, I'm sorry, but I'm going to have to bail on our trip to Cornwall."

I took a deep breath, and counted to ten, to avoid letting out the scream that was rapidly building in my chest. I was in the middle of the office, surrounded by all the other call centre staff and I did not want to lose it so publicly. I could shout at her later.

"Fine," I spat, quietly but venomously. "I'll go on my own."

"Oh Jess, please don't be like that."

"Well, how the fuck else am I supposed to be?" I snarled. "You said you would go with me, you said I wouldn't have to take the holiday on my own, and now here you are, ditching me." I took another deep breath; my voice was in danger of rising above the angry whisper I was trying to maintain.

"I'm really, really sorry. I'll make it up to you somehow, I promise."

"Fine, whatever," I replied, knowing it sounded childish, and not caring.

"I'll call you later when you've had a chance to process this a bit."

I grunted and hung up, just about resisting the urge to hurl my phone across the room, slamming it into my handbag instead. I sank back in my chair, and dropped my head back, gazing at the ceiling above me.

"Hey," said a quiet voice nearby, and I almost catapulted out of the chair in my haste to get upright. That voice belonged to Lisa, a fellow team leader here at the call centre. Beautiful, funny, caring Lisa, who had become a very good friend these past couple of months. Gorgeous, sexy Lisa, who had unknowingly lit up my days since the darkness of Trudy leaving. *Straight* Lisa, with the boyfriend.

"Hey, yourself," I said, aiming for cool and coming up with dork.

She smiled, and I melted, as always.

"I couldn't help overhearing a little piece of that." She flicked her head left and right to make sure no one could overhear our conversation. "Has Samantha just done what I think she has done?"

I nodded, unable to verbalise it without every second word being the one that started with 'f'.

"For fuck's sake," she hissed, which made me laugh out loud, and then clap my hand over my mouth to stop the sound from escaping too far. "Sorry," she continued, a sheepish grin on her cute face. "But this trip was so important for you, and she's let you down."

I sighed. "I know, but hey, it's not the first time she's done something like that. Admittedly, this one hurts a bit more than some of the other things." I looked away, suddenly aware of tears building, and I so did not want to cry in front of Lisa.

She, being the amazingly intuitive and caring person that she was, said nothing, and gave me a couple of minutes to pull it together. I took deep breaths until the sob that had stalled in my throat eased itself out and left me wiping at the few tears that were leaking slowly out of the corners of both eyes.

"Coffee time?" Lisa asked quietly.

I turned back to face her, and nodded, a weak smile on my face. "I guess it's too early for alcohol?"

She giggled, and held out her hand. I stared at it, momentarily flustered at the concept of actually touching her. We'd never done that before. Fantasies of touching her in all sorts of ways had started to play a regular role in my waking hours. This last month or so, I realised I now thought about Lisa more during a day than I did about Trudy. Given that Lisa was straight and therefore completely unobtainable, moving from fantasies about my ex to fantasies about Lisa wasn't much of an improvement in my overall mental health. I knew this, and yet I couldn't get her out of my head. And here she was, offering me her hand, offering me our first physical contact. I was scared I would blush, or react in some way, and gave myself a stern talking to as I reached out, took her hand, and let her pull me from the chair. Her hand was cool to the touch, and soft, but her fingers were strong as they clenched around mine to pull me upwards. I didn't outwardly react in any way. But inside, my nervous system went into overdrive at the thought of what those strong fingers could do to me.

We left the office and walked down to the coffee shop on the ground floor of the building. She insisted on paying, and pushed me off towards the sofas to find us a spot to sit. She appeared a few minutes later with two large mugs of steaming latte, and sat herself down next to me.

"I've been thinking, while I was over there in the queue, and I may have a solution to your holiday problem." Her voice had an edge to it that I couldn't fathom.

I wriggled in my seat to face her. "Oh yeah, what's that?"

She took a deep breath. "How about I go with you?" Her face, for the most part, still looked as calm as it always did. But as I looked into her eyes, in shock at what she'd just suggested, I saw something else. She looked a little scared. Me, I was in a complete panic. Spend a week, alone, with Lisa, just the two of us? My brain started a loud warning klaxon of terror. A tidal wave of petrifying thoughts spun through my mind in an instant. *Don't even think about it, don't be ridiculous, this is so beyond dangerous. You'll probably make a drunken pass at her, you'll make a complete fool of yourself and it will all end horribly and you'll have to leave your job and it will just be a total nightmare. Do not do this.*

"Yes, that would be really nice", I found my traitorous mouth replying.

And so, here we were, two hours' drive from home, my shift about thirty minutes in. We'd left Brighton early, both wanting to avoid holiday traffic as we exited the city and headed west. She'd taken the first shift, as it was her car we were using. After that fateful decision in the café, the arrangements had fallen into place relatively easily. I think I spent the rest of that week in shock, still completely bemused as to how my mouth had acted independently of my brain and committed me to this course. I had gone home that night and downed three bottles of beer in quick succession while I tried to process what had happened. I'd gone in to work the next morning convinced I was going to tell her I'd changed my mind, but she'd come in with a bloody guidebook, asking me if it was possible to go to the Tate at St Ives while we were down there. It was the only thing she really wanted for herself, the rest of the trip could be all about me. And she looked so adorable standing there with her thumb in the right place in the book, that I crumpled instantly, completely at the mercy of my crush. At some point during the day, however, I did finally ask the two logistical questions that were at the forefront of my mind.

"Two questions?" she asked, smiling. "Is that all?"

I stumbled then, realising I had a whole heap of questions, but lots of them were completely inappropriate at this time. "Uh, yes, just two. For now." She nodded, waiting. "Well, firstly, I'm not sure I get how you managed to get the same week off as me? We're both team leaders, so how did you swing that?"

"Ah, easy—I worked last Christmas as a last minute request from someone else, so Brian owed me. Besides, you know as well as I do that August is our quietest time, so they don't really need all of us here then."

I grunted. It made sense. Couldn't use that as an excuse to get out of it then.

"And question number two?" she prompted.

"Ok, bit personal this one. How come you don't want to spend the week with your boyfriend instead?"

Her face fell slightly at this one, and she hesitated before responding. "Hmm, was hoping that wouldn't come up till a lot later actually. The thing is, he and I split up."

"What? When? You didn't tell me." I was hurt, actually, that she hadn't been able to share that bit of news with me. I thought we were friends enough for that, never mind anything else I was feeling for her.

"It was nothing, to be honest. It had drifted on and on, and then we just realised that's all it was doing. There were no tears, it was all pretty friendly. I didn't tell you because, well, you were still upset from what happened with Trudy, and I didn't want you thinking you needed to worry about me as well. Sorry, I should have said, shouldn't I, because now you're hurt I didn't, aren't you?" God, she was good at this intuition thing.

I nodded. "I am a bit, I'll be honest, but now you've explained it, I get why you didn't. It's okay."

She smiled then, and with that smile everything was all right, and I was going on holiday with her and I was suddenly more excited about that than anything that had happened to me in the last three years put together.

* * *

Lisa woke from her doze just as I joined the slip road onto the M5. We swapped places again at the first service area we came to, and she drove the final stretch to the cottage. As we neared Polperro, I felt my heart rate increase ever so slightly. It was really happening now. In about twenty minutes, we'd be unpacking in the cottage, getting ourselves settled in for a week together. I started wondering all sorts of stupid things at that point, concerned about the amount of wardrobe space available. Did Lisa rise early or late? Would my culinary skills be sufficient? What did she want to spend our evenings doing? Somehow, in the midst of this, one startling new thought pushed its way to the front, sharply elbowing all other ones out of the way, and making me sit bolt upright in my seat when it did so.

"What?" Lisa asked, glancing at me quickly, presumably checking to make sure I wasn't having some kind of seizure. Which, actually, I almost was.

"Ah, well, the thing is, I just remembered something about the cottage," I stammered, not entirely sure how to word this.

"Yes?"

"It's… well, the thing is… sorry, I don't know how I forgot this part."

"Would you just spit it out, for fuck's sake!" She was laughing, clearly enjoying my moment of discomfort.

"It's one bedroom. One double bed."

She stopped laughing.

"Oh," she murmured, after a heavy pause.

"Yep."

"Sofa bed?"

"No."

"Oh."

"Shit, sorry." I rubbed my hands over my face in an attempt to stop the blush that was now creeping over my cheeks. "Obviously, the first time this holiday was arranged, it was for me and Trudy. Second time it was for me and Samantha, and we used to share a bed on family holidays so I didn't think anything of it. But now…"

"I know," she said softly, breaking off to deal with a busy roundabout. Neither of us spoke for a couple of minutes.

"Look," she said, eventually, as I directed her down the lane that led to the cottage. "There's bound to be a sofa anyway, so even if it doesn't roll out, I can still sleep on that and you can take the bed. And worst case scenario," she continued, as she pulled us up outside the gorgeous-looking cottage, and switched off the engine, "we can always share a bed—we're grown-ups, we can handle it. I don't snore that much." She caught my eye, and winked, and I was aware of my stomach making a rapid journey down to my toes and back again, and I swallowed.

* * *

We met with Susan, the owner of the cottage, and she gave us the run-through of the dos and don'ts. After she left, we smiled shyly at each other and set to unpacking. We found plenty of space for our clothes and food, but neither of us mentioned the obvious lack of sofa—the seating arrangement in the small living room was just two armchairs facing a cute open fireplace. When we climbed the narrow staircase to the bedroom, we each unpacked our small suitcases in silence. The elephant in the room— which was actually a rather lovely looking antique pine double covered in crisp white linens—was not mentioned, even when each of us laid our sleepwear out on the bed. I had, without thinking, chosen the side nearest the window, as that was where I always slept at home. Realising what I had done, I quickly asked if that was okay, without actually meeting her eyes, still finding this part of our situation incredibly uncomfortable.

"It's fine, Jess, don't worry."

I looked up at her, and her face was so understanding, her expression so warm, I found tears welling up, and had to turn away.

"Hey," she whispered. "What's wrong?"

"Nothing," I mumbled, unable to articulate the myriad of emotions I was experiencing.

To my mortification, she walked around the bed and wrapped her arms around me. I resisted, not wanting to feel how wonderful it would be to be held by her, but she persisted, and my resistance disappeared like smoke on the wind. I sank into her embrace, and oh God, it felt so good. Her arms, like her fingers, were strong, and her body fit to mine like a second skin. I tried to focus on the comfort she was giving, and not on the way my body was responding to the feel of her pressing against me from breast to thigh. How long we stayed like that I couldn't tell. I cried, my tears leaving a damp patch on the shoulder of her t-shirt, but she didn't move an inch. I cried for the loss of Trudy, for the anger I'd had towards Samantha, and for the ridiculous, hopeless feelings I had for Lisa, the woman who held me so tightly, so platonically, now.

* * *

We opened a bottle of red once we were downstairs again. We had said nothing about the emotional moment upstairs. There was no need. We made pasta together, opened the French doors at the back of the kitchen that led out onto a small patio, and ate our meal outside. Crickets chirped, the sun set lazily behind us, and it was one of the most beautiful evenings I could ever remember having. We talked, and laughed, and I relaxed, properly, in her company for the first time since I'd been aware of my feelings for her. All that seemed set aside for now, as if I knew deep down that it would be enough to have evenings like this with her. We planned our next day, our first proper day of the holiday, and then each retreated to a book, still enjoying the warmth of the evening out on the patio.

At eleven we called it a night, both tired after the early start, the long drive and the bottle of red we'd polished off over dinner. She used the bathroom first, and I tried very hard not to think about her getting naked in there before she appeared in her t-shirt and shorts. Willing my eyes to behave themselves, I still couldn't stop myself sneaking a glance at her tanned legs as she walked across to the bed. I nearly choked on the thoughts that leapt into my head at that moment, and quickly grabbed my sleepwear and strode off to the bathroom. I stood in front of the basin cleaning my teeth, lecturing myself not to ruin this holiday by doing anything stupid in the next eight or so hours. My biggest fear, of course, was that I wouldn't be able to stop my body from seeking out hers in the bed during sleep, something I wouldn't be able to control, but which would probably make for a very uncomfortable morning when she woke up and found she had a lesbian wrapped around her.

* * *

As it was, I needn't have worried. My body was extremely well-behaved, and actually, I had the best night's sleep I'd had in ages. When I'd returned to the bedroom, she was already half asleep under the sheets, the glow of the light on my side of the bed highlighting her features, making my stomach do that little flip again. But I got in beside her, turned off the light, said a sleepy goodnight, and found myself drifting off much easier than I'd anticipated.

The next thing I knew, it was eight thirty, bright sunlight was streaming in through a chink in the curtains, and Lisa was already up. I found her down in the kitchen, still in her shorts and t-shirt, making a pot of coffee. We smiled a greeting, and set about making breakfast together.

"Sleep well?"

"Like a log," I replied. "I guess I really needed that."

She nodded, and smiled warmly, and we started talking about the day we had planned.

* * *

We had an amazing time that day, and the next, and the one after that. We saw some beautiful countryside, walked the wild coastline, visited cute little villages tucked into the back of nowhere, and we talked and laughed non-stop. Each night we'd make a meal back at the cottage, drink some wine, talk some more, and then fall into bed and sleep like babies. My thoughts and my body mostly behaved themselves. They were happy to be sharing this with her, even if I knew I would love to have more, but just being with her was so healing, warming my soul and my heart. There were only a couple of moments when I let my guard down, and got caught, but she seemed unperturbed by them. Out on a walk, I spotted a bird of prey hovering overhead, and without thinking took her hand to pull her closer so that I could point it out, and then held on to her hand as we walked on afterwards, because it felt like the most natural thing in the world to do. She never mentioned it, and never took her hand away. It was I who suddenly realised what I was doing and pulled away, apologising profusely. She just gave me a smile I couldn't read, and walked on without saying anything.

* * *

After our third day of sightseeing, we needed a break from rushing around the countryside, and with the Cornish summer weather in full glory, we decided to spend a lazy afternoon at the cottage. The patio was small but south-facing, so we pushed the furniture around until both the rattan chairs were facing directly into the sun, and slapped on sunscreen. Neither of us had brought bikinis, but shorts and strappy tops were good enough. We opened some cold beers, and escaped into our books.

After an hour or so, I could feel my skin on the edge of burning, and thought I ought to take a break. I turned to ask Lisa if she wanted me to get her anything from inside the house, only to find she had drifted off to sleep, her book forgotten in her lap. She looked so stunning at that moment, it nearly stopped my heart. Her dark hair was loose around her shoulders, her skin glistening from the sunscreen, her long eyelashes fluttering slightly against her face as she chased a dream. Her lips were slightly parted, and looked ready to be kissed, and I had to grip the sides of the chair to stop myself from launching across the patio and into her arms.

I was falling for this woman, I knew it, and I knew I should stop but I just couldn't. I let my gaze wander down her body, taking in the curve of her breasts, the roundness of her belly, the long, tanned legs. And as my gaze drifted slowly back up that same landscape, I found myself trapped by deep brown eyes gazing back at me. Startled, and embarrassed at being caught lusting, I tore my eyes away and stood up quickly. I made to step past her and into the house, but she reached out a hand, wrapped her fingers around my wrist, and held me in place next to her chair.

I couldn't look at her; I was terrified I'd see anger, or disgust, or disappointment, but she tugged on my wrist until I had no choice but to meet her gaze. When I did, I caught my breath. Her face was open, a little vulnerable, and a little scared, but mostly her expression was one full of desire. My heart suddenly thumped so loudly in my chest it hurt.

"Jess," she breathed, her grip on my wrist tightening, pulling me, her eyes not wavering from mine for a second.

I resisted, my brain trying to catch up with events, this change in the dynamic between us throwing me completely. This wasn't part of the plan—part of the fantasy, yes, but surely my attraction couldn't possibly be reciprocated. I started to speak, to ask a tumble of questions, but she pulled at my wrist again, and finally my brain released me from its shackles and let my body go where it desperately wanted to. As if in slow motion, I bent at the waist, gripping the back of the chair behind her head to steady myself, and watched her mouth get closer, and closer, and then my eyes were closing and my lips were on hers, and they were just as soft as I'd imagined they would be. Our kiss was gentle, tentative, but at the same time searing with a heat that shot down my chest, past my belly, and settled somewhere deep between my legs. When her mouth opened, and she let my tongue slip against hers, I couldn't stop the moan that escaped my throat. I placed my free hand, its wrist still held firm in her grip, on the side of her face, stroking her skin with my fingertips as the kiss deepened. I felt her fingers tighten around my wrist, and she pressed her mouth even closer, suddenly devouring me with a passion that was equal parts unexpected and unbelievably exciting.

We pulled back, panting for breath, and I stared at her, my hand still cupping her face. "I… I don't understand," I whispered.

Lisa shook her head, and smiled wryly. "Nor do I, if I'm honest," she whispered back. "But I have wanted to do that for the longest time."

I let out a deep breath, thinking about her words, their meaning. I stood up, letting go of her face. I was suddenly scared, and bordering on angry as a result.

"I can't be some experiment for you. Don't do that to me." My voice sounded harsh even to my own ears. I stepped back. Her eyes widened, and then I saw realisation dawn, and she stood as well, still keeping hold of my wrist.

"God, no, that is *not* what I meant! I would never do that to you, you must know that?"

I paused, watching her, her expression so honest, so hurt that I would think something like that of her. She was right, she had been nothing but kind and truthful to me the entire time we had been friends.

"But, if it's not that, then…?"

She exhaled, and released my wrist to push both hands through her hair. My fingers twitched, aching to follow hers.

"I have… feelings for you," she said, eventually, looking at me shyly, exposed. "It took me a while to figure out that's what was going on, and I had no idea what to do about them. Then the chance came up to spend this time with you, and I thought, why not? Why not see how it was to be this close to you. I'd kind of got the impression you might… well… feel the same way." Now she was blushing, suddenly unsure, and I needed to rescue her, as she was being far braver than I would ever be. I took her hand, and gently pulled her towards me, slowly nodding as I did so, and letting a small smile break across my face.

"Your impression was right," I said, carefully placing my hands on her waist, marvelling as she willingly stepped into that embrace. She smiled, obviously relieved, and tentatively lifted her hands up to place them on my shoulders, and the touch of her soft hands on my warm skin sent me reeling. I leaned forward and kissed her again, and it was her turn to moan, and her fingers squeezed at my shoulders. I pulled her closer, and her hands slipped round to the back of my neck, and my arms tightened, pressing our bodies together. We lost ourselves in that kiss for quite a while, holding each other so close in the heat of the afternoon sun, our tongues and lips sliding deliciously across each other's.

When we eventually came up for air, we stood, breathing deeply, with our foreheads touching, our arms still wrapped tightly around each other.

"You are amazing. I would never have had the courage," I whispered, pressing my lips to her forehead, her eyelids.

She chuckled softly. "God, you have no idea how many sleepless nights I've had trying to work out what it was I was feeling, and then trying to work out how the hell to tell you. I almost didn't—I'd decided, by the end of yesterday, that you just wanted me as a friend, and that I'd misread all the signals I thought you were giving out."

"And here was I thinking I was being so bloody careful not to give it away!"

She laughed. "You were doing fine until you ogled me just now," she said, winking, and I laughed out loud. "That message was loud and clear," she murmured, and suddenly there was a tension between us, and my body was humming with anticipation.

There were probably many reasons to wait, to take our time getting used to this new 'us', to not rush her into something so new. But I couldn't think of a single one of them as our lips met again, this time slowly, sensuously, exploring taste and texture. And then the kiss deepened, and hands trailed over arms, and down backs, and I cupped her arse and pulled her in tight, and she gasped. I backed off, meeting her eyes, suddenly fearful I'd got too carried away. But even in the sun her eyes had darkened, and she didn't resist when I took her hand and walked us back into the house.

In the bedroom I pulled the curtains, shutting out the brightness, leaving only a soft sepia glow to see by. As I carefully lifted her top over her head and dropped it to the floor, the muted light showed in perfect relief the contours of her neck, her collar bone, the tops of her breasts spilling out from the lace cups of her bra. I let my tongue trace those lines, revelling in the sound of her breathing becoming ragged. She put her hands on my hips to steady herself, tilting her head back to give my mouth greater access to her neck, which I took, kissing and licking until she shivered. I raised my head to take my own top off, and thrilled at the sensation of her fingertips caressing my ribs as my skin was revealed. Her lips found mine again, and she surged against me, fingernails raking my back as she pulled me close. I was lost in a maelstrom of sensation, and needed to touch her, all of her.

I reached between us to tug at her shorts, and she helped me push them down, stepping out of the puddle of material once it hit the floor. I pushed my own shorts down, and then reached behind her to undo her bra, my tongue thrusting against hers as my body was overwhelmed by my desire. When my hands stroked up her ribcage to feather over her full breasts, she groaned, long and deep, and the ache between my legs intensified to almost painful proportions. I ran my thumbs over her nipples, feeling them harden underneath my touch, and I nudged her back towards the bed. Laying her down, I let my mouth capture a nipple, and I pulled on it with my teeth, her wrenching gasp making my clit throb. I reached down and pulled off her underwear; she lifted her hips to help and I tossed the lacy material onto the floor behind me. I stood straight and ripped off my own bra and knickers, and watched, beyond aroused, as her eyes roamed hungrily over the length of my naked body.

She reached out for me then, and my heart skipped a beat. This amazing woman, who had been quietly, surreptitiously, sneaking her way into my soul for the last three months, was laid out in front of me, wanting me. It was all I could do to remember to breathe. She smiled, and I eased my body down on top of hers, and kissed her tenderly, one hand running trembling fingers through her hair, the way I had wanted to do countless times over the past weeks. We gazed at each other, and she ran soft fingertips up my spine, leaving goosebumps in their wake.

"Touch me," she whispered. "I want you."

I felt tears prick at the corner of my eyes. The road I'd travelled this year to reach this point had been so rough, so soul-destroying, that to find myself here, now, was almost too much to take. But then her hips were pushing up into me, her legs opening beneath me, allowing my thigh to drop between them and press against her, and my tears abated, and my want consumed me. I didn't hesitate; I moved my hand between us, and slipped a finger into warm wetness, stroking, staring into her half-lidded eyes as I entered her, pushing hard and deep, claiming her as mine. She thrust against me, whimpering with pleasure as I met her thrusts with another finger, and another, filling her, setting a steady rhythm that had her throwing her head back, fingers digging into my shoulder blades. I moved my thumb gently onto her clit and the moan that escaped her lips tore through me, stripped me bare. When she came she held me so tight I didn't want her to ever let go, and I kissed her, capturing her gasps in my mouth.

* * *

The sun had set by the time we stumbled from the bedroom down to the kitchen in search of food. We stood naked in front of the open fridge, the cool air crinkling our nipples, making us giggle like teenagers. We grabbed a tray full of cheese and olives and bread, a bottle of wine, and raced back up the stairs for our naked picnic. She fed me olives dripping in rosemary oil, and licked the spilt drops from my breasts. Our mouths met in hungry kisses in between bites of food and sips of wine, and when we had eaten our fill, she pushed me back onto the sheets and ate her fill of me, her tongue probing deep and driving me over a precipice I never wanted to climb back up from.

Sometime in the early hours, we wrapped ourselves up in each other to sleep. I held her warmth against me, and her sleepy eyes looked deep into mine.

"This doesn't end tonight, does it?" she asked, in a whisper, her nervousness crystal clear, and I was astonished she would think something so ludicrous.

"God, no," I breathed, and her smile lit up the room.

She drew me close, and I trembled at the promise her touch conveyed.

A MOST SPECTACULAR VIEW

LUCY FELTHOUSE

There was an energetic buzz amongst the small group gathered on the tarmac. Morgan completely understood why—she was feeling it, too. The day was dry and warm—pretty much the norm for Lanzarote—the sun bright, and they were about to go and explore a volcanic landscape. On foot.

The Ruta de Tremesana was a 3.5 kilometer walk through the Timanfaya National Park, and a trek Morgan had been looking forward to ever since booking the trip to the Canary Island several months previously. Granted, it would have been better had her best friend, Jenna, been coming too, as originally planned, but her gran's sudden illness had scuppered that.

It was too short notice to try and reschedule or refund the holiday, so Jenna had insisted she go without her.

"Go on, Morgan, I'm not ruining your holiday too. You go, have an awesome time, meet a hot girl or two, take lots of photos and get a wicked tan. We'll book something else once Gran is better," Jenna had said.

Morgan didn't have the heart to tell her friend that holidaying alone was about as appealing as moldy cheese, so she went along with it. By the time she boarded the airplane bound for the land of sunshine and sangria, she'd convinced herself it wouldn't be that bad. And she had the Ruta de Tremesana trek to look forward to, if nothing else.

She'd been fascinated with volcanoes ever since she was a little girl, so delving into Lanzarote's volcanic landscape was a dream come true.

Now she was actually here, ready to embark on the two-hour trip, she was raring to go. Her boots were firmly tied, her camera fully charged, her backpack loaded with water. All the assembled tourists needed were a couple of tour guides and they were sorted.

When two outdoorsy-looking locals stepped out from the visitor center everyone had been waiting in front of, Morgan knew immediately which of the two groups she wanted to be a part of.

The young man, dark-haired, hazel-eyed and athletic, was handsome enough, if you liked that kind of thing. But Morgan didn't. Much more to her taste was the raven-haired, brown-eyed goddess beside him. She was tall and slim, with curves in all the right places. Her shorts and t-shirt left plenty of olive skin on show for Morgan to ogle, and her mind immediately wandered down a path lined with nudity and sun cream.

Before she could get too entrenched in her fantasy, the woman—who Morgan guessed was around her age, so in her early thirties—spoke. "Okay, everyone! We're all here, so we're going to split into two groups. Half of you will come with me. I am Riya. Half of you will go with my colleague, Tulio."

As subtly as possible, Morgan shuffled left, to ensure she was on the correct side of the division when it was made. Her movement paid off, as Tulio pointed at eight people in turn on his side, and said, "You are with me. The rest of you are with Riya."

Everyone moved accordingly, and those who remained with Riya moved closer to the woman, ready to hear what would happen next.

After explaining the plan and ensuring everyone was properly kitted out—apparently, in spite of very thorough instructions, people sometimes turned up to these walking tours in sandals or high-heeled shoes—Riya moved off, leading them to the beginning of their trek.

Morgan fell into line, deliberately making sure there were a few people between herself and Riya. She didn't want to be directly behind her, because she knew she'd end up spending more time gazing at those lovely long legs and delicious arse than the scenery—and she'd come a very long way to miss out on the volcanic landscape.

Once they'd moved into the national park proper, Riya stopped and gathered everyone around her again. "I will not go too fast on this walk. This is so you can appreciate what is around you, take photographs and enjoy yourselves. If you need me to stop, please call out. It is hot, so please make sure you drink plenty of water. I will also be stopping at certain points on the walk to point out places of interest and to tell you more about them. Does anyone have any questions?" She paused, but nobody spoke, so she nodded. "Okay, then. Let us begin."

About twenty minutes into the trek, Morgan was already having the time of her life. The place was truly amazing—a multitude of rocks and dirt, in reds, browns and blacks, it wasn't the desolate place she'd expected it to be. Sure, it was devoid of human life, of buildings, but there was plant and animal life. Some of which, Riya had explained, couldn't be found anywhere else on the planet. Great big mounds of rock and earth marked places where molten lava had broken through and erupted—the craters and slopes looked so serene now, but they were reminded that the volcano was dormant, not extinct.

Morgan was soon glad she'd fully charged her camera and made sure her memory card had enough capacity. By the next time they stopped, she'd already taken well over a hundred photos. Some of them would probably need deleting—errant sunbeams and an unsteady hand would render them rubbish—but then, that was the beauty of digital photography. You only kept the shots you were happy with.

Their route had just taken them to a high point, and everyone was out of breath—or at least huffing a bit— when they reached a flat area. Riya, though, clearly used to this trek, to doing exercise in the heat, sunshine and humidity, looked just as fresh as she had when they'd set off. If Morgan didn't fancy her so much, she'd probably have hated her.

"It is a most spectacular view," she said, breaking into Morgan's thoughts.

Yes, Morgan thought, raking her gaze up those endless legs, *it damn well is. Truly spectacular.*

She continued drinking in the sight of the sexy Canarian chick; toned tummy beneath her form-fitting t-shirt, pert breasts and up to her—

Shit. Riya was looking right at her. She had been caught out. Quickly breaking their eye contact, Morgan spun on her heels, lifted her camera, and began snapping shots of the surrounding craters and lava fields, paying particular attention to anything that wasn't in Riya's direction. Despite her hurried movement, she'd still embarrassed herself royally, and her cheeks radiated heat that had nothing to do with the climb, or the sun.

Bugger, bugger, bugger! Now Riya probably thought she was some kind of perv. Which she was, of course, when it came to gorgeous girls, but she was normally much more subtle. Sighing, she reassured herself that at least once the walk was over, she'd never have to see her again, and her embarrassment would fade into distant memory.

Fixing her mind on the reason she was here, Morgan shoved aside all other thoughts and allowed the stunning landscape to capture her imagination. It wasn't difficult—she'd never seen anything like it in her life. Looking around, she saw the rest of the group was equally entranced, with cameras being pointed every which way, and happy murmurs filling the air.

Smiling, Morgan tilted her head back, closed her eyes, and let the sunlight caress her face. *What a wonderful place—Riya and Tulio have the best bloody jobs in the world.*

A voice right next to her ear made her gasp.

"We are moving now. I would like you to walk at the front with me."

Morgan's widened eyes took in the olive-skinned goddess, and she managed to answer, "B—but why?"

Giving a lazy smile, Riya replied in a low voice. "I think... you are interesting. We can talk, find out more about each other."

Unable to think of an excuse, especially when deep down this was exactly what she wanted, Morgan replied, "Um, okay."

"What's your name?" Riya asked as Morgan fell into step beside her.

"Morgan."

"*Morgan.*" The way the Canarian said Morgan's name made all the hairs on the back of her neck stand on end. The sexy accent, the way she rolled the 'r'... Morgan was half in love already.

"Yes."

"I like it."

"Thank you."

Riya said nothing more, leading them past the group and back to where she'd been standing when they'd stopped at this point. "Okay, everyone!" she said loudly, immediately commanding attention. "We are going to move on now. Is everyone okay? Recovered from the climb?"

Everyone replied in the affirmative, and Riya smiled and nodded before turning around and continuing the trek. The track was a more gentle slope now, but narrow, so they had to walk in single file. Naturally, this meant that Morgan got quite the eyeful of Riya's swaying backside, encased in tight shorts. It was hypnotic.

Damn. She'd have to start paying more attention to where she was putting her feet, otherwise she'd end up plummeting off the path and tumbling dozens of feet to the rocky ground below. Granted, having Riya's peachy arse as her last memory would be a pretty good way to go, but she'd much rather find out what the other woman wanted from her, if anything. She may just have wanted someone to talk to, but why choose her? Especially after catching her staring. Her gaydar was bleeping vaguely, but she just couldn't be sure. And she'd already made enough of an idiot of herself today. She'd just wait and see what happened. If nothing did, then at least she'd have the delectable mental images she was capturing right now.

When the path widened out, Riya encouraged Morgan to walk beside her. She did so, and Riya immediately began asking her questions. It felt a little like being interviewed; where was she from, what was she doing in Lanzarote, was she holidaying alone, where was she staying. The suspicious, cautious part of Morgan's brain couldn't help wondering whether Riya was going to organize a robbery of her apartment or something while she was out, but she quickly dismissed the idea. She hadn't said anything to Riya that indicated she had anything worth stealing—which she didn't. Her passport and money were in the safe, so the only things in her room that could be gotten hold of were clothes and shoes. And none of them were even remotely designer.

Relaxing a little, she turned the tables on the Canarian, and soon found out that she was as interesting as she looked. They were indeed about the same age— Riya was thirty-two to Morgan's thirty-three; she had been born on the island, and, unlike many of her peers, loved it. Others wanted to leave, go to the bigger Canary Islands of Tenerife and Gran Canaria, mainland Spain, elsewhere in Europe, or North Africa. Just anywhere that wasn't here.

Riya, on the other hand, appreciated the beauty and unique nature of her home and had always wanted to show it off to others. So she'd gone to England and studied for a degree in geology at Leicester University, graduated with a first, then moved back and had learned on the job ever since. Now she was one of the island's leading experts on volcanology. She was also well known in her field the world over, and got many opportunities to travel to conferences and seminars.

"So," she said, smiling, "I have the best of both worlds, as you English say. I have my home here, in the place that I love, doing the job I love. But I also get to travel a lot, to different places all over the planet. And I am paid to do it!"

Morgan nodded, impressed. "It sounds idyllic to me. And the fact you studied in England explains why you speak English so well. You've even got some of the slang down."

"Yes. Being able to speak good English is very useful—it is what allows me to travel to all these conferences and communicate with other people easily. It seems no matter where people are from, they have at least a grasp of the English language. I certainly could not learn the languages of all the places I have visited. I would not have time for anything else!" She laughed, and the lively, full-bodied sound caused a pleasant buzz deep down in Morgan's abdomen, and heat flared between her legs.

Christ, but this girl was hot. Gorgeous, sexy, funny, incredibly smart… now if only she was a lesbian, then she'd be Morgan's ideal woman. Oh, and if she didn't live a couple of thousand miles away. But still… if she was indeed into girls, and was single, then a holiday fling could be on the cards, perhaps?

She'd just have to wait and find out.

They continued talking as they walked, pausing every time Riya had something else to point out or to explain to the group. Morgan, at Riya's prompting, spoke about her job. After explaining what she did, she was suddenly overwhelmed with a need to find something else to do, something fulfilling, that filled her with excitement and passion every time she spoke about it— like Riya and her volcanoes. She didn't have an unhappy life, but fuck, was it dull.

When the trek was over and they headed back to the visitor center they'd started at, Morgan was both bitterly disappointed the trip was finished—she could have wandered in that stunning landscape for weeks on end and not gotten bored—and buzzing with anticipation of what would happen next. Would Riya simply wish her goodbye along with the rest of the group, or had walking beside her and chatting meant something more than just a simple conversation? She hoped so.

Mercifully, she didn't have to wait long to find out. Morgan was just putting her camera into its case and then into her bag, ready to head back to her hire car and the resort she was staying in, when Riya appeared beside her.

"Hi," the Canarian said, smiling.

"Hi," Morgan replied, a little hesitantly. Was she just being polite, was she teasing… what?

"Are you going back to your accommodation now?"

"Yes."

"Can I come with you?"

"Um, don't you have work?" *What are you saying, you stupid woman? Why the hell are you trying to put her off?*

Riya shrugged. "My hours are… fluid, shall we say. I do this trek three times a week. Aside from that and specific meetings and conferences, as long as all my work is done, nobody minds what hours I work. It's not a typical office job."

"Fair enough. Then sure. I'm in a hire car. Do you want to follow me in your car?"

Riya nodded. "Okay."

Well, that was something, at least. Clearly the drive back to her apartment was going to be tough to concentrate on, given the hottest, smartest woman she'd met in forever was following her back for… well, she still wasn't sure what. But it'd be slightly easier to keep her focus on the road without Riya sitting right next to her in the tiny car, just inches away. She might even make it back in one piece.

But then what? By now, she was pretty confident she and Riya were on the same page. But there was just that little niggle of doubt in the back of her mind— maybe she was just being friendly? If that was the case, though, wouldn't she have just invited her to a local café for a drink, rather than asking if they could go back to Morgan's apartment?

There was only one way to find out. Smiling, she picked up her bag, slung it over her shoulder and headed to where she'd left her car at the side of the road. Riya signaled that she'd meet her back there, and Morgan enjoyed the view once more as the woman turned and walked away to collect her own vehicle.

Morgan barely had any memory of the journey from the centre of the island back out to the coast. It seemed to zip by in a blur, and the next thing she was really conscious of was trying to get out of the car and realizing her seatbelt was still on. Thankfully, Riya was busy manoeuvring her car into the space behind and hadn't seen.

After successfully exiting the vehicle, Morgan grabbed her bag, locked the car and waited on the pavement for Riya. When she appeared, she gave a nervous smile and turned and headed for her apartment. Seconds later, as she unlocked the door and let them into the relative cool of the room, she shivered.

"Are you cold, Morgan?" Riya said, with a look of concern.

She wasn't entirely sure *what* she was feeling at that moment in time, but it definitely wasn't cold. Shrugging noncommittally, she replied, "Would you like a drink?"

Glancing around and taking in her surroundings, Riya then looked back at Morgan. "Maybe later. Right now, there is something I would like much more."

"Oh?" The word came out as little more than a squeak, and Morgan's cheeks heated. "W—what's that?" *Way to go, Morgan. You are the queen of seductive conversation. Be careful, or you'll blind the hottie with your dazzling wit.*

"I think you know." Riya stepped closer, and put her finger beneath Morgan's chin as she tried to stare a hole in the tiled floor. Tilting her head to force eye contact, Riya continued, "I saw you looking at me, Morgan. You were looking at my legs, my arse, my tits. Then you got embarrassed when I caught you doing it. But you should not be embarrassed—I was looking at you, too. But perhaps I was more… subtle about it."

"You were looking at *me?* But w—"

"Shh." Riya moved her finger to press against Morgan's lips. "Come on. Let us go and do more than just *look.*"

Taking Morgan's hand, she walked towards the two doors opening off of the main space. The bedroom door was ajar, and she strode in, with Morgan trailing speechlessly behind.

God, was this really happening?

Her confusion and disbelief soon turned to full-on arousal when, seemingly all in one movement, Riya shut the door, steered them both towards the bed, then shoved Morgan onto the mattress and immediately clambered on top of her. Instead of trying to process what the hell had happened, Morgan let go of everything and threw herself into the moment. There was a gorgeous woman on top of her, and they were about to have sex… what else mattered?

Riya's beautiful brown eyes glinted with mischief as she looked down at Morgan, and Morgan couldn't stop the lascivious grin from taking over her lips. "You're fucking gorgeous."

Riya's response was to lean down, covering Morgan's body with hers, and kiss her. Morgan kissed her back immediately, reaching up to slide her arms around the Canarian's neck and pull her closer. Already, their hips were grinding together, and Morgan moved her legs so they could rub their heated crotches on the other's thigh as their tongues tangled.

And tangle they did. Riya had an incredibly talented mouth; soft lips, agile tongue, wicked moves. They pressed and licked and sucked and caressed until they had to break away to pull in a dizzying breath. Then they repeated the process, their movements becoming ever more frantic, bucking against each other's legs, eager for friction on their clits and cunts, their lips mashing together, teeth clashing. The room filled with the sound of feminine grunting and groaning, gasping.

The next time they came up for air, Morgan grasped Riya and flipped them over so she was on top. She couldn't remember the last time she'd been this hot for someone, and she had to exercise all her self-restraint not to tear both their clothes off and dive between those beautiful olive thighs. Much as she wanted to, she didn't want to rush things, either, and have it all be over too soon.

After moving in for another pussy-soaking, toe-curlingly erotic kiss, Morgan pulled away and stood, only to remove her boots, socks and t-shirt. Riya did the same, and the two women drank in the sight of each other as more skin became revealed.

Getting in first this time, Morgan shoved Riya back onto the mattress and began using her lips, teeth and tongue to explore the flesh that had been exposed. There was the faintest taste of salt, of sweat, and Morgan lapped eagerly at the smooth, soft skin, delighting in the gasps and giggles coming from Riya as she teased her. She licked, sucked and nipped her way down Riya's throat, décolletage, lingering for a good long while on her breasts, taunting them through the material of her bra, before moving onto her toned stomach. As she explored the area just above the waistband of Riya's shorts, she caught the unmistakable scent of a wet, aroused pussy.

With a growl, Morgan immediately shuffled down the bed and made short work of removing Riya's shorts and the barely-there g-string she wore beneath it. To hell with not wanting to rush things... the best thing about being a woman, in her opinion, was the ability to have multiple orgasms. And she was sure that both of them would enjoy that particular capability in the very near future.

The tantalizing smell of Riya's cunt almost drove Morgan to distraction, but she managed to retain just enough self-control to reach up and help the other woman remove her bra. Now she was completely naked, and Morgan spent a few moments drinking in the sight of the long-limbed beauty, before pushing apart two of the limbs in question. Very lovely limbs. Now she feasted her eyes on the waxed pussy before her. With no hair to hide it, Riya's luscious sex was on full display—all swollen, pouting lips, an already distended clit, and shimmering juices covering her outer and inner labia.

With a happy hum, Morgan ran a finger up Riya's slit, gathering some of those juices, and stuck it in her mouth. Tangy, musky flavours assaulted her tongue, and she grinned widely up at Riya before settling in to taste more—directly from the source.

Before long, sexy little sounds began emanating from Riya's lips, and Morgan had to press down on her thighs to stop her from wriggling too much. Clearly she was pushing all the right buttons, so she decided to up her game. Soon, the sexy little sounds became louder moans and groans, and occasional random words in Spanish. Morgan had no idea what Riya was saying, but, given the woman's body language and the increasingly wet pussy she was licking, she had a pretty good idea.

Slipping one finger inside Riya, Morgan gasped against her wet flesh at the heat emanating from her core—it felt as hot as the lava she spoke about so often. Hot, slick, and welcoming. Adding another digit, she began pumping them in and out slowly, then faster as she continued to tease Riya's clit.

The Canarian's reactions grew wilder, more forceful. Morgan responded by angling her fingertips so she could press against Riya's G-spot as she finger-fucked her, and sucking her swollen nub into her mouth. She suspected the other woman's climax was close, and she was determined to make it good—like a volcano blowing its top.

Suddenly, Riya's hands grasped Morgan's hair, and she was pulled even harder against the Canarian's groin. She was so close that any finesse was nigh-on impossible, but apparently Riya was past finesse, past teasing. She wanted to come, and Morgan was more than happy to oblige.

Sucking and thrusting harder against Riya's respective erogenous zones, Morgan delighted in the wonderfully responsive woman beneath her; the sounds she made, the increased pressure on her scalp, the delicious juices bathing her taste buds. She'd always been a big fan of cunnilingus—both giving and receiving—but this was something else. Riya was so wild, so abandoned. Nothing like the more repressed English girls she'd been with before.

Maybe that was it—maybe it was a cultural thing. Either way, Riya was a woman Morgan would never, ever forget. And she hadn't even come yet.

Soon, though, she did. Morgan's heart pounded as Riya's body tensed, and her cunt clenched almost painfully around her fingers. But she didn't stop what she was doing—no way was she risking it now. She wanted to be absolutely sure that this beautiful creature was going to come apart beneath her.

Riya obliged like a star. With an almighty tug of Morgan's hair—which sent delicious sparks of pain dancing across her scalp—and a scream, the Canarian came. Her body undulated, her tits jiggled, and her cunt fluttered crazily around Morgan's fingers. She had, by now, had her lips shaken from Riya's clit by her jerking movements, so she could at least lift her head to enjoy the vision of the climaxing woman on her bed. And enjoy it she did. As passionate and unselfconscious in climax as she was in everything else, Riya rode out her orgasm in style.

Eventually, she stilled. Breathing heavily for a few seconds, she then seemed to summon the energy to open her eyes. With a sexy smile, she beckoned to Morgan. "Come here, Morgan. I would like to talk to you."

Talk? She'd just had what had looked like an earth-shattering orgasm, and she wanted to *talk*? Confusedly, Morgan did as she was told and scrambled up the mattress, settling down beside Riya and waiting expectantly.

It seemed the other woman had picked up on her confusion. "Don't worry, Morgan. We are not done here yet. Not even close. But I have had an idea."

"A—an idea? But you were just, we were just…" Christ! She'd thought she'd been doing a good job at pleasuring Riya, but apparently the Canarian had still had time for thinking!

Shooting her a look, Riya continued, "I had the idea while I was driving over here. But I just wanted to be sure. Of you. Am I right in thinking that you are not particularly happy in your job?"

Her lust-fogged brain struggling to work out the relevance of the question, she blurted out an honest answer. "No, not really. I'm not *un*happy, though. Just… it's not very exciting. It's just a job, something I do to earn money to pay my bills. Today, talking to you, I realised that some people are truly passionate about their work. So much so that it doesn't even seem like work. And… well, I'm jealous."

"It is as I suspected. But you *do* have passion, Morgan. I have seen it."

Heat infused Morgan's cheeks, and Riya threw her head back and laughed. "That's not what I meant! But yes, your passion was very obvious there, too. And I appreciated it, very much." She paused. "What I mean is, you are passionate about the same thing as me— volcanoes. It was that which drew me to you, and what brought us here, now. A mutual love."

Nodding slowly, Morgan said, "Yes, that's true. I've always been fascinated by them, ever since I was very young. I would love to do your job."

"And that, Morgan, is exactly what I am proposing."

"What?" The fog was clearing, but she still couldn't make sense of what Riya was saying.

"You cannot have *my* job, exactly. It is mine. And you are not qualified. But I do need an assistant. I have needed one for some time. I have the budget, but have not been able to find anyone worthy of the position. For many people, it would be just a job, as you have said about your own. I want someone who really cares about the position. So, I would like to offer it to you, if you are interested."

"Me?" The dazzling wit was back, it seemed.

"Yes, you. Now, I have made my proposal, and I want you to think about it. In the meantime, I have my energy back, and I would like to continue what we were doing…"

"But—"

Her reply was cut off by Riya's lips against hers. After an all-too-brief kiss, Riya moved away and crawled down the bed. "No more talking for now. You are in Lanzarote for a little while longer, yes? Then let me know when you have decided."

It was the nicest way anyone had ever told Morgan to shut up before. And, as Riya removed Morgan's underwear and set about returning the favour, Morgan found she had nothing to say. Nothing meaningful, anyway.

As for thinking about Riya's proposal? Not necessary—she'd already made her decision. A dull, dead-end job with no prospects, and no love life to speak of, versus an exciting job that could lead to even better things, and getting to spend a lot more time with the Canarian beauty currently between her thighs?

Well, there was absolutely no contest, was there?

SUMMER STOCK
EMILY L. BYRNE

I'd seen almost every show at the Playhouse for a week, and it wasn't because I was that big a fan of *Grease*, believe me. It also wasn't how I'd imagined this vacation would go, not by a long shot. But I was newly single and the friend who'd planned to go with me on this trip had been forced to cancel at the last minute so I was at loose ends.

In my twenties, I might have canceled the trip. But I was older and wiser now, and I knew that a good vacation package in a pleasant resort town where I could walk on the beach, and go whale watching and antiquing wasn't to be sneezed at. Or maybe I was just older and not that much wiser. Whatever the reason, I decided that some alone time would help me lose my worst memories of the breakup with Mara. The ticket to the Playhouse came with my room at the B&B and the rest was history, at least in terms of how I had spent most of my evenings and one matinee so far.

As to why I kept going back, it wasn't the pretty young blonde playing Sandy who had caught my eye, still less so the chiseled male lead. Nope, it was Rizzo, the resident Bad Girl, for me. The actress playing her was the spitting image of Liz Taylor in her salad days and I would have been more than happy to be her Richard Burton, given half a chance.

Not that I was actually making any effort to achieve that end, beyond buying a lot of tickets and putting forth a bunch of appreciative applause, of course. Younger Me would have said that I was chickening out. Older Me just didn't want to deal with the drama if she turned out to be straight.

No, that wasn't very honest; I was afraid that she'd never go for an old broad like me, even if she were available. I had twenty years on her, plus a few pounds and some wrinkles, and I just didn't have the confidence that Younger Me had possessed in abundance. Not after Mara. Even thinking about dating made me want to curl up in a little ball and hope that it went away.

No, better to just admire her performance, her black jacket, the way her sheath skirt hugged her ass... Those eyes, that voice. Okay, so maybe I had more of a crush than I wanted to admit. But since I only had two days of vacation left and one of those would be spent driving, I wasn't too worried about it going too far.

I wrinkled my nose at my book and finished my lunch. There'd be time for me to wander a little before I caught today's matinee. Though, on second thought, given the amused way the ushers watched me the last time, maybe I should take a day off.

I sighed at the thought. I had nothing waiting for me but an empty condo in Brooklyn and the job that was burning me out. Mara had even taken our cats, pointing out that since I was never home, she'd be a much better food monkey for them than I was. It still hurt like hell that she'd been right and that depressed me enough that even seeing Rizzo again wasn't as appealing as it had been a few moments before. Maybe I'd just cruise the shops on Main Street until my feet got tired instead, and then head back to the hot tub in my room. There was a movie downloaded on my laptop and a half bottle of wine in the room fridge.

I was so lost in my thoughts that I collided with another woman as I turned the corner. The shock of unexpected contact would have been enough to jolt me back to reality on its own, but the realization that I had made her drop her grocery bag put an extra layer on my embarrassment. "I'm so, so sorry! Let me help you. Is anything broken? I'll replace it," the words spilled out like I'd been bottling them up.

I was crouching on the ground next to her, reaching for an orange before it could roll away when she looked up. I fell into a pair of lively gray eyes in a too familiar face before I could stop myself. "Rizzo!" I yelped and she grinned.

"Ah, our most faithful audience member. How lovely to see you outside our humble Playhouse." The wry twist of her full lips sent a set of butterflies in a tailspin through my midsection, then downward from there.

I felt my cheeks flush and looked away as I handed her the orange. "I really enjoy your performances," I said at last. Then I reached for a package of crackers to hide my blush. A quick shake of the box told me all I needed to know. "They're broken. Let me buy you another."

She was still watching me, her expression appraising and amused, and her fingers brushed my hand as she took the crackers from me. "I'm Larissa Elton." She dropped the box in the bag, and reached out her hand to shake mine. Then she used her grip on my hand to haul me upright.

I got closer to her dazzling smile and the curves under her formfitting shirt and choked out something about oranges. Or maybe clumsiness. I felt like a teenager all over again and I couldn't say I was enjoying this particular trip down memory lane.

With a desperate effort, I stepped backward and took a deep breath. "It's wonderful to meet you. I'm Regan Brooks and I love your voice. Now, can I replace any of your groceries? Take you to coffee to make up for this disastrous first impression?"

Larissa grinned. "A cup of tea would be really nice, now that you mention it. There's a great little place around the corner, unless you had somewhere else in mind?" Dark eyebrows rose inquiringly over those amazing gray eyes and I found myself starting to spiral off into fantasy.

I made myself gesture her forward and wandered after her, my brain full of pictures of what it would be like to kiss her, to thrust my hands under her shirt, to... I bumped into her again outside the coffee shop. This time, I covered my lust and embarrassment with, "Guess I need that caffeine more than I thought I did. I'm not generally so klutzy." I could feel myself blush when she swung the door open and ushered me in with a wry smile.

The aroma of tea and coffee swept over us, warm and spicy and suggestive of far more distant climates than this little seaside resort could boast. I glanced at the menu hanging above the register and was immediately overwhelmed by the choices. The coffee drinks, I expected, though there were a few things I'd never heard of before. But the teas, in all their black, green, white and herbal glory, took me by surprise. Larissa grinned when she caught my expression. "They have an amazing selection. Do you have a kind of tea you like? Would you like me to recommend something?"

I nodded mutely, swallowing a sudden stab of despair. I didn't have a chance with her as it was, but did I have to prove myself a novice tea drinker in the bargain? Still, another glance at the options, and I decided to concede defeat and find out what she'd pick. "Yes, please. I like fruit-flavored teas."

She nodded and picked out something involving apricots and vanilla. I paid for it and added some ginger cookies on impulse while she got us a table near a window. I joined her a moment later with our tray, determined to make grownup conversation that wouldn't make me sound like more of a fool than I had already made myself appear.

"How long have you been with the Playhouse Theater?" I tried to make my tone casual, as if I hadn't gone from reading her bio in the playbill to reading her bio online. I had drawn the line at looking for online dating profiles or anything more personal than that, something I had been quite proud of. Until now. When I actually wanted to know that level of detail.

We wandered around in a maze of small talk while I entertained fantasies of running my hand up her thigh, coaxing a response from that flawless skin, that gorgeous body. I wondered if she'd smell like the leather jacket that she wore when she was playing Rizzo. While I was at it, I wondered if I could somehow get her to serenade me with a few numbers from the show.

Then I wondered how disgusted she'd be if she could read my mind. And my fantasies went up in the steam from our cups. I was here to try and make a new friend and have a nice chat, one that would ease the slight stab of loneliness I'd started to feel as my ten day vacation went on. Looking into Larissa's gray eyes, I found myself hoping that this would be the best summer vacation friendship ever. I did my best to ignore the stab of desire that radiated up from my pussy.

She had to leave much sooner than I wanted to see her go, especially after she leaned over and squeezed my arm, her thigh brushing against my leg under the table. She got close enough that I could smell lavender soap and something that reminded me of lemongrass. I was pretty sure that I smelled like pure lust and wondered if it was a giant cloud surrounding me. If so, she didn't give any sign of it, and even invited me to join the cast and crew for a party after tonight's performance.

My brain said that wasn't a great idea, that I'd feel

like a fifth wheel, that I needed my rest. But my brain wasn't making my decisions for me today, and what came out of my mouth was, "Yes, that sounds like fun. I'll just hang around after the show tonight, then?"

She told me that she'd let the house manager know and that she looked forward to seeing me later. I realized that I was watching her ass as she walked away and made myself bury my face in my tea and my book. Then, I flipped the book back to the sex scene I had read last night and enjoyed it again, letting my imagination populate the page with Larissa and me, letting my nose fill with her remembered scent, my mouth fill with her imagined taste.

I stopped short of ducking into the bathroom to live out my fantasies, choosing to let everything get all warm and moist and squirmy as I sat there, looking prim and proper and middle-aged with my tea. I hadn't felt this way in ages and I'd missed it. If I got nothing else from this vacation but rest and lust, it would be a summer to remember.

I drifted off to the B&B and grabbed an early dinner with a nice straight couple I'd met at breakfast. We made small talk about antiques and local vineyards while I channeled all my fantasies, my longing, my nerves, into amiable normality. It was next to impossible to sit with Ellen and Chad and think racy thoughts.

They went back to their room, leaving me standing outside the theater. The realization that I was going to see her again clobbered me. Did she have a lover in the cast? Would I find out? For a moment, I just wanted to turn away, to keep my fantasies intact. Why end this lovely vacation on a disappointed note?

But what if she was single? What if she liked me, as in *liked* me? I'd promised myself that I would try new things, be open to possibilities, after Mara left. I walked slowly up to the box office with a smile on my lips and nerves tingling throughout my body. "Should be a full house tonight. Larissa told me to save the last ticket for you." The usher at the box office smiled cheerfully at me as she pushed the ticket over to me.

I took it and swallowed, hard. I made myself smile back at her before I followed the crowd into the theater. Somehow, I was going to enjoy a reasonably good production of a musical... that I'd seen seven times in the last week. I was starting to hum the songs in the shower, which was much less enjoyable than other things I was doing in there while thinking about Rizzo.

I settled into my seat with a sigh and remembered that I was going to get to watch Larissa again and that was worth the earwormy songs that would be in my head for hours to come. And she delivered. This was the company's second to last performance and she gave it everything she had: hot, angry, fierce Rizzo, at her most memorable. In fact, she put so much sexy into her role that she gave me what might have been hot flashes off and on for the whole last hour.

I sat through the curtain calls and stayed put as the theater emptied out. My stomach squirmed with nerves and even a quick run to the restroom and the judicious application of cold water to my overheated face didn't settle it. But I made myself go out anyway and walked down the line of cast members in the lobby congratulating them on their performances.

Larissa gave me a devilish grin. "Best one so far? Excellent. Give me fifteen minutes and we can head down to the beach." She did a quick pose for a photographer, then vanished, leaving me to chat with the crew and sundry partners and relatives.

The sidelong appraising glances didn't do much for my stage fright. I could feel their thoughts. Aunt? Family friend? Sugar momma? Pretty much anything except girlfriend, or even lover. It depressed me, that litany of things I might be, but wasn't. I thought about claiming I had a headache and going back to the B&B. But then what? I wanted something more, something different. Something potentially hotter than a warm bath and a hot toddy.

By the time Larissa came back, I'd dug in my heels and was talking shop with the stage manager. True, I hadn't stage-managed a play since college, but I still knew some of the terms, and she was happy to share some new ones with me. Quite happy in fact, though that didn't occur to me until Larissa walked up. "Thanks for keeping my friend entertained, Beth. Learn any new tricks?" The last comment came my way on a wave of rippling tension.

I said something noncommittal and gave Beth another once-over. Short-cropped hair, earrings running all the way around her ear, a couple of visible tattoos and a look of frustrated desire that sent warm tingles down my thighs. Interesting. And, oh, so relatable! I wondered if I was looking at Larissa the same way. I hoped not; I obviously hadn't been at it as long.

Larissa was determined to ignore her, even going so far as to tuck her arm through mine and tow me away. The contact of her body against mine drove Beth clear out of my mind and I found myself laughing at Larissa's jokes, even the ones I couldn't remember. The pressure of her arm, her hip, her thigh against mine trailed fire down my skin and I wanted her naked in my bed. Or in my car. I wasn't that fussy.

Somewhere in that whirl of fantasies and lust, I became sure that Larissa was interested in me, at least for tonight. And that might be enough for a summer fling, enough to call this a real vacation, the kind my friends thought I needed, but wouldn't just tell me to take. But I was torn, pulled apart between conflicting desires. I could attempt to work my wiles on the beautiful young actress and see where it went or I could enjoy a nice sedate mature lustful, yet unfulfilled, crush.

Larissa decided it for me. One minute, I was sitting around a roaring bonfire on a beach, drinking beer from a bottle and talking to the actors from the Playhouse, the next, I was taking a walk down the beach with Larissa. The moon had just risen over the horizon and the waves created a music all their own, and it was enough to make me giddy and let my guard down. The first kiss was tentative and lovely and sweet. The second one had a lot more oomph and tongue to it.

And things progressed from there. I pulled her up close to me, pressing against her until she pulled me down and we both got mouthfuls of sand. No one ever talks about all the sand when they talk about sex on the beach. Sand in your mouth, your hair, your unmentionables. And I remembered why now.

Larissa's tongue scraped down my neck and she turned her head aside and spat. Our eyes met and we both started laughing. "This always sounds so hot and intense in pop tunes. The beach, the moonlight, though. Makes me want to break into song. Shall I serenade you with something from the show or have you had too much of that this week? What's your favorite song?" She grinned at me, adjusting her arms around my waist and tilting her head back.

"Ooh, do *There are Worse Things I Could Do*! I love that one!" I gushed like the fangirl I was. And it was true; she sang it with verve and skill and it sent chills down my spine every time. Especially when I changed the lyrics from "boys" to "girls" in my head every time I heard it.

It was as if she read my mind. She crooned it into my ear until I nearly shuddered with pleasure at the sound of her voice, the warmth of her breath on my skin. And she changed the lyrics, just the way I hoped she would. We rocked together back and forth, breathing in the salt waves and the warm air and the beautiful sound of her voice.

I might have fallen in love, a little, at that moment. Even though I knew it couldn't really be love, not with someone I barely knew. But it was lust and like and comfort and desire and longing and far, far more than I had hoped to find on this vacation. Larissa crooned the song to its end and nibbled on my ear, sending shivers down my spine. "I love the way the moon glints in your hair," she murmured.

"It's all the gray," I said, without thinking. I cursed myself for reminding her about the difference in our ages, like maybe she'd have forgotten under the influence of the moonlight and the waves. I almost had. I was feeling younger tonight than I had in years, at least up until now.

"If you're fretting about being older than me, don't. I like older women. Sophisticated, smart, sexy and with excellent taste in musical theater, that's what I like." Larissa tilted my face so she could look into my eyes. "You hear what I'm saying?"

"It's not the hearing, it's the believing," I found myself responding. "But I do like hearing it. You are the most gorgeous and talented woman I've met in ages." I stroked her cheek with one finger, admiring its perfect curve like she was a work of art. "You should be on Broadway."

"I like the way you think," Larissa purred into my ear, then nipped my earlobe between her teeth, sending a wave of heat through me that made me want to strip off all my clothes and hers, too. We could run into the waves and make furious love like something out of an old movie. Just the thought was enough to make me feel like a new woman.

"I love your laugh lines. I think experience is hot." And my fantasy of recovered youth went up in smoke. She must have felt me pull away because she murmured something that might have been an apology. Then, as if she'd been reading my mind, "Can you swim? If we go down past that outcrop, we can go in and they won't be able to see much from the bonfire."

"Much?" I didn't want them seeing anything. I wasn't even sure I wanted Larissa seeing anything, either. Unless it was her own gorgeous curves in the moonlight.

Larissa laughed, a low sexy growl of a chuckle. "There are currents out there. We don't want to be completely out of sight, unless you want to go back to your room. I've got a roommate; makes it easier to afford to do theater in the sticks."

There was something she wasn't saying and I mentally penciled in that her roommate was Beth, and that Beth had been more than a roommate. Maybe still was, but I wasn't sure how much I cared. I gestured down the beach and bowed with a grin of my own. We didn't have to go far out into the water, after all. Just enough to be bold, to be daring. To get in touch with my inner Rizzo.

Or to get in touch with her outer Rizzo, if that came first. I started giggling as we trotted around the rocks and she laughed with me. We were both laughing as I tugged off her shirt and she yanked mine up and our skin was hot and soft against each other. And our mouths were hot and everywhere.

Clothes went flying in all directions, even the bra and panty set that I'd bought new and was really going to want to put back on later. The sand still warm between our toes as we walked, or rather, rolled into the surf. The cold shock of the waves, was another story, for the first few minutes, at least. But then it was gone, overwhelmed in a flood of other sensations, as we tumbled into the water.

Larissa rolled me over so I was on top, and buried her tongue in my mouth. Our thighs twisted together, rubbing skin against skin, nerve endings against nerve endings, until there was only the slightest of differences between our wetness and the wetness flowing over us. Then, her fingers were between my legs and I could feel my back arch as I rode her touch.

I ground my hips against her, laughing and gasping as a wave swept over us, filling our open mouths with warm salt water. "You are so beautiful," Larissa whispered against my skin as she drove her fingers deeper inside, thrusting, rubbing, coaxing. I rocked and rode and tried to slip my fingers inside her only to have her move away. "You first." She ran her tongue down my neck and my back arched as I shook and groaned my release into her arms.

Just in time for a big wave to drench us both. We came up sputtering and laughing and coughing. I rolled us over a few times so that we were more on shore than in the surf and stroked her cheek. "I could get to like this."

Larissa laughed. "I think that you already do." I growled in response and lowered my face to her breasts. Her nipple was hard in my mouth as I tongued it against my front teeth. I pressed until she dug her fingers into my scalp, then switched to the other breast, sucking and nipping until her hips were rocking against me, begging for release. I lowered my mouth into the salty sweetness between her legs and sucked her flesh, caressing every nerve I could find with my tongue.

She rocked up into me, thighs twisting and wrapping around my shoulders. I felt her legs go rigid, then her entire body convulse in release, once, then again a few minutes later. But when I went to try to coax a third orgasm from her, she caught my face and pulled me up to her mouth for a long, hot kiss.

I laughed when we broke off the kiss, grinning at the moon, the waves, Larissa. Beth, when her face loomed up above us like a second moon. Until she kicked sand at us both before storming off in tears. I wiped the sand from my face and grimaced at Larissa. "Just how much of an 'ex' is she?"

"A lot more of one than she likes, unfortunately. We broke up two months ago, but I couldn't afford to move, and she said I didn't have to. Guess we know how that's working out. I'm so sorry about this." Larissa wiped her face and sat up, her eyes going hard and Rizzo-like for a moment as she looked after Beth.

Then, I ran my hand up the silky skin over her ribs and her face softened again. "How about we go back to my room? I'll fix it up with the innkeeper in the morning."

Even as I said it, I could tell the mood was lost. A string of emotions crossed her face in the moonlight and I could see her settle on graceful brushoff, then hesitate and reconsider. I wondered if I should say anything to convince her, tell her that this was just for the night. Because it was, wasn't it? And I was okay with that. Maybe.

It was just that it was disappointing watching her pull back and away. I wasn't looking to get married or move in or anything, but maybe coming to every performance of *Grease* for a week wasn't sending that message. "Look—," I started.

"I—," Larissa gave me a sidelong grin and reached for her clothes. "You first."

"I don't want to give you the wrong impression." I reached over for my own clothes. "I'm not looking for... I mean, it would be nice if... but... this is going fabulously." The last part popped out of my mouth spontaneously, the way the rest of it was refusing to do. Sigh. It was easy to see I hadn't dated for a while. "What I'm trying to say is that I'm not a stalker or about to announce that I'm madly in love with you or anything like that. I do think you're beautiful and talented and I'm thrilled that we got to have fun doing... this." I ended with a vague gesture at the beach and the waves and our abraded skin.

"Me, too. Even though I have to go back to my apartment and deal with Beth. But this was totally worth it. Thank you." She reached over and squeezed my arm. "This is the most fun I've had in months." She finished getting dressed and gave me another long look. "And I think that maybe I'd like to start over and get to know you better. How about lunch tomorrow?"

"I have to head out around noon to drive home. Not a lot of time for starting over," I said regretfully, trying to cover up my sudden flair of dismay at losing this chance. "I have to be back at work on Monday." I scrambled back into my sandy clothes and wished that I hadn't. It was going to be a long, itchy walk back to the B&B. And that was just the state of my clothes.

"Breakfast? I really want to see you again before you go. There's something I'd like to tell you, but I want to check my email first. You know how you mentioned Broadway..." She hesitated and I saw her catch her lower lip in her teeth. "I mean, unless you're just being polite and you don't want to see me again?"

My heart melted, terror at being rejected shedding itself along with any other lingering concerns about our ages. "I'm not sure that I'm ever that polite. Is the email about a part?" She nodded and I kissed her enthusiastically. "That's great! I'll hope for good news tomorrow." I beamed at her and we made a date. Her answering grin was enough to make me risk a goodnight kiss, molding our bodies together once again before I walked off to the B&B and she went back to the bonfire to say goodnight to the other actors.

It wasn't until I was falling asleep in a blur of fantasies later that night that it struck me: this was what it felt like to have possibilities. Hope, even. It was something I hadn't felt for a long time, long enough that I almost didn't recognize it. I didn't know what kind of news she'd have in the morning, but my stomach whirled with butterflies and heat and an utterly glorious crush. And who knew where it was all going to lead? Larissa wanted to see me again and there was a chance of something more. I hummed her song from *Grease* as I drifted off into sweet dreams.

M I S T R E S S
BROOKE WINTERS

She looked different without the leather and the whip and the six inch heels. She wore her hair loose and it fell in soft blond curls to her shoulders. It was nothing like the severe ponytail that I was used to. She was sporting a pink bikini, so different to her usual black. Although I guess maybe the pink bikini was her usual wear, at least on holiday, and the black leather was just something she wore to James's private parties.

I recognised her immediately. Even though I had only met her a few times before, there was no mistaking her. I would recognise Mistress Marie in a dark room.

I'd barely spoken to the woman. She left me so flustered that it was all that I could usually do to greet her politely. I always knew when she was at a party. Even without seeing her I would always know that she was there. It was as though, when it came to her, I had some kind of sixth sense.

I paused at the entrance to the pool area when I sensed her. I knew that I must be mistaken, that she couldn't possibly be here in Spain. Still, I looked around. Just in case. And sure enough, there she was. Not just there at the pool, but sitting with my friends.

"What are you doing?" Erin asked me when she arrived at the pool. I'd been in such a rush to get as much sun as possible that I had left her in the room because she was taking too long to decide which bikini to wear.

"Just looking for a sun bed," I lied. "I think we're

out of luck. Maybe we should try the beach."

"Kit and Lily have already saved some for us," she replied. "Where are... Ah, there they are."

I followed Erin to our friends. To Marie. I wished with every step that I could turn around. That I could get back on a flight to London. But that would look silly. I would just have to get through this morning and then avoid her.

I kept my eyes to the ground as I walked. The last thing I wanted was to trip over in front of Marie. I wished desperately that I had worn a one-piece or that I had a t-shirt or something to wear over my bikini top. If only I was wearing a corset. It would tuck me in in all the right places and make it look like I had cleavage.

When we got to the sun beds, Erin took the one next to Kit and I was left standing with nowhere to sit. So much for saving us both sun beds. I could feel the panic beginning to settle in my stomach, work its way up my chest to my throat. I looked around for an exit, any way to leave the situation without looking like a complete twat.

"I've got you a sun bed here," Marie said, indicating the lounger on the other side of her—away from my friends.

"Thank you," I mumbled as I settled myself on it.

"Sorry," Kit said. "Marie, this is Erin and you know Danielle, don't you?"

"Nice to meet you, Erin," Marie said. "Good to see you again, Danielle."

"You too," I muttered.

Marie turned onto her side to look at me. I tried not to let my gaze linger on her chest but it was difficult. I dragged my eyes up to her face and found her grinning at me.

"I didn't realise you knew Kit and Lily," I said.

"We were at uni together. In fact, it was Kit who

introduced me to James. You left early last week."

I shrugged. I didn't want to explain to her that I was sick of watching her spank other women. Or that since she had started attending, I hadn't wanted to play with anyone else. When Marie was in a room everyone else may as well have disappeared.

"A shrug isn't an answer," Marie said.

"You didn't ask a question," I responded and then felt my cheeks burn as I realised how insolent my comment was.

Except we weren't at a play party, we were on holiday. And she wasn't my Domme.

"Why did you leave the party so early, Danielle?"

I dropped my gaze. It was difficult to maintain eye contact with her when she fixed me with that serious stare.

"I just wanted to go home." When Marie didn't respond I said, "I don't think it's my kind of thing."

"I was under the impression that you've been attending regularly since before I started going."

I wanted the conversation to end. A voice in my head told me that it was none of her business and that I should just tell her to drop it. Instead I said, "I wouldn't call myself a regular. I just go sometimes."

"Even though it's not your thing?"

"I don't go for sex," I blurted out and immediately wished that I could take back the words. "I mean…" I stumbled on. "It's not like… I just—"

I could feel tears pricking at my eyelids and my cheeks burned hotter than ever. I couldn't believe that I had made such a fool of myself in front of Marie.

This is why I left early, I wanted to tell her. *I can't talk to you.*

I didn't trust my ability to walk away from her any more than I trusted my ability to talk to her, so I didn't do either. I shut up and closed my eyes, hoping that when

I opened them she would have turned her attention somewhere else and I could just slip away and spend the rest of my life avoiding her.

I felt her hand on my arm before she said, "You're looking for something."

It wasn't a question, but I answered anyway. "In the wrong place."

"That depends on what you're looking for."

"I don't know what I'm looking for," I lied.

I opened my eyes to look at her. She smiled and I found myself smiling back.

"I don't think that's true," she said. "I think you know exactly what you're looking for. Have dinner with me tonight."

"Dinner?"

Marie sat up and leaned over. She whispered, "I plan to at least buy you dinner before I tie you up and fuck you."

* * *

I was 30 and I had never been on a date. I'd had girlfriends, of course. One-night stands and fuck buddies. I'd played with dominants at James's party, though it was never sexual. But I had never been on a date. And it wasn't like I had packed for it either. I had clothes for a week sitting by a swimming pool. I made do with one of the dresses that I had packed for the evening, wishing that I had brought something a little more glamorous.

As I made my way down to the lobby to meet Marie, I wondered if she really intended to tie me up tonight. The thought excited *and* terrified me. My heart seemed to beat erratically as the lift descended and I felt butterflies flutter in my stomach.

She was waiting for me in the lobby and I felt my breath catch when she turned towards me. She smiled and I smiled back at her, my cheeks heating as they always seemed to do when she was around.

She walked towards me and when we met, she kissed my cheek. "You look beautiful," she told me. I wanted to return the compliment, but I couldn't seem to make my voice work.

She escorted me out of the hotel and we walked the short distance to the restaurant, her hand on my back. We made polite conversation about how lovely the weather had been and what the others intended to do with the evening but all I could think about was what would happen later. Was she really interested in me?

By the time the waiter brought our wine and took our food order, I was feeling calmer. Not entirely at ease but confident that I could at least have a conversation with Marie.

"James told me you're a barrister," Marie said. "What kind of law do you practice?"

She probably doesn't believe it, I thought. *Or she thinks I'm the most incompetent barrister in the history of the bar. The kind who can't even string a sentence together.*

"Family law," I told her. "What do you do?"

"I lecture in Social Policy."

"That sounds interesting," I said honestly.

"It is, but I want to hear about you," she reached across the table and took my hand. "You said earlier that you don't have sex at James's parties."

I could feel the blush rushing up my face. Heat engulfed my body. I had hoped that we could forget about my earlier comments. "No," I mumbled and dropped my gaze.

"I prefer it if you look at me when I'm talking to you," Marie said. I dragged my gaze back up to her face and she rewarded me with a smile and a squeeze of my hand. "BDSM isn't sexual for you?"

"Not with men," I told her. "And all of the women at James's parties are submissive or straight."

"I'm neither submissive nor straight."

I nodded and went to lower my gaze again but caught myself. I was well aware that she was a dominant woman interested in other women. I had watched her spank, flog and finger other women. I had watched other women worship her while I did so silently, from afar.

"You've avoided me," Marie stated. "Yet you accepted my invitation tonight which makes me think that I'm not wrong to think that you might be interested in me."

My face burned and I felt like I was in flames. I didn't say anything.

"I think that a highly regarded barrister would be able to say no to a date that she wasn't interested in so that makes me wonder, why have you been avoiding me, Danielle? Why did I have to fly out to Spain just to get you to talk to me?"

"I've talked to you before," I responded.

"Barely."

"You're always with other women."

"I always come to you first and you always make an excuse to be anywhere else."

"I'm sorry. I don't know…" I could feel myself getting flustered again. I could feel the words seeping out of my head as I tried to string a sentence together.

"You don't need to apologise. I just want to know if I'm wasting my time chasing you. Am I?"

I shook my head. "No. You're not wasting your time. I—I haven't had much luck with Dommes," I said. And then I found myself telling her everything. I told her about my ex cheating on me and the string of women I had played with since then who didn't know the meaning of aftercare. "I prefer to play with the dominants at James's and know that I will be taken care of after, even if they are all men," I finished. "The sex isn't that important anyway."

She had listened throughout, never once

interrupting me. Suddenly I felt vulnerable. I couldn't believe that I had shared it all with her.

"Sorry," I said quickly. "I shouldn't have told you all of that…"

"I'm glad you did." She lifted my hand to her lips and kissed it. "I haven't had much luck either. My exes were all either vanilla or not into monogamy."

"And you are? Into monogamy, I mean." I had seen her with so many women that I wasn't sure. My heart sped up in anticipation for her answer.

"Yes, I am. I require total fidelity from my partners. Are you?"

"Yes. I don't like to share."

We spoke for hours about mutual friends, films, music, museums. I was surprised by how easy she was to talk to, pleased by how much we had in common. It was easy to feel comfortable with her, easy to forget that she was a Domme.

After the meal, we walked back to the hotel and I could feel the butterflies returning to my stomach.

"Will you come back to my room?" she asked as we approached the elevator.

"Yes," I managed to squeak out.

She put her hand on my back and guided me into the lift and then down a corridor.

I kept up a nervous chatter as we walked to her room. "Emily, Jane and Jess are arriving tomorrow," I said. "And on Saturday there are six of Erin's friends coming. At this rate, we'll have the whole hotel."

"A lesbian invasion," she joked. "Didn't Emily and Jane just have a baby?"

"They're bringing her," I replied.

It felt like the longest corridor ever created. Like I had walked into some kind of parallel universe of never ending hotel doors. We finally got to Marie's and into her room.

I didn't have time to feel nervous, to wonder what I should do, where I should sit.

"Take a seat on the sofa," she said. "Make yourself comfortable. Would you like some water? Tea?"

"No wine?"

"I think you've had enough wine for what I have planned."

My heart thudded in my chest, excitement and nerves settled in my stomach.

"What have you got planned?"

She gave me a wicked smile. "Do you really want to know?"

I nodded as she took the seat next to me. She leaned towards me and captured my lips with hers. I melted into the kiss, opened my mouth to let her in.

She pulled back and said, "Pick a safe word."

I told her my safe word and she caught my lips in another kiss, this one harder, more demanding. I could feel myself getting wet just from her kisses.

"First," she said when she pulled away again, "I'm going to tie you up." She ran her hand down my neck and settled on my breast, gently brushing my nipple over my dress. "Then I'm going to play with these gorgeous tits of yours, I'm going to suck them and squeeze them and bite them." I moaned as the pleasure pooled in my pussy. "You're going to lick my pussy. Would you like that?"

"Yes," I said breathlessly. "Please. Please, let me lick your pussy."

"I love it when you beg. I think I'll let you beg some more. Get on your knees."

I obeyed immediately, dropping to my knees in front of her. She pulled her skirt up slowly, revealing inch after inch of her long legs. She pulled her panties aside, exposing the place that I desperately wanted to kiss.

"Beg," she said. "Beg me for the pleasure to eat my pussy."

"Please," I said. "Please, let me eat your pussy. Please, let me lick you."

She grabbed the back of my head and pulled it between her legs. I reached out my tongue tentatively and licked her clitoris. She let out a moan and I eagerly lapped at her pussy. I let her wetness coat my tongue, satisfied that I had caused it. That she was aroused by me.

"One finger," she told me and I slid a finger into her. "Keep licking. Don't stop."

She moaned my name as I licked her to orgasm and then gently pushed my head away from her.

"Stand up." I stood. "Remove your dress."

Suddenly nervous, I let my dress slide to the floor and stepped out of it. Uncertainty filled me as she stared at me.

"Remove the bra and panties." I removed them. "You look beautiful."

I felt myself blush and lowered my gaze.

"Get on the bed, on your back."

I did as she asked and she secured my arms and legs to the bed with scarves. She climbed onto me, straddling my waist. She leaned down and kissed me again. Her hands found my nipples and pinched them. Pleasure and pain flared. She kissed her way down my neck and her lips found one of my nipples. She licked at it before engulfing it in her mouth.

"Please," I begged, unsure if I was begging her to stop or to keep going.

I whimpered when she pulled away from me. She turned herself around and offered her pussy to my mouth. I licked and lapped at her wetness. When she lowered her mouth to my pulsing clit the pleasure shot through me and I cried out. I felt her add one finger and then another as I continued to lick her. I screamed out my orgasm and felt myself drift away, light-headed and floating. I felt her move from on top of me but I was floating on ecstasy and couldn't muster the energy to open my eyes.

I felt her thrust into me a minute later. She whispered the dirtiest things while she fucked me, telling me that I was her slut, that she would use me in any way she wanted to.

Afterwards, she untied me. I didn't move. I was still floating on the high of her dominance, on the thrill of submitting. She kissed my eyelids, my cheeks, my lips. She pulled the sheets down and I mustered the energy to lift myself so that she could pull the blankets over me. She climbed under and pulled me into her arms. I leaned my head against her breasts and smiled.

"Thank you," I murmured.

"You were perfect."

I felt myself drift off into sleep and as I did I thought I heard her say, "My perfect submissive."

* * *

The week seemed to go by too quickly. Marie and I alternated our days between the beach and the pool. At night, we would have dinner, sometimes alone, sometimes with friends, and then retreat to her room. We discovered a shared love of bad American reality shows and good wine.

I remember the first night we watched television together. She took a seat on the sofa and placed a pillow on the floor at her feet. I lowered myself to the cushion and rested my head on her knee. As she tangled her fingers through my hair I felt perfectly comfortable, perfectly content. Occasionally, she would ask me to sit next to her so that she could hold me, but I felt happiest at her feet.

Despite the power exchange, things felt relaxed. We would laugh together, talk together. She was interested in my opinions, my experiences. I think perhaps it was because of the power exchange that I felt so relaxed. I didn't have to worry about anything. She would make the decisions. She would choose when I stopped drinking. She would decide when I'd had enough chocolate. All I had to do was obey and I was happy to do that.

By the last evening, we still hadn't discussed the future. We hadn't discussed what would happen when we got back to London. I was trying not to think about it. I didn't want to imagine what I would do when I saw her with some other woman at a party. In fact, I was pretty sure I wouldn't go back to one.

At dinner, I couldn't think of anything else. I kept imagining her with a slim blonde woman I had watched her spank at a previous party. I kept imagining her being polite to me, acting like I was just an acquaintance.

All evening, I could feel tears pricking at my eyelids. I struggled to force my lips into a smile. When the waiter brought the wrong dessert I waved him back over.

"This is not what I ordered," I told him.

"I am sorry, I will…"

"It's not difficult to deliver the right dessert."

"Danielle," Marie warned. "Apologise."

"For what?" I snapped. "I didn't give *him* the wrong dessert."

"I'm sorry for her behaviour," Marie said. "Please, just bring us the bill."

"I'm sorry," the waiter replied. "You will not be charged for the dessert."

"Please don't apologise," Marie said. "Danielle is the one who should apologise to you and please do charge us for the dessert. It's not the restaurant's fault that we are leaving early."

She paid and as we walked out of the restaurant I could feel the anger seep away, leaving the familiar feeling of guilt and another, less familiar one. An anxiety. A feeling that I had let her down, that Marie would be disappointed in me.

"I would like to apologise to him," I said quietly.

"Good," Marie said.

She walked me back to the waiter and I apologised to him for being rude.

As we made our way to our hotel I said, "I'm sorry for the way that I behaved."

"We will discuss it in our room."

I felt a tear leak out of my eye. I had disappointed her. I had ruined our last night together. She would always remember me as the sub who was rude to waiters.

"You can cry all you like," she told me. "That won't get you out of your punishment."

"Punishment?"

"Of course. What do you think happens to submissives when they misbehave?"

My mind raced as fear and misery warred inside me. How would she punish me? What would happen after she punished me? Would she send me away? How could I make it up to her? I had already apologised.

The walk to our room seemed to take longer than usual. In the time it took us to get there I had already imagined a dozen different scenarios involving Marie breaking up with me.

When we got to the room she ordered me to take my clothes off. I did as she asked, hoping that my obedience, my submission, could somehow undo what I had done. That she would smile at me again, stroke my hair, kiss me. Maybe if I took whatever punishment she had to give me, that would be enough.

I didn't believe it, though. I had messed up, made her angry.

I stood in front of her, naked and unsure of what to do next. I had never felt so vulnerable. My heart hurt as I stared at the floor, waiting for her to say something. It seemed like I stared at that floor for hours while she stood in front of me saying nothing.

"I am so disappointed in you," she finally said, her voice soft.

"I'm sorry." I wanted to beg her for forgiveness. I wanted to tell her that I would be a better person, that she could make me a better person.

"Do not speak unless I ask you to. Your behaviour in the restaurant was unacceptable. Do you want to tell me what was wrong with you in there?"

"He brought the wrong dessert and it made me angry," I whispered the words past the lump in my throat.

"You reacted like that because he brought you the wrong cake? Really?"

I nodded. I wasn't going to tell her that I loved her, that the thought of being apart from her, of not being her submissive, was killing me. It would only make it more difficult, for both of us, when she rejected me later.

I watched her feet move away from me, worried that this was it. That my punishment was over. I could feel panic clenching around my aching heart.

"Come here," Marie said.

Relieved more than scared, I looked up to find her sitting on the sofa. I walked towards her.

"Over my knee," she said.

I felt myself flush with humiliation, but I did as she asked, hoping that I looked more graceful than I felt.

Her hand came down on my ass. I whimpered at the sting, but she didn't stop. She rained down blow after blow, occasionally stopping to stroke my abused flesh.

"I'm sorry," I sobbed as the punishment continued. "I didn't mean to disappoint you."

"Shush. You've already apologised. You are not to talk during your punishment."

I didn't say anything further. I didn't tell her how desperate I was to make it up to her, that I would do anything to make things better between us, that I would do anything to please her. That I would *be* anything she wanted me to be.

The tears continued to fall as Marie spanked me.

I didn't notice at first that she had stopped. The sting dulled to a warm ache and Marie's fingers traced circles around my ass cheeks. She ran her hand up and down my back and it was then that I realised that it was over. That my punishment was done.

That *we* were done?

The tears had slowed, but they came back in full force at the thought that it was all over. I began to sob and Marie ran a soothing hand over my hair. She helped me up, off of her lap and I slid to my knees. I let my head hang, not wanting her to see my tear-stained face, and waited for her to dismiss me.

"Come here," she told me. I looked up at her and she held her arms out to me. I scrambled up onto the sofa and let her pull me into a hug.

"It's okay," she told me. "Your punishment's over. You took it well. It's all okay now."

I let her hold me against her chest as I cried, her hands running soothingly over my arms.

"Will you tell me what's wrong?" she asked after a while.

"I'm going to miss you," I blurted out.

"Miss me?" She sounded confused. I didn't look up at her. I didn't want to see pity in her eyes when she realised that I had imagined a future with her and she had just seen me as a holiday romance.

"I'm sorry that I ruined our last night."

"You didn't ruin it, pet." She continued to stroke my hair. "All subs need a little discipline now and then. Next time you do that you won't have an orgasm for a week. Do you understand?"

"Next time we'll be back in London."

"Are you expecting this to become vanilla when we

get home? I thought we were both clear on what kind of relationship this was going to be."

I pulled back to look up at her. She reached out and ran a finger down the wet tracks on my cheek.

"I didn't realise that you wanted this to continue."

"What?" Marie frowned at me.

"Well, you haven't mentioned anything about when we get home and I know that there's a lot more choice back in London and that you have all those other subs from James's parties and I don't expect…"

"Danielle, I've chosen you. I flew out to Spain to be with you."

"You did?"

"Did you think it was a coincidence that I happened to be on holiday with your friends?"

I nodded.

"James suggested it. Danielle, I've wanted you from the minute I met you. There aren't any other subs for me. I just want you. I love you."

The tightness around my heart dispersed and I felt my heart flutter like it was coming back to life. "I love you too."

She leaned down and kissed me. When she pulled back she smiled.

"When we get home, I'm going to buy you the prettiest collar. Something discrete and beautiful."

I couldn't stop a smile from spreading across my face. "I can't wait to wear your collar."

"Then you need to start calling me Mistress."

"My Mistress," I said.

"All yours, pet," she replied. "Only yours."

I snuggled back into her arms, content in the knowledge that she was as much mine as I was hers.

My Mistress.

A GOOD READ

RJ LAYER

Popular lesbian romance writer Bryce Kaylin dabbed perspiration from her brow as she stepped into the long line waiting to check in at the Royal Suites Plaza Hotel. *Who's hare-brained idea was it anyway to have the Romance Writers Conference in Dallas in the middle of summer?*

At ninety-eight degrees it was literally hotter than blue blazes. A trickle of sweat raced between her breasts. The temperature had been a very pleasant twenty degrees cooler when she'd departed her Minneapolis suburb of Richfield. She dabbed again at her damp forehead as she stepped up to the counter and faced an African-American woman with a wide welcoming smile.

"Good evening, Ma'am, how can I help you?"

"I have a reservation. Kaitlyn Bryce."

Sherise, as her name tag read, tapped beautiful French tipped nails on the keyboard. "Here we go." Within seconds she reached down and pulled a sheet off the printer. "Oh, I see you were updated to a late arrival. I hope your delays haven't ruined any of your scheduled trip." She slid the paper across the counter pointing out the signature line.

"Well, I'm here," Kaitlyn said with exhaustion. "Although, I'm sure I missed the 'get acquainted' cocktail party."

Sherise narrowed an eye. "If you're with the writers conference, I believe they're still tipping them back in the Kennedy room."

Kaitlyn scratched her signature.

"I can hold your suitcase if you want to pop in now. I'm here until eleven."

Kaitlyn looked down at her rumpled blouse and Capri pants with a frown. There was someone she was hoping to catch up with before tomorrow. "That would be lovely. I think I'll take you up on your offer." She gave a tired smile.

Stepping away from the check-in desk Kaitlyn's eyes fell on a most attractive androgynous creature seated at the bar across the large lobby. The stranger quickly averted her gaze and turned back to the counter. Kaitlyn gave a sideways glance as she passed the bar on her way to the cocktail party. Definitely attractive.

* * *

Inside the Kennedy room, which was only a part of the larger conference area that would be transformed tomorrow for the writers and publishers, Kaitlyn plucked her blouse away from her chest to allow the cool air to dry her skin. Tomorrow in this space they would have tables at which to sell their books, do author signings and then later the area would essentially become a ballroom where awards were presented followed by a social event that would include book professionals and their readership. The previous conferences Kaitlyn had attended gave her an emotional boost she couldn't find anywhere else. There was something so inspiring about connecting with the fans of her novels.

Her eyes continued to roam the room looking for her old college chum. She heard Sarah's Texas drawl before she saw her and gravitated in that direction. Talking, laughing and tipping back a cocktail with a group of what appeared to be lesbians. If they weren't, well then Kaitlyn knew her gaydar needed to be tuned up. She managed to catch Sarah's attention as she approached.

"Kai," she squealed, handing off her drink to the

butch standing closest to her. She then wrapped Kaitlyn in a firm hug. "I'm so glad you made it, darlin'. I was afraid I was gonna have to send one of these brave butches on the hunt for you." She gave a wink and watched with a grin as the color rose in Kaitlyn's cheeks. "Come, come meet my groupies for the next few days. Oh," she touched her fingers to her lips. "I suppose I shouldn't say things like that to a single lesbian." She lowered her voice. "You are still single, I presume."

Kaitlyn nodded with reluctance. After introductions to the women, who in fact were a good looking bunch, Sarah excused them and steered Kaitlyn to the bar for a much needed drink. With a double gin and tonic in hand, Kaitlyn's confidence in her ability to survive the remainder of the evening rose substantially.

"So darlin', what held you up this evening? You always arrive to these things before me. A mile-high adventure perhaps?" She waggled her brows.

Kaitlyn took a drink and savored the warmth all the way to her empty stomach. One drink would be all she required to sleep like a baby tonight.

"There was a storm in Chicago that delayed flights for a good hour and you know how it is flying these days. Everything just backed up from there. I ended up flying here via Baltimore, believe it or not. Talk about wasting precious fuel." She looked over Sarah's shoulder at the group of women she'd been entertaining moments before as she took another drink. "It appears that writing a romance with lesbian characters in leading roles gets you into the Les Club."

Sarah looked over at the women too. "They swarmed me. They wanted to know how a very straight southern gal, married with three children, could write such realistic love scenes between women."

Kaitlyn grinned. "And what did you tell them?"

"I did go to college."

They laughed in unison and for another twenty minutes caught up on each other's lives since last they talked. Kaitlyn finally placed her empty glass on the bar. She was more than ready for a soft pillow. After picking up her bag from Sherise at the desk, she turned to head for the nearest elevator and met the eyes of that gorgeous woman still at the bar, who was seemingly checking her out. She caught a glimpse of what appeared to be a nervous smile as the woman again averted her eyes. Kaitlyn smiled to herself as she passed en route to the elevators, sensing the woman's gaze on her backside.

She fell into an exhausted sleep, but it wasn't long before dreams of soft lips caressing her skin and the sensation of heated flesh woke her in a sweat. Staring at the ceiling lit by the ambient glow of the pool's lights three floors below, she could conjure up that gorgeous face from the bar earlier. Maybe, she imagined, there might be a chance that more than the weather would be hot for the conference. It was a long night with restless sleep.

* * *

Kaitlyn devoured a nutrition bar from her travel stash, grabbed a bottle of water from the mini fridge and headed to the hotel's workout room. After some stretching, she commandeered a treadmill and set about running her usual sixty minutes. An hour and a half later she finished with weights for her upper body and some core work. Her workout complete, she sat cooling down and emptying her water when her late night dream gal strolled in wearing spandex shorts that showed off long muscled legs and a tank top that revealed small breasts and nicely developed biceps. Kaitlyn hurriedly slipped out before the woman noticed her. She knew she looked atrocious. Her hair was damp and partially plastered to her forehead and her shorts and t-shirt clung to her sweat-covered skin. She indulged in a long hot shower before rushing down to meet Sarah in the restaurant for breakfast at eight o'clock. They had an hour to catch up a bit more before reporting to the large conference room where they would set up to sell books, and meet readers and fellow authors.

* * *

It was nearing noon when Kaitlyn's stomach reminded her lunch would soon arrive. As she waited in line for a pre-made salad, a bottle of water and a yogurt, she spied her fantasy woman seated alone at a table across the room from the vendors' tables. She looked back and forth several times from where her friend Sarah was seated. It was time to make an introduction. *What's the worst that could happen? I've declined an offer or two, and no one died as a result.* Surely she could handle being shot down.

"Excuse me." She made certain her most charming smile was in place before the woman looked up from one of the many books she had stacked in front of her. "Would you mind if I shared your table?" The woman quickly gathered her books into one pile.

"Uh, no." She gave a wave at the table before nervously running her hand through her short blonde hair.

"Are you expecting company?"

Her head shook. "I'm, uh, here by myself." She gave another wave. "At the table."

Kaitlyn pulled out the chair, leaving one between them, and took a sip of water. "I'm Bryce Kaylin. Thank you for sharing your table."

"Uh, Hayden Carter. I… uh, recognized you." Her cheeks turned a rosy hue as she picked at the corner of the book in front of her.

Kaitlyn took a bite while she gazed at the woman staring at her books. "Is this your first Romance Writers Conference?" She knew before asking that she would never have missed, or forgotten such a gorgeous face.

"Yes," Hayden stuttered.

She ate more of her run-of-the-mill Caesar salad. The silence was a little unnerving. "You said you recognized me. Have you read any of my books?"

"I, uh…" She cleared her throat. "I've read a few of them."

Kaitlyn stood gathering her lunch debris. "I have a selection of all my books here today if you want to stop by my table and check them out." The other woman gave Kaitlyn a bashful smile. "It was very nice to meet you, Hayden."

She popped up from her seat, rubbing her hands over her shorts before shoving them in her pockets. "Uh, it was nice to meet you, Ms. Kaylin."

Kaitlyn extended her hand and marveled when the nervous Hayden took it in hers. "Please, call me Bryce." She winked before she drew her hand away and made her way back across the room.

With all the people milling about she couldn't see the table where she had left Hayden sitting. But she didn't have to see her, to *see* her. She could close her eyes and perfectly envision those bright baby blues in that gorgeous face, and those full, kissable lips. She suppressed the urge to groan.

"Excuse me."

Kaitlyn's eyes flew open to meet those familiar bright eyes. "What can I help you with?" she asked with a smile.

"I, uh, wanted to get one of your books that I haven't read. Is there one you recommend?"

"Which ones have you read?" Kaitlyn fought the desire to grin like a schoolgirl.

"*Wait For Love* and, uh…" Hayden looked at her feet. "*Take Me Tonight.*" Her cheeks colored a deep crimson.

She is so damned gorgeous. Kaitlyn selected her latest

release, *Hold On For Love.* "I think you'll enjoy this one." She picked up her slim Cross pen and flipped to the title page. "To Hayden—Love happens when you least expect it!" she wrote and signed her pen name.

Something happened when Kaitlyn took Hayden's credit card. A jolt of excitement passed through her. She guessed that Hayden felt it too, judging by the way she suddenly appeared more nervous. Hayden's hand trembled slightly as she took the book and credit card. Something was definitely happening.

Kaitlyn packed up at five o'clock and hauled only one box of unsold books to her room. There was a cocktail party at seven thirty that preceded the awards presentation, which would be followed by more socializing. Sarah was out dining with her publisher and several other authors so Kaitlyn returned downstairs to dine alone. The place was packed, but there was one small table in the corner, which offered a view into the bar area and the main hall to the north wing of the hotel.

She looked up from the menu to see Hayden waiting at the hostess stand. She had changed out of her cargo shorts and polo shirt, and was now decked out in a pair of snug black jeans and a blue oxford shirt that seemed to match her eyes. Kaitlyn sat hidden behind her menu, staring at Hayden leaning casually against the low wall, people watching. The hostess finally led Hayden to the upper level and out of sight. Kaitlyn rushed through dinner and back to her room to shower, put up her hair and dress for the final event of the conference.

Downstairs, she located Sarah standing with several of the women from the previous night. Sarah waved her over, looped her arm through Kaitlyn's and steered her toward the bar.

"I asked that you be seated at our table, darlin'. I hope I wasn't being too presumptuous in doing so since we're up for the same award." They ordered drinks.

"No, it's fine. I wanted a chance to catch up some more."

Sarah turned from the bar, drink in hand. "So… are you going to fill me in on your hot lunch date?"

Kaitlyn paid for her cocktail. "It wasn't a date."

"Oh? Well that's a shame because you two made a perfectly adorable-looking couple."

Kaitlyn hid behind her drink as heat rose in her cheeks. She'd been thinking of nothing but seeing Hayden tonight.

Sarah hooked her arm through hers once again. "Let's get seated and chat."

She selected a chair at their table that gave one of the better views of the stage and Sarah talked of her kids while Kaitlyn's eyes wandered around the gradually filling ballroom. She held hope against hope that Hayden would show up, but as the tables filled up, there wasn't a sight of her anywhere to be found.

The awards presentation went off without a hiccup and, not surprisingly, Sarah won the Lesbian Romance category for her maiden voyage into the world of lesbian fiction. Afterwards the hotel crew moved with precision, as if the task of moving chairs, tables and laying the hardwood dance floor in place was a daily one. In the time it took fifty or so women to pass through the ladies room, the ballroom was transformed.

Sarah guided her to a table between the dance floor, which held the DJ stand against the wall, and the bar. After several of Sarah's groupies commandeered chairs around their table, two of them made a trip to the bar for drinks. Kaitlyn again scanned the room. For reasons she couldn't quite comprehend, the desire to see Hayden overwhelmed her. She wanted to drag her off to the darkest corner in the room. Something stirred in her at that thought. Something primal. She wanted to kiss those luscious lips and, well… so much more.

Thirty minutes after the music started, a number of couples—straight and gay—had taken to the dance floor. Kaitlyn's breath caught when she finally spotted her. There she stood casually leaning against a pillar not far from the bar, looking right back at her. Hayden smiled and gave a nod. Kaitlyn's blood pulsed hot in her veins. *It's a good thing I'm sitting.* Hayden was dressed in black trousers and a matching tailored jacket over a crisp white shirt. The look, well… Adonis was the only thought that came to mind. She was, without question, the most handsome woman Kaitlyn had ever laid eyes on. If one could consider a woman handsome.

I Bet My Life by Imagine Dragons began playing and Hayden's body responded to the beat, but her eyes never left Kaitlyn's. Kaitlyn finished her gin and tonic in two swallows, then excused herself from the table. Nervous as a school girl going on a date, in heels for the very first time, she weaved her way between tables to the back of the room. She watched as Hayden's eyes traveled down her slinky black knee-length dress to her peep-toe heels and very slowly back up again to meet her gaze. Her mouth went dry and a flood of heat settled between her thighs.

"Hi." Hayden's eyes sparkled in spite of the dim light.

"Hi yourself." Kaitlyn gazed at Hayden's lips. "I'm dying for a drink." Hayden turned toward the bar, but Kaitlyn caught her arm before she got away. "What are you having?" She indicated the glass in her hand.

"Just club soda."

"May I?" When she reached for the glass Hayden put it in her hand. She felt the same excitement from earlier as their fingers brushed. She sipped slowly, more nervous than she recalled ever being in her life. Hayden's eyes remained intent on her. "Thank you." She held out the glass.

"I'm good," Hayden said. "Have as much as you like."

You're good… what an understatement. More like great, or incredible or astounding. Some kind of energy, like wildly firing electrons, bounced everywhere around them.

Hayden leaned away from the pillar and closer to her. "You are…" She showed that bashful smile again. "I just have to say that you are drop dead gorgeous."

She was close enough that Kaitlyn could smell her cologne. Sandalwood and something earthy. Mysterious and intoxicating like the woman before her. She wanted to slip her fingers under the lapels of Hayden's silk jacket, then move them down to her hips. But more than anything, she wanted to kiss those lips. It had obviously been far too long since she'd been intimate with a woman. As much as she loved writing, it was, unfortunately, a solitary task and always with a deadline. Novels, shorts, blogs and occasional articles for *Curve Magazine*. She didn't have time to hit the social places to look for love, or even a simple affair.

Hayden took the empty glass from her and placed it on the nearby table. "I really…" She dropped her head and averted her eyes. "I'd give anything to dance with you." She shoved her hands in her pockets. "Do you… dance with women?"

Kaitlyn answered with a smile as she tugged Hayden's hand from her pocket, entwined their fingers and led her to the dance floor. She linked her hands behind Hayden's neck. Hayden placed noticeably shaking hands on Kaitlyn's hips and her steps were stiff and unsure.

"Relax, sweetie. I won't bite… unless you want me to." Hayden gave a nervous chuckle. "You have danced with women before, haven't you?"

"I, uh…" She looked away. "No, not really. Never with a woman as beautiful as you."

"Thank you. I'm flattered. And might I say that I've never danced with a woman as gorgeous as you. You make me feel like swooning."

Hayden's step faltered. "That sounds like something you write in your books."

"Fiction mirrors real life more often than you would think." She tightened her arms around her neck. "I was hoping I would see you this evening. I wanted to talk some more."

Hayden met her eyes. "Would you like to go somewhere quieter to talk?"

Kaitlyn stepped back, took Hayden's hand and led them from the ballroom to where she'd first spotted her the night before.

"Buy a girl a drink?" Kaitlyn slid onto a bar stool.

"It would be my pleasure."

The dark-haired bartender, apparently familiar with Hayden, gave a wide smile as she asked, "What can I get you?"

"I've had enough alcohol. Just a club soda for me."

Hayden nodded. "Same here."

Kaitlyn turned sideways to face her. She couldn't get enough of looking at Hayden. She made her feel all tingly inside. "I don't detect any Texas drawl, so I'm going to assume you're not from around here."

Hayden took a slow sip from her glass. "Uh, no. I'm from the Midwest. A small town up in Wisconsin."

"Small world."

"Oh, yeah. Where do you live?" When Kaitlyn didn't answer, Hayden shook her head. "Sorry. Stupid question. I mean, I could be some crazy stalker."

Kaitlyn placed her hand on Hayden's thigh. "I don't believe that for a minute. I too am a Midwesterner. I live in a suburb outside Minneapolis." She shivered at the thought that they lived so close to each other. Hayden shrugged out of her jacket and helped Kaitlyn slip it around her shoulders. There wasn't a single thing not to like about this woman. She hoped with all her heart Hayden wasn't a stalker.

The conversation flowed and Hayden seemed to finally relax. They talked until the bar closed, moving to the grouping of couches adjacent to the bar and continued to talk until 3 a.m. when Kaitlyn had to stifle a yawn.

"It's really late." Hayden stood, offering a hand to her. "Come on, I'll walk you to your room."

At the door of room 426, Kaitlyn slipped off the jacket and handed it over. "I thoroughly enjoyed our time tonight. You're an intriguing woman, Hayden Carter." She couldn't take her eyes off Hayden's lips.

Hayden's hands moved to her pockets. "Maybe we can meet in the morning for breakfast?"

There was that bashful smile again. She curled her fingers around Hayden's forearm. "Call my room and we'll do that." Unable to resist, she leaned in and brushed her lips over Hayden's. She wanted to invite her in. She wanted Hayden in her bed. But instead she slid the key card into the lock and met Hayden's heavy lidded eyes.

"Goodnight, Hayden. See you in the morning." Hayden bounced her head and stepped away.

* * *

Inside the room, she leaned against the door and mentally beat herself up for letting Hayden leave. She had never picked up a woman before while traveling. No one-night stands, but she certainly wanted to make an exception for Hayden.

She stripped off her dress, bra and panties then pulled on the thick terrycloth hotel robe. The moment she reached to turn on the shower, a knock sounded on the door. Through the peep hole she saw Hayden, hands in her pockets looking uneasy and unsure. She opened the door and met her eyes—and silence. She arched her brows.

Hayden looked at the floor where she toed the plush carpet. "I, uh…" She finally met Kaitlyn's eyes.

Kaitlyn's heart beat a fast staccato. "Tell me what you want, Hayden." She could barely breathe. When Hayden leaned in the doorway, a longing so intense swept through her, it stole her breath.

"I…" her head shook. "I couldn't make myself go back to my room."

"Would you like to come in?"

Hayden nodded so Kaitlyn stepped aside to allow her entry. She closed the door and turned to find Hayden a mere breath away. Hayden's hypnotic gaze held her. Her distinct scent tantalized all of her senses. When Hayden stroked her fingertips over her cheek, she closed her eyes, absorbing the many sensations her touch evoked.

"You're so beautiful," Hayden whispered. Her fingers slid into Kaitlyn's hair at the base of her neck. "I… I want to kiss you," she said breathlessly.

Kaitlyn moved her hands inside Hayden's jacket and held her waist. Her legs grew shaky. "Yes," she murmured as Hayden's lips captured hers.

Although the kiss was tender, Kaitlyn felt it all the way to her toes. Hayden pulled back after a moment, gazing at her, as if asking permission. Kaitlyn tightened her hands around her waist and pulled them together. They kissed feverishly, Hayden backing her against the door and snaking a hand under the robe to stroke her bare hip. A moan escaped before she could stop it. She was wet. Desire devoured her—consumed her. She wanted Hayden. She wanted Hayden to take her. But Hayden obviously had other ideas. She broke the kiss and leaned her forehead to Kaitlyn's, breathing heavily.

"We hardly know one another."

Kaitlyn's eyes searched Hayden's. She wanted her

more than she wanted her next breath, but only if Hayden wanted her too.

Hayden touched her fingers to her cheek once again. "It's so late, Bryce. I should go. I have a breakfast date in the morning."

"Kaitlyn." Hayden tipped her head, her brows furrowed. "My real name is Kaitlyn Bryce."

"Kaitlyn," Hayden said in a breathless whisper. "Beautiful, like you." She stepped back. "So… Kaitlyn, I'm going to go now, and I'm going to call room 426 in the morning. Maybe for brunch so we can both get some sleep. Unless you have a flight…"

Hayden had become somehow more confident, or at least she appeared that way. *Or maybe I'm on hormone overload.* Kaitlyn smiled. "Brunch it is then." She stepped aside and opened the door. "Goodnight again, Hayden."

She leaned down for a quick kiss. "Night, Kaitlyn."

Kaitlyn leaned out the doorway and watched her disappear down the hall.

* * *

Kaitlyn startled awake at the sound of the ringing phone. The bedside clock read 10:08 a.m. She could swear she'd just checked the clock a moment ago at a little before 7 a.m.

"Good morning!"

Hoping her voice didn't betray her exhausted state, she replied, "You sound awfully chipper for someone who didn't go to bed until this morning." Kaitlyn had tossed and turned for hours even after taking a cool shower to douse her libido.

"What time would you like to meet downstairs?"

Kaitlyn resisted the need to moan as she pushed herself from the bed. "I need to jump in the shower. How about thirty minutes?"

"Works for me. See you soon."

Once downstairs, Kaitlyn spotted Hayden right off,

in her now familiar stance of hands in her pockets of a pair of worn, faded jeans into which she had tucked a bright blue button-up shirt. Kaitlyn bit the inside of her cheek. Hayden Carter made her blood run hot and gather in a torturous pool between her thighs. They were seated promptly and placed their drink order. She generally only drank caffeinated coffee when she wrote, but today was a needed exception. It was as if her eyes were bleeding.

Hayden on the other hand seemed much more relaxed. And interesting conversation wouldn't change the inevitable—they would be parting sooner rather than later. Hayden insisted on paying for their meal.

"How often do you think I get to take a famous author to brunch?" She flashed a grin.

Out in the lobby, Kaitlyn fumbled her phone from her small purse. "We should exchange email addresses so we can stay in touch."

"You should already have mine, um maybe. I wrote you after I read *Wait for Love*." Color rose in Hayden's cheeks.

Their information exchanged, Kaitlyn asked, "What time do you have to leave?"

"Whenever I want. I'm already checked out and my car's packed. How 'bout you?"

"I have a five twenty flight."

Hayden tucked her hands in her back pockets and rocked back on her heels. "I have an idea."

Kaitlyn's heart rate picked up.

"I'll give you a lift to the airport. I passed airport exit signs on my way here."

"That's so sweet, but I already scheduled the hotel shuttle, and I don't want to impose." *Even though I'd like nothing better.*

Hayden lowered her head. "Betcha won't think that when they pack you like sardines in that van with a bunch of sweaty people."

Kaitlyn's mind flashed back to Friday's arrival, and feeling like a dishrag. "I'll agree only if we leave when you were originally planning to."

"Better get to packing then." Her lips lifted into a mischievous smile. Lips Kaitlyn wanted to kiss something fierce. "Need any help?"

Kaitlyn opened her mouth, then quickly closed it. Sure, she could invite Hayden up to the room while she packed her things, but she didn't trust herself in a room with a bed and Hayden looking so... delicious. It wouldn't look good if she were suddenly compelled to rip that pretty blue shirt open, would it? Still, if Hayden wanted to follow her up, she could hardly stop her.

"It won't take me long. Why don't you relax here. You've got quite the drive ahead of you."

Hayden gave a nod.

* * *

Twenty minutes later Kaitlyn rolled her bag to the end of the couch where Hayden sat with her head leaned back into the cushion. "Do you need a nap before we hit the road?" Hayden's eyes popped open. "I booked a late checkout if you want to use my room." *Oh, God, stop talking now.*

"I'm good." She stood and stretched.

"Okay. Then I only need to check out. Watch this for me, please?" She patted the handle of her suitcase.

"I'll do you one better. I'll take this and pull the car up out front."

Kaitlyn was all too aware when she stepped outside and the hot humid Texas air assaulted her that she'd not been out of the hotel since her arrival, and was eternally grateful she wouldn't be packed like a sardine in the hotel van. She slid into the comfort of Hayden's air-conditioned Subaru. Perspiration had accumulated along her hairline in a matter of thirty seconds.

"How in heaven's name do people live in places this

hot?" She pulled the seatbelt across her as Hayden shifted the car into gear and turned the fan up another notch.

"I imagine they're used to it. Kinda like us freezing in the winter. Let me know if you get too cold."

Kaitlyn hoped they could discuss something more than the weather in the limited time they had left to share each other's company. After all, they *had* made out last night.

"We've talked about so many different things, but I still don't know what you do for a living."

Hayden glanced at her. "What do you figure I do for a living?"

Kaitlyn studied her intently before answering. "Hum, maybe you're one of those computer programmers who write all those code things I use on my computer."

Hayden chuckled. "Not even close. My family owns property around Lake Hayward. We have rental cabins and I'm the designated handy/maintenance/fix-it person since my dad developed MS. Mom does the books and all the financial stuff, and my cousin takes care of housekeeping. Me and Dad handle everything else. He knows everything about everything. He's a great mentor." Kaitlyn loved the enthusiasm and conviction with which Hayden spoke about her family and her job. "I imagine you spend your days in a posh penthouse writing. Isn't that what famous writers do?"

She shifted to look at Hayden, lightly touching her hand to her arm. "I really hate to burst your bubble, Hayden, but I actually work a full-time job to support myself. Writing is what I do because I can't *not* tell these stories that play out in my mind."

"Oh, wow! I just assumed writers made lots selling books."

"Maybe the *New York Times* best sellers, but us little old romance writers, not so much."

It seemed like in no time Hayden was taking exit 121N toward the airport and asked which airline she was flying. Kaitlyn stared out the window not seeing what passed by. She had almost skipped this conference in lieu of one scheduled in Atlanta. She likely would have never met Hayden, and the thought that they were about to part ways was saddening. They stood at the back of the car, hatch open and her suitcase beside them.

After a moment of unblinking eye contact, Hayden wrapped her in a hug. "Safe travels."

Hayden's first kiss she'd felt to her toes, but there was something so intensely intimate about this embrace, she felt it in her soul. She didn't want to let go. And as it turned out, she didn't have to.

"God, I miss you already, and I don't want to let you go."

Kaitlyn leaned back. She wanted... no, needed to burn Hayden's image into her memory. "I know. Me too." She brushed her lips over Hayden's cheek. "We'll talk soon."

Hayden slowly released her and rested her hand on the suitcase handle. "You know..." she grinned. "I could just buy your ticket and drive you home myself."

Kaitlyn's mind raced. "I can't let you do that." Hayden frowned. "Pay for my ticket that is. I wouldn't let you. And the only way I will agree to riding all the way to Minnesota is if I can share the expense."

Hayden's face lit up with a smile as big as Texas. In a swift move she hoisted the suitcase back into the car. "Deal!"

Once they were back on the road they fell into conversation as easily as two long-time friends. Kaitlyn talked about her job as an executive for Best Buy in Richfield and how the stress led her to begin reading romance as an escape, and ultimately to writing it because the voices in her head kept getting louder.

Surreal was the only way Kaitlyn could describe this trip. There were few gaps in conversation between them, and she felt completely at ease entwining her fingers with Hayden's when she rested her hand on her thigh. She'd had a few lengthy affairs over the years. Lengthy in that they lasted more than a few months. But, she'd never met a woman who made her feel the way Hayden made her feel. She'd never quite believed all the romantic notions that she wrote about love at first sight, and there being a perfect someone for everyone. Now though, she was a dyed-in-the-wool believer.

In no time they were passing exits for Oklahoma City and the next thing she was conscious of was Hayden shaking her awake.

"Hey sleepyhead, we're here."

She shook the cobwebs from her head. "How long have I been asleep? And where's here?"

"I don't know, maybe a little over four hours and Kansas City."

"Which one?" She scrubbed her hands over her face and pushed her hair behind her ears. "Which Kansas City?"

Hayden turned north on Main Street. "The one in Missouri."

"And you haven't stopped since we left Dallas?"

Hayden pulled into the parking lot of the Fairfield Inn at Union Hill. "I did, but you were sleeping so soundly I didn't have the heart to wake you up."

"That would explain why I have to pee so bad."

"Sorry." Hayden turned off the car. "This is roughly the halfway point. I just can't seem to make myself drive fifteen plus hours anymore without a good long break. I hope this is okay."

Kaitlyn exited the car and gave her body a cautious stretch. "As long as the water is hot and the beds are soft, it's perfect."

They hauled their bags into the lobby, Kaitlyn hanging back while Hayden registered them.

She waggled the plastic card. "Top floor. I got us the penthouse." She winked.

As the elevator rose, Kaitlyn's excitement accompanied it. She was going to spend the night with the first woman she'd ever craved like a drug.

Hayden stopped in front of the room. "So, the good news is free breakfast, an indoor pool, hot tub and fitness room." She ran the key card along the seam of her jeans. "Um, there's another thing, uh… you should know." Kaitlyn looked up into her eyes. "The room only has one bed."

"Really?" Her heart skipped a beat. Hayden's head bobbed. Kaitlyn pulled the card from her hand and slid it into the lock. "Then what are you waiting for?" She practically pushed Hayden through the door. This was fate—destiny. She smiled broadly. And the best damned vacation she could ever have hoped for.

O R C H I D   R A I N
ERZABET BISHOP

Kim gripped the wheel, steering around a slow moving car ahead of her. Under construction, the highway was red lights and bumper-to-bumper at this time of night. Summer was here and everyone was apparently behind the wheel. The additional fact that it was raining made her even less excited about being on the road. Her phone rang but she ignored it, trying not to hit someone in oncoming traffic.

"Thanks for coming with me, Sis. I really appreciate it." Chrissy sat in the passenger seat, mirror down, applying makeup like there was no tomorrow. Her little black dress barely reached her thighs and the strappy black heels were gorgeous. "Jonathan will be there and I promised him a dance."

"Why didn't he bring you?" Kim was curious. The two seemed to be spending more and more time together and when Chrissy had asked her to drive she'd said yes, if for no other reason than to meet this mysterious boy.

Chrissy swiped on a layer of lip gloss and grinned. "He and the groom brigade had wedding things to do before the ceremony and I didn't want to hang around getting in the way. Besides… I knew you needed to get out of the house and have a little fun. I know you and Maggie had a fight and well…"

"So you thought going to Maggie's wedding gig would be what I needed, huh?"

She glanced down at her own attire and smiled. The

gray lace dress was one she hadn't worn yet but she had to admit it showed off her legs to their best advantage. Paired with her new sparkly silver strapped heels, Kim knew the outfit was at least one her sister wouldn't give her lip about. She'd bought the dress six months ago but hadn't had an opportunity to wear it.

Maggie. Just thinking about her caused her panties to dampen and her stomach to twist into knots. Last night had been perfect. Dinner, a movie and some curl-your-toes sex back at their apartment. Then Maggie got up to do the bills and they'd had a major fight.

"I see your paycheck from work went into the account but what is this electronic transfer?" Maggie advanced into the bedroom, regarding Kim with a frown.

Kim shrugged, climbing out of bed. Joint accounts were helpful in most circumstances, but difficult in this particular case. It was hard to surprise someone with a summer vacation when your partner did the bills. Not to mention she was the owner of her own business and an ace with accounting. Kim sidled over to the dresser and ran a brush through her hair. "Oh... you know. Expenses..."

"What expenses? Jesus, Kim." Maggie waved the checkbook ledger in her direction. "Where did it go? You entered the dollar amount but only put down 'M.C.'. What does that even mean?"

Kim took in Maggie's guarded expression and reached up to run her hand down the side of Maggie's face. "Can we talk about this later? I kind of wanted to continue where we left off."

"No. Five hundred dollars is missing from our account. What gives?" Maggie slipped out of her reach, her focus intense.

Hindsight being what it is, Kim realized she should have told Maggie her plan but instead she'd gotten irritated.

"It's my money too. I don't give you the third degree when you spend money on yourself. Why can't you extend me the same courtesy?"

"You're not going to tell me?" Maggie shot her a wide-eyed look that screamed hurt. "Wow." She slapped the ledger shut and

vacated the bedroom.

Shit.

"Maggie…"

"No. You don't want to tell me and suddenly I don't want to know." She waved her hand at Kim wearily and sat down at her desk where her laptop glowed in the dim light. *"If you'll excuse me, I have a wedding to plan for tomorrow night and an article to write about Texas travel destinations. Despite your nine to five life, my work doesn't stop."*

Ouch.

"Mags. Please."

Kim wrung her hands and tried to think of a way to tell Maggie her plan without giving away the surprise. She opened her mouth to speak but Maggie headed her off.

"No. Just go to bed Kim."

And she had. The whole night she tossed and turned thinking about how she could've told Maggie the money had gone to a deposit on their summer vacation. She'd been wound way too tight lately. With all the weddings and Bridezillas she had to contend with, it was no wonder. And that didn't even count the blog.

But that was just it. She knew what Maggie's schedule was and she'd made plans around it. In fact, she'd marked off some specific days in her calendar starting next week and hadn't told her why. Well, to be accurate, her assistant Terrance had marked them off for her when she'd explained what was going on.

"Yes. Get her out of here. If she doesn't get some time off I'm going to lose my mind."

And now here she was heading to the wedding with a brochure for Mermaid Cruises in her purse. It would do both of them good. She needed to get away from her deadlines for a couple of days and Maggie needed to just enjoy life without the breakneck speed of the Houston wedding circuit. It made her dizzy every time she even thought about all the things Maggie fit into one day. Taking some time for themselves would be perfect. If she could get Maggie to agree. Hell, she was even considering hog-tying her and dragging her on board the ship.

Chagrined, Chrissy slid her makeup bag into her purse. "Look, I know you've had a rough time. You never not text me at night. I'm worried about you. You hardly ever go anywhere and if you're not at work, you're working on another one of those novels of yours. Life balance, Sis. Didn't you always tell me that?" Her elegant eyebrow tilted up in question, her perfectly glossed lips bowed into a smile.

"Chrissy…" Kim groaned. The swishing sound of the windshield wipers was loud in the sudden silence. Summer rain in Houston could go from a light mist to a gully washer in moments.

"You'd better not just drop me off either. I know it's Maggie's event and all but the emcee for this thing is going to be awesome and Candace's sister Grace is supposed to be there. Remember, you met her two years ago at that freaky company picnic with the chili cook-off Mom dragged us to?"

Lightning flashed in the Texas skyline, illuminating the new construction of the Grand Parkway rising into the sky. Kim used to recognize where she was going but since they had started working on the new toll road, everything was a mess and all of her landmarks were hidden behind giant walls of concrete.

"Erm. Yeah." She pressed the navigation button on her phone and listened to the droning female voice guide her to the next stop on her journey.

"Besides, Jordan is a cop and the place will have all kinds of sexy guys… um, I mean people in uniform, if you want to give Maggie a reason to be jealous."

"In two hundred feet, take a right onto State Highway 290. Then take a left to Brower road," the mechanic voice said.

"Chrissy you're incorrigible." Kim chuckled.

She guided the vehicle along, making the required turns. It was times like these when Kim missed her mother. Their father had passed away when they were both too young to remember much, but their mother's death was still fresh. Cancer had taken her way too young and Kim still found herself reaching for the phone to tell her about her day, only to replace it with a frustrated sigh.

Her younger sister had by some miracle just graduated high school. They were separated by ten years and sometimes it made Kim feel like she'd inadvertently stepped into the role of being Chrissy's mother, like it or not. The girl was a wild spirit and keeping her on track was as close to a full-time job as her real one at the software company. When she wasn't at work, she tried like hell to keep up her passion for writing, but lately that was taking a back seat to real life.

"In fifty feet, turn left onto Stone road." The metallic voice startled her and Kim blinked, reacting quickly to the last minute direction. She dove into the left lane, earning her a long honk from a car nearly on top of her.

"This phone…" Her heart was beating fast and the icy prickle of hyperawareness slithered down her back. "God, I hope they have an open bar." She turned left and the highway was replaced by a two-lane, badly maintained road with potholes and no street lights.

Chrissy giggled. "Oh my God, Kim."

"Turn right in twenty five feet and you have reached your destination."

Kim grimaced and followed the directions. Up ahead was a plantation style home with trees wrapped in twinkle lights. The rain had become a sparse drizzle.

Two police officers stood at the entrance to the parking lot waving the guests to where they were to park their vehicles. Kim pulled in and with a sigh, turned off the engine.

"We made it. In Friday rush hour traffic, no less."

Chrissy rolled her eyes. "Come on." She collected her purse from the floorboard and exited the Kia. "Hurry, before it starts raining again."

Kim angled the rearview mirror down to check her lipstick, the new Mac color making her lips pop. 'Sin' was her new favorite color. It went with nearly everything, especially gray and black. Her long black curls were left to their own devices for a change, making her look younger than her twenty-eight years.

Knocking on the window, Chrissy startled her. "Come on, glamour puss. Let's go."

"I'm coming." Kim snagged her purse and opened the door. She stepped out of the car and slammed the door, pressing the lock button on the key fob. Chrissy was pining to head inside. "Go ahead. Just text me later if he doesn't bring you home, okay?"

Chrissy squealed and enveloped her in a floral scented hug. "You're the best!" She released her and tottered off down the pavement toward the lit up house where groups of tuxedoed men and elegantly dressed young women clustered. Her sister would have fun. If the place was loaded down with cops, there wasn't likely to be any underage drinking.

Kim took her time making her way inside. The sky was clearing up and she wanted to enjoy a moment of quiet before she went inside. Since she had been dating Maggie, she'd been to dozens of weddings. This venue was one she'd been to before. The Stone Planation. It dated back to the 1800s and was a popular location for parties.

In the winter and during rainy days, they had a gorgeous glass paneled room, but for days when it was sunny, the gazebo was absolutely perfect. It was a shame the night was rainy, but in the summer months most sensible brides would choose air-conditioning for the party and the gazebo for the photo op.

The exterior was well lit. Trees wrapped with sparkle lights paired with spotlights made the landscape pop. The lights of the window-lined event space glowed bright and with the first droplets of rain, Kim scurried for the walkway leading to the back door.

She entered the house and immediately inhaled the citrus scent of hot spiced tea. With low ceilings and wooden floors, she remembered why she wasn't fond of the place. It was lovely for the time it was built, but for today's standards it was a confined space. The bar was crowded and people were making their way into the event space to the rear of the house.

Chrissy had vanished into the fray of glamorous teens, but that was fine with her. She would get a ride with Jonathan and be home before midnight. Kim wasn't worried. The girl had sense and would never do anything to compromise her safety.

Kim wandered out of the house and took the first step down into the atrium extension. The room had been made up in silver and purple, the stunning table settings located around the ring of the room absolutely beautiful. Orchids in glass containers winked with candles and twinkle lights. Silver napkins were folded into glassware. Silver accent plates with purple party favors were laid out waiting for their guests to arrive after the ceremony. For now, silver bows wrapped around the backs of white folding chairs arranged to face the front dais. Draped in white shears with twinkle lights and vines cascading down, it was a sight to behold. The ceiling was covered in textured white paint with more sheer white fabric drawn together in long draped sheets centered by a tastefully done chandelier.

"Nice," she breathed.

"Thank you."

Kim swiveled on her heels. Maggie. "I should have known Chrissy was up to something," she said wryly.

"You didn't answer the phone today and well…"

"I was driving and before that I had meetings."

"Okay…. well, I asked her to bring you." Maggie blushed, her fine porcelain skin turning an attractive shade of pink. Her curly mass of auburn hair was drawn up, the curls cascading down the side of her face to her shoulders. The little black dress she wore accentuated her very womanly curves, the heels making her legs look like they ran on forever.

Because they did. She'd mapped every inch of them with her tongue, her lips. The rush of desire pummeling through her snapped Kim back to reality like a glass of cold water.

"Really? And why would you do that?" Kim couldn't keep the chill from her voice.

Maggie winced. "I deserve that."

"Damn right you do." Kim crossed her arms and regarded her lover.

"I'm sorry, Kim. I shouldn't have left it the way I did. Will you stay and talk to me after the wedding? I don't want to fight."

Kim found herself nodding, half curious as to what she would say.

"Good. Great. Okay… Look, why don't you sit anywhere and we'll get these kids married and then I can leave things to my assistant. He loves it when I let him get a little crazy with the receptions." Maggie grinned and scooted off toward the microphone.

"Okay, everyone. Let's find our seats for the ceremony."

Kim wandered over to the seating area and lowered herself onto one of the end spaces toward the back. A small lantern was placed at the end of the aisle and as the row filled, young men came and placed battery-lit votive candles inside. A young woman in a black dress approached, sprinkling blue and purple rose petals along the main walk.

Music from the Piano Guys trailed through the space and soon the ceremony was well underway. Bridesmaids in purple off-the-shoulder tea length dresses and silver heels paraded down the aisle with stunning groomsmen in dark gray suits. The bride entered and everyone in the room got to their feet. Glamorous and model pretty, she strode down the aisle supported by the arm of her father, her shapely form covered in white satin and pearls.

The minister appeared and as the bride approached the dais, her father handed her over to the young man who would become her husband.

There were reasons Kim sat in the back row. It was easier to remove herself without a lot of people noticing. All she could think about watching the couple was that she would never be able to pledge her love to anyone if she lived here in Texas. At least not yet. Someday… she was determined that would change. She and Maggie would be walking down the aisle one way or another. The Mermaid Cruise was just the start. What she hadn't told Maggie was that the advance she'd gotten from her last contract had gone into a special account she'd used just to buy her a ring. She carried it with her everywhere, waiting for the right time to ask for her hand.

She made her way back inside the house and decided to walk out next to the lake. It wasn't raining and she needed some fresh air. The path was well worn and lit, making it a pleasure to walk along.

"Where are you going?" Maggie caught up with her, obviously out of breath from running. "You aren't leaving are you?"

Kim shook her head. "No. I just wanted to see the

lights and watch them from out here. You did a good job."

"Thanks."

Kim gestured toward the wedding. "Aren't they going to miss you in there?"

"No. Terrance has everything well in hand. He's been just itching to run one of these."

Kim smiled. "Good. Do you want to walk for a bit? It seems like the rain has stopped."

"Sure."

"What did you want to talk to me about?"

"I really just wanted to say I'm sorry for interrogating you like that." Maggie sighed. "I'm sorry."

"It's okay." Kim's stomach fluttered and she turned her gaze up toward the sky as warm summer rain began to fall in earnest.

"Good thing the kids had their event inside."

"I know. She almost changed her mind on me at the last minute. I had to argue with her that the weather was going to be rainy all night."

"Do you have anywhere for us to talk that isn't crawling with wedding people?"

Maggie nodded. "Follow me."

She led Kim back to Stone House, but instead of going into the main portion, she showed her a stairwell against the back of the building.

"Handy."

"It works when you have a persistent groom who won't take no for an answer about seeing his girl before the ceremony."

Kim giggled at the visual to that one. "Hazards of the job, I suppose."

Maggie rolled her eyes and started climbing. "You wouldn't believe half the stuff I've seen people do. Some of these women... total Bridezillas."

"What about the one downstairs?"

"She's something else. Not sure yet really, but I hope for that boy's sake she's more real for him than she's been around here."

Kim followed Maggie as they carefully maneuvered the rain-slick outdoor stairs. "What do you mean?"

Pausing mid-climb, Maggie peered down at Kim. "It's like she's plastic. Acting for the camera, like a model on a shoot. After a few of these you just get a sense about people."

"I suppose so."

Maggie opened a door and led her inside what looked like a bedroom. "This is where some of the girls change when there's a large bridal party. This one isn't too big so we have the room to ourselves." She flipped a switch and a muted light illuminated the room.

Kim entered, instantly charmed by the cozy surroundings. The ceilings in this part of the house were high, with fresh white paint and crisp baseboards. Cherry wood furniture graced the walls and a queen-sized bed with an old fashioned purple orchid and green leaf quilt reigned over the space.

"Beautiful."

Maggie grinned. "It reminds me of my grandmother's house."

"I hope that's a good thing." Kim laid her purse on the dresser and sat down on the edge of the bed.

Joining her, Maggie smiled. "It is." She smoothed her hands along the lines of the dress and lifted her eyes to meet Kim's. "So, I kind of flew off the handle. I'm sorry. You don't have to account to me every cent you spend."

"Mags…"

She held up her hand. "No. Let me finish. I sounded like my mother and as the words were coming out of my mouth, I heard it and couldn't do a thing to stop it. My father used to run through her checks like they were water on beer and cigarettes. I just panicked, I guess."

"I'm not your father."

"I know." Maggie offered her a flimsy smile.

Kim held out her hand and enveloped Maggie's in her own. "I have a confession to make."

"What?"

"I've been worried about you with all the pressure you've been under lately. Terrance agreed to watch over things while I take you away for a vacation. That's where the missing money went. At least part of it anyway."

Maggie blinked, drawing her hand out of Kim's grip. "What do you mean? I have deadlines and there is the McDougal wedding coming up."

"No." Kim shook her head. "Terrance has it. You have only one job this next week."

"What?"

"Making me happy." Kim reached for her purse and pulled out the brochure and after a moment to consider, a small velvet box. She handed Maggie the brochure and smiled. "You've heard of these guys, right?"

"Oh my God, yes!" Maggie beamed. "They are so hard to book a cruise with. You have to call so far ahead."

"I've been planning this for a while." Kim grinned and cleared her throat.

"What?"

"There is one other thing…" She nibbled on her lip, her hand clutching the small box.

Maggie cocked her head. "What?"

Kim held up the small velvet box and presented it to the woman she loved. "This was the other part of the money you didn't see. It was from my last book advance, and well… I …" Words failed Kim as happy tears welled in her eyes. "Will you marry me?"

Maggie's mouth opened and a soft startled sound

escaped. She took the small velvet box and opened it, a gasp immediately following. Her startled gaze went from the contents of the box to Kim's eyes.

"I never thought." She closed her eyes as a single tear slid down her cheek. Opening them again, she took the ring out of the box and slid the platinum and diamond antique ring onto her finger.

Maggie nodded.

"Are you sure?" Kim swallowed and licked her lips, which had gone bone dry.

Maggie moved forward and pressed her lips against Kim's. She leaned back and regarded Kim. "I've sat back and arranged wedding after wedding and a small part of me wondered if I'd ever get to have my day. When I could call you *my* wife." She grinned and wiped a tear from her face. "But I will. Thanks to you."

"I love you, Mags. Now come on this cruise with me and let's have some fun."

"That sounds wonderful, but first…" Maggie grinned, pulling Kim back into her embrace. She reached for the zipper on the back of the lace dress and lowered it, letting the garment fall to the floor.

"I want to see you. Please…"

Kim's bra and panties were the next to go, landing in a heap on the floor next to the dress. She kicked off her shoes and was glad her legs were smooth enough to not wear stockings.

"Maggie… I…" Kim pressed her lips against Maggie's, sinking into the sweet and familiar taste of her. "This is how I feel. Every day, every hour."

Maggie groaned and swayed in Kim's embrace. Kim's fingers twined in Maggie's hair and her mouth hungrily devoured her, moving from her lips to the soft spaces on her neck and behind her ear. Her kiss was urgent and exploratory, sending her stomach into a wild swirl of longing. Kim pushed Maggie back toward the bed, lowering her down onto the quilt. She let her gaze travel over Maggie's body and tenderly appraised her.

"I've loved you for better or for worse every day since I met you while saving that stupid cat from the sewer grate in front of the bookstore." Kim smoothed a tear from Maggie's cheek. Her lips claimed Maggie's once more, Kim's hand slipping beneath the dress. "Let me hear you say the words. Let me love you forever."

"Oh Kim…" Maggie nuzzled her neck, her breath warm against her hair. The touch was like a whisper urging her on. "Yes… a thousand times yes."

Laughter and sounds of people in the hallway jolted them both.

"The door's locked." Maggie murmured. "Don't worry."

Kim pressed a kiss onto her thigh and pushed the dress upward. "Good." The small triangle of fabric covering the apex of Maggie's thighs was little more than a wisp of black lace. Her fingers edged along the elastic, teasing the silken folds hidden within.

Maggie's body squirmed beneath her. "Kim! You're killing me."

A wicked smile curled her lips upward. "I haven't even started yet." She lowered her lips to the lace and pressed a kiss onto Maggie's mound. Her own pussy dampened at the musky scent and she hungered to savor the sweetness between Maggie's thighs. It had been too long and she was starving for her. Hours felt like centuries and she clamored for her touch.

"I want these." She hooked her thumbs on the lacy black panties and tugged them down Maggie's creamy flesh, past the lace edges of her smoky black hose and over her shoes.

"Here. Let me take them off." Maggie reached for the heels and Kim waved her hands away.

"No. I want to look at you, legs spread and heels

digging into the bed when I make you come."

"Do it then." Maggie watched her with bright eyes, her lips parted with desire.

Kim placed a kiss on the top of one creamy thigh. "Show me your breasts."

With shaking hands, Maggie reached into the bodice of her dress, tugging it down to reveal the swollen bounty of pearly rose-tipped flesh. Maggie's breath was coming faster now, the rise and fall of her chest tantalizing to Kim. She leaned forward and took the tip of one of the mounds into her mouth and sucked. Maggie writhed beneath her as she switched from one to the other, the rock-like points glistening in the half light.

Easing her finger along the slick folds of Maggie's heat, she slid a digit inside of her hot wet sheath. Her hand cupped Maggie's sex, rubbing lightly against her clit and Kim smiled as she watched her lover twist against the quilt.

"More…"

"Mmmm. Soon." She slid first one finger, then two inside of her and placed tender kisses down the rounded curve of her tummy. Delving into her delicate softness, her thrusts made Maggie buck forward, a cry on her lips. Kim trailed kisses down Maggie's stomach, placing a final kiss on her mound as she withdrew her fingers.

"So beautiful."

She urged Maggie's legs wider. Kim slipped to the floor, giving her the perfect view of Maggie's pink womanly center, slick with the evidence of her desire. She slid her palms up the outsides of her thighs and Maggie shivered. Leaning in, she placed a kiss on the creamy flesh traveling inward until she reached her destination.

Her tongue dipped into the moist folds and Kim lapped at Maggie's warm entrance. She slipped inside, penetrating her throbbing core. Kim's nose nudged her clit. Maggie bucked against her as she took the delicate nub between her lips and began to suck.

Maggie shrieked and her body tensed. Kim sheathed her fingers inside of Maggie's slippery softness, filling her as far as she could go. She drove her higher and as the first tremor of orgasm wracked her body, she added yet another digit to push her over the edge.

"Oh God!" Maggie's legs wrapped around her, her hands reaching to pull her closer as the shivers subsided.

Kim withdrew and joined her on the bed, enveloping her lover in her arms. Her body pulsed with need but she was content. Her eyes began to shut when she felt Maggie's fingers slide between her thighs.

"Are you falling asleep on me?"

Her eyes flew open, senses hyperaware. "Not on your life."

"Good," Maggie chortled, her face still flushed. "Because I have plans to make you scream all night."

Kim grinned. The patter of rain against the glass and the scent of orchids in the air lulled her into the purple spirals of her own passion as Maggie began to map her flesh. The evening had just begun, her body awakening to her lover's lips. The future was theirs, but first there was the night.

THE BOI WHO CRIED WOOLF

ALLISON WONDERLAND

"Where shall we go this summer? The Rubyfruit Jungle? The Whistle Stop Café? In deep waters where we can hear the mermaids sing?"

I turn away from the bookshelf and come face-to-face with a pair of eyes that are Rita Mae Brown and round like typewriter keys. "How about to the lighthouse?" I suggest, emulating a Woolf in sheep's clothing—whatever that means.

"Come on, reading material girl, you can't go against the season. If we take a holiday, everything will be okay."

Bernadette nudges my side. It's friendly but flirty, although I wouldn't recognize coquetry if it winked at me from the cover of a pulp fiction novel, especially if it's the one about *The Bashful Lesbian.* We have that queer—er, here—in the library, which I should specify is specific to the LGBT community. Sandwiched between a beauty salon and a sub shop, we're kind of on the small side, when compared with your average athenaeum, anyway. I manage the Chick/Chick Lit section, an archive of lesbian literature we want to save, share and… Wait a minute. *If* we take a holiday, everything *will* be okay?

In spite of the synthetic breeze, courtesy of our enfeebled air-conditioner, beads of perspiration ease down my back. "Um, are we not okay?"

Bernadette's hands parenthesize my hips. "First of all, Fallon, those were not heated words, so stop sweating. You read way too much into everything."

In an attempt to improve (and disprove) my image as a femme with stone butch blues, I touch her too, making my wrists droop daintily over her shoulders. "So… what *are* you saying?"

"I'm saying let's make like a bastard and get out of Carolina."

I'm about to put her in her place, so to speak, but when her eyebrows curve like the drawer handle on a card catalog, I'm the one who stands corrected. "I'm just more of the head-trip type," I tell her. "Like that proverb, you know—East or Vita Sackville-West, home is best. I like to keep it local. What was that vintage children's book series we were reminiscing about recently? *Something Queer Is Going On.* At the ballpark, at the lemonade stand, at the library." I gaze longingly at the Sapphics in soft covers on the shelves. "We can go anywhere and everywhere right here, just by reading the rainbow. We can even—"

"Books are transportable in more ways than one," Bernadette counters, and I don't mind the interruption. Her voice is Adrienne Rich with vibrancy and certainty and I could listen to it all day every day and then some. "But it's fine," she continues. "We don't have to go anywhere this summer. I do want to, uh… take you places though, okay?"

Her gaze Nat Burns me more than the sun ever could. "Um, okay… um… cutie." It doesn't come out like a term of endearment, of course. More like an arbitrary noun filling in the blank that my mind has drawn.

Bernadette's look is a hyphenation of amused and confused. I feel like an incomplete entry in a card catalog: untitled, unauthorized, subject—to ridicule.

I attempt to chortle charmingly, but alas, a rolling ladder makes sexier sounds than I do.

Fortunately, Bernadette lets it slide. "All right,

Fallon, well, I'll just keep browsing until closing time."

So saying, she drifts over to the Action/Adventure section on the opposite wall. Her selection isn't surprising, given that she's not getting either with me. Ours is a women-in-the-shadows-who-whisper-their-love sort of romance. It's not that we consider our feelings forbidden or our urges unnatural. It's just that, as much as I know about lesbian fiction, I know next to nothing about lesbian friction—and this lack of carnal knowledge is really starting to rub me the wrong way. I don't know why I feel so queer about intimacy. I *have* the urges. I just don't have the courage to act on them. And I don't want Bernadette to make the first move, or feel like she has to just because she's the boi. *I* want to make it.

I pick up the pulp classic *The Heat of Day*, whose garment-deficient cover girls proclaim their preparedness for a 'summer of awakening'. Will I ever be as ready for Bernadette? I mean, in theory, I'd rather get her off than put her off, but in practice… I'm out of it. I think of myself as a prurient prude, meaning I think about sex mentally and, you know, manually. But as far as hands-on learning, actually putting my hands on someone else, I can count the number of times I've done it on one finger.

On the one hand, I'm kind of proud of the fact that I've kept Annie (and Chloe plus Olivia) on my mind instead of in my bed—if I were straight, I'd be a good girl, but since I'm gay, I'm just a lesbophile. On the other hand, I fear I'll never truly transition from lone star lez to full-fledged Dykewomon if I continue to refuse the acquisition of sinister wisdom.

That's when I notice that Bernadette has moved on. Not from me, thank goodness. Sarah may have Patience, but Bernadette has patience—although she *is* in LGBT History now, so I hope this isn't her subtle way of telling me we're history. No, she wouldn't do that. She wouldn't leave me just because I treat her like a banned book, a restricted country, a fried green tomato that spoiled because I waited too long to eat it. And shame on me for thinking (again) that she would.

Returning my mind to the gutter where it belongs, I check Bernadette out like a good librarian should. Her figure is... Well, she looks, to put it bluntly, and without benefit of the color purple prose, genderfucking good. Her baseball jersey separates the bois from the men, its body tight and bright white and its raglan sleeves a brash yellow that reminds me of those Curious George books I used to read as a kid. Her red hair is concisely and precisely cut, much like her jean shorts. To sum it up, she resembles a grown-up version of my childhood literary heroine, Cam Jansen. Like the baby dyke detective with the photographic memory, we just click.

Which is why I shouldn't be so shy about intimacy. If we're compatible in every other way, why wouldn't we also be simpatico sexually? But what if we're so compatible that we become a couple of Diana Cage rattlers who are constantly on our backs and never do anything but each other? Let's say we go to a resort and, after exhausting all other forms of recreation, resort to the one called lovemaking. We may never leave the room! That's a real thing, isn't it? Never leaving the room?

It won't even matter where the room is. Once Bernadette and I move past chaste to experience another kind of love, we'll go at it until we Bern the candle at both ends and our relationship regresses to an evil friendship because 'unsatisfied' is a synonym for 'insatiable' and... Sheesh, if I could just extract the *n* and the *u* from *neurotic*, I'd be as good as nude.

You know what? I can do it. Because if I can do it, then we can do it. And today's the day.

Actually, the next day is better—a tribute to that novel *Tomorrow Wendy*.

Or perhaps, to honor the Sapphic scribes of

speculative fiction, I shouldn't speculate on the specifics but just be content with my intent to do it sometime in the future.

I know, I know—the more I think it over, the more I overthink it. Before Bernadette gets on the case of the good-for-nothing girlfriend, we need to get it on. And so, I am going to make my journey to a woman and Nancy Clue her in: after eight months of us going to bed together, only to engage in purely puritanical pursuits like reading and sleeping, I am ready to Joan Nestle against her in a duet in darkness.

As if reading my thoughts, Bernadette turns toward me, and the look on her face is that of an odd girl out and about to ensnare me in the trap of Lesbos. As she makes her approach, my head starts spinning like a carousel of paperbacks, those of the lesbian pulp fiction variety, to be exact.

"Stop looking at me like that," Bernadette scolds, and holds my gaze.

"Like what?"

"Like you want to finish what you can't start."

"I'm not looking at you like that," I insist, instantly defensive when I should be aggressively agreeable. Great—instead of springing on her a stimulation of her box at its leakiest, what do I do? Give her a simulation of a box spring at its squeakiest. I'd be Phyllis lyin' if I said I wasn't disappointed in myself.

I clear my throat and try again, opening my mouth in anticipation of a flow, however slow, of words, each of which will coalesce into something torrid, maybe florid, but hopefully not horrid. Instead, all that comes out is a hot puff of breath. Just call me The Draggin' Lady. A rainbow of opportunity knocks and I blow it like… like pencil shavings. I just completely erase my desires with that little pink knob, which kind of reminds me of an erect nipple.

Or a clitoris, if it's been well rubbed.

From her expression, I can tell Bernadette is contemplating whether to eat, shoot or leave me. Her loose lips tighten into a smile, drawn-out but not drawn on. In fact, the only illustrations on her face are the freckles sketched all over her nose and cheeks. There's something delightful about those dots. They're like some sort of erratic, rebellious ellipsis. She's a girl with boi-ish good looks, and if looks could thrill…

A shiver shoots through me, rapid and rambunctious, like thumbing through a flip-book.

Without a word, she folds her arms around me, and all I can do is feel the Bern.

"So…" I begin, but I'm too warm for her form to form a sensible, let alone sensuous, sentence.

"Something you want to get off your chest, Fallon?" she queries, hoping I'll take the hint and take her.

"Not… right now."

"I figured as much," she says, more resigned than resentful. She maximizes our contact, and soon our chests are closer than a checkout card in the paper pocket of an old-fashioned library book. "At least you're upfront with me."

Regrettably, the ersatz air causes my temperature to dip a drop. Well, there's the summery summary for this chapter of our relationship: summer lovin', had me a blast of air-conditioning.

* * *

"Fallon, my love," Bernadette purrs, amorous and glamorous and unquestionably sincere, "each minute away from you is a drag king, each hour a satirical eternity. I can't stop thinking about the color of your dykes on bikes or the way you wear your books on tape. When I look at you, my tailbone skips a beat, my bellybutton leaps into my throat, and my freak flag trembles so much I can hardly exfoliate. You set my

THE BOI WHO CRIED WOOLF

fanny pack on fire. I love you from the bottom of my spleen."

Having said all that, she flips the tablet of Mad Libs closed and clips the pen to the cover, then drops the pad onto the empty swing beside her. If I'd been listening, I'd be laughing. But instead of paying attention to what she was reading, I was too busy reading by flashlight. Her lips, I mean. I love watching her mouth move and groove to the words. Bernadette has that wax lip look. Not size-wise, of course—that would make her stranger than fiction—but she's definitely sporting a deluxe, cherry confection of corpulent opulence.

On impulse, I spring from my swing and kiss her. It lasts about as long as it takes a librarian to stamp the due date into a book, and then I'm right back where I started. Good grief, I'm like the poky little puppy on tranquilizers.

Bernadette says nothing, but there's a cryptic crimp in her smile.

"Cat got your tongue?" I tease, pocketing the little flashlight. There may be no Adam for this Eve, but if I'm going to attempt original sin, I might want to try being more original.

"No, the cat has not got my tongue." Bernadette looks toward my lap. "I should be so lucky."

She doesn't add: *It's a good thing I work at a record store or I'd never enjoy a summer of sixty-nine.* But I can read her thoughts.

In the middle of my mind-reading, Bernadette hops off the swing and comes toward me, sneakers clamping down on the wood chips beneath us. She brings her knees to mine. Pretty soon, she'll bring me to my knees. After she jumps—er, bumps—my bones, she proceeds to sit on my thighs and wraps her arms around my neck. Well, I suppose since I was upfront with her the other day, it's only fair that she return the favor.

"Hey," she says, "did that lady come today?"

Because if I can't come, someone else might as well have the pleasure, she doesn't finish, but it's crystal queer that's what she's thinking.

With my rear rubbing the rough, rubbery seat and Bernadette's body heat rearranging the love letters in my head like a word jumble, it takes me a while to respond. "Um, yeah, that lady came today. She wanted to donate her entire collection of Baby-Sitters Club books. Now, I know Mallory hates boys—"

"—and gym—"

"—but what was this woman thinking?"

"Make like Kristy and get a great idea, why don't you? You should have at least accepted the books about the club president. Then you could devote a whole subsection to sporty dyke blue jean femme power lesbian dykes in training." The heels of Bernadette's hands dig into my shoulders. "And did you ever see the TV show? Those girls were so... demonstrative, way beyond typically tactile. They got the theme song all wrong. It should have gone: 'Gay hello to your friends—Budding Sapphics Club.'" Her fingers tickle my neck, lightly but sprightly, as if she's groping wind chimes.

I wait until the pleasure Berns out before replying. "Please tell me you aren't entertaining inappropriate thoughts about thirteen-year-old girls."

"First off: gross. Second: Fallon, my love, you are the modern-day gay Mary Anne: prude extraordinaire and world-class worrywart. You know, if Kristy and Mary Anne had dated, Kristy never would have made it to first base. She'd be more sexually frustrated than I am."

"You'll cover all your... or my... bases eventually."

Bernadette fondles my ponytail, making it swish like the tassel on a bookmark. "Oh, I know it," she crows. "One of these days, I'm going to get a fun home run."

"As long as you refrain from doing something awful

and unlawful with underage literary characters. You are not Bastille material, not by any stretch of the incarceration."

"Oh, and how many times have *you* been down?"

I swallow, dry all of a sudden—in the throat area, anyway.

Bernadette smirks. "I meant that the only record you'll ever have is the kind that comes in vinyl and plays on a phonograph." She circles a finger through my hair. "But you should totally go down. In fact, I'll go down—" she pauses, as if to ponder the proper preposition "—with you. We can be cellmates. I can see us now: two dames caged in a maximum-security prison, where our bond, so hot it's criminal, clicks into place like a pair of handcuffs."

"I'm… pretty sure physical contact between inmates is prohibited."

"And I'm pretty sure, Fallon the Felon, that *inmate* is two letters short of *intimate*." Her gaze blazes like a bonfire, causing my insides to get mushier than a roasted marshmallow and my cheeks to match the color of the sidewalk chalk hearts we sketched on the basketball court. "I'm also sure," she continues, caressing my face, "that you would be a model prisoner. You'd keep to yourself, but me, I'd mingle too much. I'd probably try to organize a talent show or something. On the upside, I doubt prison would ever scare me straight. I'd probably love all the estrogen energy and esprit de corps the slammer has to offer and never want to leave."

"Yeah, I bet you'll meet a girl who can jailhouse rock your world and make you forget all about me," I lament, because insecurity is such an irresistible trait in a mate. "She'll be more passionate than me and she—"

"You keep that up and I'll throw the book at you," Bernadette promises, and I have her to thank for my reduced sentence. "Besides, I already have a girl who can jailhouse rock my world. And she will, when she's good and ready."

She starts to get up, but I take my hands off her hips and slip my fingers through hers. "Something you *don't* want to get off your chest?" she teases, and squeezes my hands. Her grip is strong, like reinforced binding, but her skin is softer than the fabric in a touch-and-feel board book.

Instead of answering, I put her on lip-lockdown. There are not enough adjectives in the universe to sufficiently summarize the experience of kissing Bernadette—when it's a real kiss, not a paltry peck. When it starts, it's like cracking open my favorite book and knowing I'm in for a treat. Halfway through, I find something new to love about it. And when it concludes, my smile has more Watts than Julia does.

I'm suddenly very aware that Bernadette's legs, which are the color of a cake cone and smoother than the ice cream it holds, are bare, and mine are too. Now would be a good time to initiate some hot fun in the summertime, a season whose temperatures and fashions are designed to create and sate lust.

"Want to go to my place and knock back a few Georgia Beers?" asks one of the bois of summer.

To which I, in my inebriated state, reply, "You know I don't drink."

"Audre Lorde, have mercy," Bernadette quips, and I feel my face turn pinker than the flip-flops on my cold feet. "I'll make you some Michelle Tea. How's that?" She sticks out her tongue. "FYI, midsummer night's dream girl, I kind of feel like a book whose date of release is forever TBD. But you know what I've determined?" she asks, and leans closer until there's only one degree of separation between us. "I've determined that the reason for this interminable delay is this: you're afraid that once we start, you won't be able to stop. I know how you get when you're totally engrossed in a book—you can't put it down, you never want it to end, you're completely oblivious to everything else until it does. That's how you feel about the erotic content of our romance."

I nod. I also feel like a stripped book. She certainly knows me like one, I note, as she proceeds to gloat, "Face it, Fallon: you're easier to read than *The Hell of Loneliness*."

"*Well*."

"Well what?"

"It's called—"

"I know what it's called. I'm an invert too. And don't be ashamed—you're not the only one who's concerned about our potential immunity to Lesbian Bed Death." Outwardly, she winks. Inwardly, she thinks: *You're more warped than a water-damaged book.*

And she's right to think that.

My outlook on lovemaking isn't worth a Gerri Hill of beans.

It's a cruel summer, leaving her queer on her own.

* * *

"Stop rushing ahead, you little speed-reader," Bernadette chides, and guides my finger back to the previous paragraph.

"And if I don't, Mrs. Dilly-Dalloway?"

Bernadette guffaws. Her laugh, with its serrated edges and signature flam-boi-ance, thrives in her throat. "If you don't, there will be no pages for you," she declares, grinding her shoulder against mine.

"Fine," I sulk, and smile, my body cooling off and heating up at the same time. "But do I still Jane Rule your world?"

"Yes, Fallon, but only because my heart would be a desert without you."

As my brain gets goopier than the glue at the arts & crafts table at summer camp, I paste my gaze to hers.

Compared to everyone else—sister outsider, Beebo Brinker, the girls in 3-B—Bernadette is literally my favorite lesbian in this whole entire library.

It's getting harder and harder to ignore the invisible text written on the body in front of me. Text that says *Touch me* and screams *Take me* and reminds me why it's important to read for pleasure.

I push away Mrs. Dalloway. She skids across the blanket and comes to a stop at the edge of twilight. Normally, couples prefer to share their book and blanket in a field or on a beach under the boardwalk, but instead of being odd girls out, we're odd girls in.

Love, that is.

I meant what I said before, that we could go anywhere and everywhere right here. We don't need some sun-kissed, starfished holiday getaway in order to ride a heat wave of pleasure. Nor does Bernadette need to be a beach boi to experience good vibrations. We can enjoy each other, those lazy-hazy-crazy gays of summer, right here right now.

"Once again," Bernadette says, edging toward me, "you are undressing me the same way you always do: with your eyes."

"I'm sorry. I… Next time I'll use my hands?" I stammer, as I clamber for courage.

Bernadette's brows arc like a rainbow of balloons at a pride parade. "I think there has to be a first time, Fallon, before there can be a next time."

My heart starts thrashing around inside my chest. Jeez, it's like a lavender love rumble in there. I recognize it for the LGBT cue that it is: I'm finally ready to Bern my bridges.

Before my nerve Julie Anne Peters out yet again, I reach for Bernadette's hand, although I'm so out of it, I don't even realize I'm touching her until I see her freckles disappear beneath my palm. "I know we're in a public place," I begin, after swallowing several helpings of antiquated air, "and that means that someone could come in here—"

"Yeah, me."

"Um, however," I persevere, like the heroine in a Penny Hayes western, "we're here, we're queer, we're alone—for the time being. So there's no reason to go to the lighthouse when we already have a room of one's own."

Bernadette blinks at me, her eyes as round as inner tubes. "Is that a dare, truth or promise?" she asks, proceeding with caution, as though I'm one of those dykes to watch out for.

Before my resolve can crumble like a sandcastle, I answer with clarity, sincerity and above all, honor. "It's the truth, I promise."

Bernadette's face lights up like a reading lamp. She glances across the blanket at the neglected novel. "Now I know why you like Virginia so much: she's for lovers."

She grins at me, causing my smile to leave my cheeks and head straight for my eyes. Bernadette moves something else: her bottom, which she transfers to the top of a nearby table.

I go to her.

She leans in a little.

I lean in a lot, until I'm almost at the notch of her crotch.

The young in one another's arms, we're closer than Lillian Faderman and Leslie Feinberg on the bookshelf.

I kiss her. Her breath tastes like oranges—and they're not the only fruit. There's also a hint of honeydew and a lick of lemon, courtesy of the smoothie we shared for breakfast.

Bernadette gets her bell hooks into me, her digits digging dexterously into my sides.

I feel my nipples tighten.

She must feel them too, because she says, "I guess our conversation last week about babes behind bars really inspired you. You've become quite the hardened criminal."

At that, my clit corresponds, tit for twat.

Bernadette pops the button on her jeans, then pulls the zipper back along the track. As the tab descends, so do I.

Approaching the carpet in order to access hers, I notice the aisle marker behind her. It occurs to me then that even though we're finally moving forward, we're still stuck in the past. That's all right. After all, what better way to go down in history than to... well, go down in History?

Once her jeans are out of the way, Bernadette spreads her legs again—minimally at first, like the little nook in a hand-drawn heart; and then more comfortably, like an open book.

Her panties are the dust jacket, and I shove the flap aside like a brazen femme in order to get to the next part: her Nancy Garden of Eden. It is creased like the spine of a well-loved novel and looks juicier than boi-senberries. My mouth Sarah Waters at the sight and I experience a tinge of Venus envy.

It isn't long before I'm completely immersed in Bernadette: the gently curling hair—redder than Anne of Green Gables'; the lusty scent—sweeter than the intoxicating raspberry cordial imbibed by her bosom friend Diana; and the unctuous lips—dewier than the Decimal System.

Burrowed in the V of her Katherine Forrest, I am a naiad in her nether regions, and I concentrate exclusively on loving her, adoring her, exploring her.

She is a cross-genre softcover: romance, mystery, fantasy, thriller.

I probe the persistent desire, investigating as if I'm

Alison Kaine or Stoner McTavish.

My tongue scrubs the nub, rubs her the long way, stretching her juices from hatch to thatch.

She makes a noise: a curious whine.

The sound builds, subtly yet swiftly, like suspense, as we blend into a single perfect paragraph—my sentences, for once declarative and interrogative, mingle with her imperative and exclamatory ones.

Now I truly understand the appeal of audiobooks.

I watch Bernadette waver and savor the climax, the payoff for enduring the convoluted plot that I created.

I replace the dust jacket, pressing it against the sticky pages until the material is ensconced in her folds like a bookmark.

I lick my lips and at last identify her flavor: she tastes like trail mix. The price of salt makes it a very hot commodity.

As I get to my feet, Bernadette studies me like an unfamiliar subject she needs to read up on. "Given your… intuitive aptitude for cunnilingus—seriously, it's like you wrote the book on it—it's become painfully obvious and yet absolutely nonsensical why you waited so long to Virginia Woolf me down."

I chuckle, but my knees buckle from the weight of her gaze. She's not even touching me and already I'm twisting and turning like a crime fiction lover—er, novel—ready to burst like a water balloon. If she keeps this up, I'll never be able to take my nose out of her book. And why should I? It's the most absorbing Sapphic graphic novel I've ever read. "I can't believe I finally finished," I gush like a fire hydrant. "Started, I mean. I can't believe I finally—"

"Don't start, Fallon," she exhorts, and thwarts my regularly scheduled rambling. She presses her lips against mine. It's firm and purposeful, the way she folds the corner of a page so she won't lose her place.

In my book, Bernadette will never lose her place.

"You know," she says, "our story might not be a bawdy beach read, but it will Dinah Shore become a classic, what with its time-honored plot of girl meets boi, girl gets boi, girl gets boi off."

There's a significant pause. I hope this story doesn't end on a Radclyffe-hanger. "Um, then boi gets girl off?" I supply, helpfully and hopefully.

"Well, we don't want to make the plot *too* predictable, but yes, that's where this story's headed." She punctuates her sentence with a smile, which gradually grows into a grin, until she resembles one of those anthropomorphic beaming sun faces.

It's a face that suggests she'll be tipping the velvet, though not necessarily with a velvet glove.

A velvety, ungloved hand glides along my side, then goes on to slip 'n slide across my hip. "As you know, I don't do anything by the book," Bernadette states in the foreword, and I can't wait to acknowledge her in the afterglow. Er, afterword. "So you can expect to come out of nowhere, but don't expect a tidy resolution."

Of course—I've read enough lesbian literature to understand that happy endings are not all alike. Even so, I'm excited for the completion of our first edition. Oh, sure, it means that from now on, we'll always be out of breath.

But it also means that we'll never be out-of-print.

OLD COLLEGE FRIENDS
ANNABETH LEONG

How Callie and Andy had managed to find and rent the exact same beach house we'd used ten years before was a mystery to me. I was sort of surprised I still had the same name I did ten years ago—I'd changed so much since college graduation that memories from back then startled me when they hit.

I climbed off the Old Beast and dropped its kickstand, my boots sinking into the damp, sand-swirled dirt of the weedy front yard. The bike was a greasy, noisy, testy thing, and if I hadn't felt so vain about it, I'd have traded it for something that didn't require quite as much time undergoing maintenance. On the other hand, *undergoing maintenance* was probably a good description for my life over the past five years at least. Who was I to judge? I gave the Old Beast's seat an apologetic pat, licked lips made salty by sea air, and squared my shoulders to face the former best friends I hadn't seen in close to a decade.

The side door was open, and from it spilled a nostalgic playlist, along with the cheap, boozy smell of the alcohol adults buy when they want to remember their youth. I stepped up a short flight of stairs, not sure what I was about to see when I peered in.

Callie and Andy turned out to be eerily unchanged—she still had pale pink cheeks rounded by baby fat, and he still possessed thin, boyish hips that would have made my pulse pound had they belonged to a woman—except that, a decade ago, they'd have been so busy pressing their faces together that it would have been next to impossible to get a look at either of them head-on. Now they were shoving various boxes and bottles into an oversized refrigerator, their bodies tense and frenetic.

For a second, I panicked and wanted to run back to the Old Beast before any of them spotted me. Ten years ago, I'd had long hair and a fiancé named Jordan. Along with Callie, Andy, Jennie Parks, and her flavor of the week, we'd hung out here as couples, and I'd had no clue that only six months later, I'd freak out, call off the wedding, delete my Facebook account, and move across the country with a woman who made me feel like no kiss before hers could possibly have counted.

Callie noticed me before I could turn away. She stepped toward the screen door, forehead creased with concern. "May I help you?" Then her eyes widened. "Elena?"

I shrugged awkwardly. "Most people call me Len now." So maybe my name wasn't *exactly* the same. Callie stumbled over herself to let me in and make me feel at home, and I cringed at the awkwardness in every excessively polite gesture. I wondered why they'd invited me, not Jordan. I would have expected him to stay in touch with them.

"Jennie should be back any minute, and then we'll all be here together," Callie said. She made it sound like an item on a list that needed to be checked off, and I noticed Andy rolling his eyes behind her back.

I had no patience for whatever was going on with those two. I was busy realizing just how nervous I was about seeing Jennie Parks again. Back in college, she had unsettled me because she was so beautiful, as in better than me. Now I couldn't help wondering if there had been more to it than that.

I wanted to ask if she'd come alone, but I feared I wouldn't be able to make the question sound like idle chitchat. Besides, it was a ridiculous thing to wonder about. My girlfriend and I had married the first day it was allowed in my state, along with dozens of other couples, but a few years later I had the groundbreaking divorce to match the groundbreaking wedding. The Old Beast was the only thing that soothed the sting to my pride. I didn't need to go seeking any further humiliation at the hands of Jennie and my former college friends.

I toyed with the label on the bottle of craft beer they handed me. Callie kept giving me weird stares, and even Andy's friendly half-smile made me uncomfortable. I wasn't sure how I felt about this particular blast from the past.

"I wondered why you deleted your Facebook," Callie said. It wasn't a question. She acted like the way I looked told her the whole story.

I took a long swig, grimacing at the aftertaste. Did someone make a law requiring brewers to use too much hops? "I wondered why you made such an effort to find me," I returned, challenging her to go ahead and talk about it.

She shrugged, reaching back for Andy's hand. He made a face like she was squeezing his bones together. "If we were going to have a reunion, it had to be *right*."

Her tone made me remember her many anxieties going through college. I used to take her down to the city dock, sit dangling my feet over the water, and just let her talk at me. I never thought I was doing any good. I realized how she must have worried putting this trip together. The first beach house trip had been wonderful, an experience that had lulled me into a falsely idyllic sense of my future life prospects. It wasn't an easy thing to match or recreate, and I knew in my gut that she had lost sleep and fretted endlessly trying to take us all back to a happier time.

Setting the beer down on the counter, I reached out and squeezed her upper arm, surprising us both. "This is nice," I said. "Thanks. I'm glad you found me."

Her face was just starting to soften when Jennie arrived and all the air left the room. I snatched my hand away from Callie as if I'd been doing something wrong, and turned to face the swinging screen door.

With the sun at her back, I couldn't make out her features. For a moment, she looked like the girl of 21 she'd been the last time I'd seen her. She dressed the same, too—floral sundress with messily laced Docs and girlish plastic barrettes in her hair.

"Elena!" She flung herself into my arms as if we were long-lost lovers, and it made my heart want to pound right out of my chest.

"She says it's Len now," Callie said in a cold voice.

Jennie pulled back and looked me over. Her face had sharpened into a fearsome beauty that belied the youthfulness of her attire, unblemished, olive-toned, and pointed. This was the charisma of statecraft, the face that had launched a thousand ships because the woman who owned it damn well planned to. My mouth was too dry to let me say anything. I was pretty sure that any words I tried would come out as inarticulate creaking.

"Len," Jennie agreed with a sweet voice and a nod. She stood on her tiptoes and kissed my cheek. "Got it."

I was dizzy, almost shaking. Jennie's message was coming through loud and clear. And yet my eyes didn't follow her. They returned, for some reason, to Callie's face, where I was greeted with thin-lipped disapproval.

* * *

"Are you sowing your wild oats post-divorce?" Jennie asked. The way she cut her eyes in my direction had to be calculated—it made her look too beautiful, too carefully shy to be accidental.

We were walking along the beach, and had been long enough that, despite my sun-resistant golden-brown complexion, I worried I'd get a burn across the back of my neck and shoulders. Jennie didn't walk so much as march, arms and hair swinging cheerfully and inexorably, and I was out of breath from keeping up with her. I used that as an excuse to put off answering.

For a few minutes, I got really interested in the calling of seagulls and the crashing of waves. I hooked a strand of seaweed with one bare toe then picked up a couple of shells. It wasn't possible to ignore the way the back of her hand kept brushing mine, but I pretended that I could.

Finally, she laughed and nudged me. "Come on. Don't get all mysterious. Are you sleeping around now that you're free?"

Why? Are you volunteering? The words were on the tip of my tongue, but I thought my own throat was about to strangle me. Since the divorce, I hadn't been able to get through so much as a drunken kiss. A part of me just wouldn't let me make a move.

Taking a small step back, I tried to look casual. "Is that what you do after a big breakup?"

Jennie just laughed. "I've never really had a big breakup, so I wouldn't know. But I think, yeah, maybe I'd do that."

I cleared my throat. Jennie was looking at me like we were about to kiss. I was bending toward her like a weed in the wind, but before I could do anything, I heard my name above the sound of the waves.

I jerked upright guiltily and got irritated at myself for acting guilty. Callie was approaching, hand half-raised as if she wasn't sure whether to wave, face tight as usual, body stiff and precise. Jennie's lips twisted, inviting me to share a moment of private ridicule, but even though Callie looked ridiculous, I didn't have the heart for that.

The sight of her wearing dorky pink shorts and carrying a grocery store tote bag, hunks of brown hair forced into her mouth by the wind, inspired a sort of deep sympathy that made me pull back from Jennie even farther. I *did* wave, and the way Callie smiled to receive the gesture made me glad I had.

"I was looking for you two!" She glanced between Jennie and me. "I'm not interrupting, am I?" There was an odd wobble in her voice.

"No," Jennie said grudgingly, in a tone that said Callie very much had been.

And I ought to have been feeling the same way—something had definitely been about to happen between the two of us—but instead I felt a rush of relief that I couldn't explain. "It's cool," I said genuinely, earning myself a sharp look from Jennie and another grateful smile from Callie.

"Maybe I'll head back," Jennie said. "I'm getting hungry."

Callie lifted her tote bag. "I have snacks in here. Crackers and fruit and cheese." She looked like a child anxious to please angry parents. It made my chest hurt to see that.

Jennie shook her head. "I don't eat gluten or dairy." She shoved her hands into her pockets and leaned back slightly, so her shirt rode up to show off her slim, muscular stomach. God, she was beautiful. I was pretty sure that if Callie hadn't showed up, I'd be pressed against Jennie's perfect body at that very moment, but I just couldn't summon the disappointment that any sane person ought to have felt. She shrugged and turned her back. "It's cool," she echoed, aiming the words over her shoulder at me. They didn't hit their mark.

I dropped onto the bare sand, shaking my head when Callie tried to get me to sit on a blanket instead. I smoothed out a spot for her, clearing it of seaweed.

"Come on. I want to see what's in that tote bag."

She eased herself down as if something on the ground might bite her. "It's just grapes and whatever. Wheat crackers. Nothing special."

I squinted like the sun was stopping me from looking at her face. "Sounds great."

She handed me the tote bag. I looked inside, and everything was arranged in neat little plastic storage bags, the same number of crackers and cheese slices in each one. It was almost too sweet to bear. I took out a bag and grinned in the direction of the ocean.

"You don't have to do that, you know," she said. The edge in her tone surprised me. Callie was clutching the bottoms of her shorts, her knuckles white. Tendons stood out on her neck.

"Do what?"

"Be nice to me."

I shook my head. "You want me to be mean to you?"

"No. I want…"

I wanted to see if I could smooth out some of the tension in her body. I imagined running a hand down the side of her neck and leaving it gentled in my wake. *Oh.* That little fantasy woke me up to what was going on. I had gorgeous, *single* Jennie Parks throwing herself at me, but instead here I was sitting with Callie Holbrook, an extremely anxious woman who'd been dating the same guy for over a decade. I slid a few inches away and opened the plastic bag.

She grabbed my arm. I braced to fend off whatever inappropriate contact was coming, but it turned out she only wanted my attention. "Back in college, what were you doing? When we'd go down to the dock?"

I stared at her. "Listening to you."

"Okay," she said, in a disbelieving tone. "Fine. But why? Honestly, I got sick of listening to myself, but you'd still be staring at the water like there was nowhere you'd rather be. I decided you had to be tuning me out, but I couldn't get myself to stop talking."

Fuck, the way she was looking at me made me want to brush a lock of hair out of her eyes. I shook her hand off my arm and stood up, trying to think of Jennie. When that didn't work, I tried to think of Andy. When that failed, too, I gave myself a strict five-minute time limit. Once that was up, I'd have to get off this beach and onto the Old Beast for a long, head-clearing ride.

"I was listening to you," I repeated. Before she could protest, I held up a hand. "I remember one time you were trying to decide whether to get Andy a leather-bound copy of King Lear for your anniversary. You thought it was gorgeous, but since it was leather, the gift for the third year of marriage, you were afraid he'd think you were pressuring him. And behind all that—you weren't sure if he'd ask you to marry him after you graduated, and you weren't sure if you wanted him to." I swallowed a sudden lump in my throat. "Since I was already engaged to Jordan, you thought I might have some kind of perspective to offer."

"You remember all that?"

"More than that." I had barely thought about her for years, but now that I wanted the memories, they flooded me. "I remember the stuff about consolidating your student loans, the time you were thinking about taking dance lessons, the weird guy in your linear algebra study group."

"You know me better than anyone. Better than my parents. Better than Andy. And I don't know anything about you. Never did."

What she'd just said felt too dangerous. I didn't want to be compared to Andy, and I damn sure didn't want to confess any of my secrets to her. "I don't know you, Callie. It's been ten years."

"You do," she said. "I can see it in how you move."

She stood. Ever responsible, she kept track of the tote bag as she did, hitching it neatly over one shoulder. I was afraid she would try to kiss me, but I didn't have the guts to run. She was the one who did, and I watched her until she disappeared over the dunes. Then I ate my cheese and crackers and followed that with a long, cold swim. When I got a stomach cramp from exerting myself while I was still digesting, a part of me felt glad, as if I deserved the punishment.

* * *

I avoided going back to the house until the last possible minute, when I had no choice but to spend the night there or find somewhere else to sleep. The Old Beast hunkered where I'd left it, tempting me to just get out of this mess.

My ex-wife had asked me sometimes if I'd been interested in women before her, and I'd always told her I hadn't been. Now it seemed like things had always been complicated with my closest female friends from before.

I didn't know what Jennie wanted from me, and I wasn't sure if I actually liked her enough to give her whatever it was.

That was nothing, though, compared with the torrent of unspoken feelings that had whirled through me on the beach with Callie. For some reason, I'd never stopped to ask myself why I'd spent so much time with her in college, why I'd always been willing to lend an ear.

I tried to figure what drew me to her in the first place. She wasn't full of sexy knowingness like Jennie, and she was always wound tighter than a spring.

I leaned against the Old Beast. These people had been out of my life for so long. It wouldn't really matter if I rode away, wouldn't change anything in the present, and yet I couldn't bring myself to do it.

A sudden floral smell burst into the air near me. I

lifted my head just in time to intercept a running hug from Jennie. "I wondered why you weren't coming to bed, Len. I was waiting for you." She said that last bit with a pout so pretty it almost didn't come off as dirty as it was. Callie had the two single girls sharing a bedroom, and while that had initially given me a little thrill, it now made my stomach twist.

"I had a lot to think about," I said, trying to make a little space between us.

"You shouldn't think so much." She trailed a finger over the Old Beast's seat. "You should take me for a ride instead."

"Why?"

Jennie laughed. "Why not?"

I thought about flying through the night, air whipping past my jacket, her clinging to me with strong, gentle fingers. Of course, that would feel good, but I felt no thrill in my body at the image. "Seriously, why?"

"I'm curious." Jennie's finger on the Old Beast turned suggestive. She lowered her voice into a purr. "I've never done it before."

Ah. On paper, what Jennie was doing made sense. She wanted a new experience, and she thought I might want no-strings-attached fun. The problem was, that had never been my style, and I didn't think I wanted to change my ways now.

"That thing you asked me earlier? About the wild oats? It's really not…"

She shook her head with clear disapproval, but she did leave off caressing my motorcycle. She jumped up to straddle it instead. "Jesus, Len… You and Callie…"

That got my attention. Nobody was supposed to be able to guess what I'd been thinking about Callie. "What?"

"Both so hung up on your exes."

"I'm not hung up on my—" Then the important

part of that statement penetrated my consciousness and shut me up. Jennie was leaning closer, whispering in my ear about how it was okay, it was nothing to be ashamed of to miss my ex-wife, and maybe there were ways she could help me get some mental and physical relief…

My heart wasn't pounding for the reason I would have expected, though. I pulled back so I could see her face. The hunger on her features shone brighter as the evening dimmed, but my body wouldn't answer it. "Why were you talking about Callie? She's here with Andy."

Jennie rolled her eyes. "That's what she wants you to think. Earlier today, when I came back from the beach before you?"

I nodded.

"Andy told me everything. They haven't had sex in three years."

"That doesn't make her his ex."

"It does if they broke up right before coming on this trip." Jennie raised her eyebrows. "Callie begged him not to tell, but he told me."

"Did he want to sow his wild oats?" I asked darkly.

Jennie didn't take the question as an insult. She just threw back her head and laughed. "I think he did, Len." She curled her first finger, raising it into the air. I held my breath until it came to rest against the side of my face. Her voice dropped to a sexy purr, one that I couldn't help thinking would harmonize well with the sound of my motorcycle's engine. "But I've had sex with plenty of *men*, so the offer wasn't all that interesting…"

It would have been so simple just to take Jennie up on this. My hand would only have had to travel a few inches to her hip, and my lips wouldn't even have had to move. The slightest tilt of assent would have made her close the distance between us. I didn't want to think of Callie. I knew anything we did would be a mess of emotions—whatever we had left over from college, combined with the grief of my divorce, combined with the fresh wound of her break from Andy. Jennie didn't need anything from me but my body, and she didn't seem to want to give me anything but hers. I told myself it would be easier. Better.

But my throat tensed. I couldn't get over the revulsion I felt at her obvious desire to fuck me for the novelty of it. And I couldn't stop flashing to Callie's look of gratitude and relief when I acknowledged her on the beach. So when my hand lifted, what it did was brush her finger free of my cheek. "You're hot, Jennie. So hot."

This time, her chin dipped as she laughed, the throaty sound sinking into her lower register. Her eyes glinted. "But not hot enough."

I didn't know what to say to that. Jennie, however, had hardened her face and stepped away from me, retracting her offer as if flipping a knife blade closed.

"You stay here, then," she said. "That motorcycle of yours shouldn't go to waste."

Blinking, I stood and waited, not quite making sense of what she'd said. It was only when she reappeared at the door dragging a reluctant Callie by the wrist that I realized what she had in mind. My stomach tensed, and I searched Jennie's face for any sign of what she was up to. Had she guessed what I was feeling? Was she setting me up?

Callie wore a denim jacket that fit oddly on her frame—Jennie must have loaned it to her. Her hair was up in an unsteady bun. She was shaking her head.

"That thing's not safe," she was saying.

"Jennie, I'm not going to make her ride with me if she's not comfortable."

"Shut up, Len." Jennie turned to our old friend with a fierce expression that masqueraded as sweetness. "Callie, you're going to get on that motorcycle, and you're going to enjoy it." She muttered something else about

Callie needing to feel some power between her legs, but if I'd let myself really hear that, I would have blushed.

"She probably doesn't even have an extra helmet. Besides, she doesn't want me on that thing with her."

Jennie turned to me and rolled her eyes, obviously wanting me to back her up on this. *Oh, hell.* I didn't think she had a clue of what she was doing to me by creating this situation. I was taut and hot everywhere thinking about exactly how much I wanted Callie on the Old Beast behind me, her body curled around me, her breasts pressed against my back, her thighs to either side of mine. Everything I hadn't been able to get my body to do in response to Jennie was starting up at the thought of this, then roaring off down the highway of my imagination at a terrifying speed.

I locked eyes with Callie, but I couldn't read if she wanted me to convince her or turn her away. It wasn't just the darkness. Her forehead was creased with worry, but the parting of her lips looked like desire to me. So I left the choice to her. I lifted both the helmets I carried to show her that she could, in fact, ride with me if she decided to take one.

Callie shook free of Jennie, and I held my breath, uncertain of whether she'd step forward or backward. Her foot seemed to hover in midair. Then she came to me.

* * *

The way Callie held onto me wasn't sexy or comfortable. She squeezed me in a full-body death grip, and it didn't seem to matter how carefully or slowly I rode. Without having to look, I knew just the expression on her face, and I couldn't bear the thought of it.

After about fifteen minutes of that torture, I pulled the bike over. Air whooshed from her lungs as soon as I came to a full stop, and she threw herself off the seat as if from a sinking ship. Her knees must have been weak, because she stumbled and fell. I dropped the kickstand and followed her to the ground, taking the helmet off her head, pulling her against me.

"Callie, Callie. I'm so sorry. I shouldn't have let Jennie talk you into that. I'm sorry. I'm so sorry."

She was apologizing to me, too. "I just wanted… I thought you would want… I just wanted…"

She wouldn't let me draw her to her feet, so I stayed there on the ground. It was fully dark by now, and there weren't many cars passing us. None of them seemed to notice us. The only things in the world were the heat of the summer night, the big sky, the scent of the ocean, the distant sounds of engines and waves, and this woman.

"Stop apologizing," I told her, my voice sharper than I intended. "I don't need that from you."

"Why not?" I heard tears in her voice. "I don't get why not."

"There's nothing to apologize for," I said, but I felt angry, and so a part of me wasn't surprised when she insisted there was something to apologize for. "Well, what then?" My voice sounded commanding, like I was demanding an answer from the entire night, not just from her.

Her body changed in my arms, becoming stronger. She didn't just come to my mouth—she *grew* toward it. Her breath tickled my upper lip. Her face was so close to mine that her eyes crossed slightly as she held my gaze. "I'm sorry I never did *this*."

The kiss she pressed into me was a living thing with veins of fire. It made the night seem bright. I was sure the others would see us from all the way back at the beach house. There was that death grip again, but this time it was mine. I clung to her as if my whole life were blacktop flowing past me at a hundred miles an hour.

"God," she whispered, while the light of that kiss was still pulsing in my temples. "I'm so sorry. So, so sorry."

"You don't have to," I was saying between kisses. "You don't owe me this."

"You think I'm apologizing to *you*? Len, I'm apologizing to *me*." Callie dragged me off the shoulder of the road, into the scraggly weeds beyond, and then farther, onto the beginnings of beach. Sand crunched under my leather jacket. Her body was light on mine, but her weight was decisive nonetheless.

She reached for the hem of my shirt, and I got the last shreds of my brain together just in time. "Jennie told me you and Andy broke up. That's true, right?" *Please tell me it's true.*

I both hoped and worried that she wouldn't stop, but she did. "Jennie told you that, huh? I wonder how she knew."

Her tone suggested she had a guess, but I didn't want to take the bait. I bit my lip, and Callie caged my head, her arms to either side of it and her face pressed close. "Why don't you tell me about Jennie?"

"There's nothing to tell."

"She wanted there to be, though. Didn't she?"

I shrugged. "It doesn't matter."

"It does." She gripped my chin. "I need to know why you're here with me, not her."

I growled. "Why do you think?" I reached for her shirt, but she arched away from me and slipped it off along with her jacket, then unclasped her bra and tossed it aside. Done with talking for the moment, I buried my face in her neck. Her sides were smooth, just warmer than the night. I felt a mole on her back beside her spine, and she shivered when I stroked it.

It was like I'd imagined. I could feel her letting go in the wake of my touch, as if I was easing her into a different space, as if I was changing her. It went to my head, and pretty soon it felt like she was changing me.

I kissed the hollow of her throat, then pressed my cheek to one soft breast, her nipple hardening against my ear. My abs protested at the way I arched up to get to her, but when she slid her nipple to the corner of my mouth, that dull ache faded from my consciousness.

It felt like we were still wearing so many clothes. I fumbled with my jacket, not wanting to take my mouth off her breast. Callie laughed and pushed me down flat, then clambered over me undoing everything. I hadn't been naked with a woman since my ex-wife. I was a bit shocked at myself that I was letting her do this. I'd felt utterly unable with Jennie, and yet for all Callie's awkwardness, this seemed natural now.

"You're so beautiful," Callie said fervently, and I couldn't help shaking my head.

"I'm not beautiful, honey. I'm just not." I'd never been the kind of woman people called *beautiful,* not even with long hair. My ex had called me *handsome.*

But Callie said, "You are," and the kiss she pressed to my left inner thigh made me half-believe her. "I always thought so, even before I knew what I wanted to do to you."

I sat up, blinking. "Huh?"

She leaned back onto her heels. "Come on, Len. I'm not like Jennie. I can't do something like this on a whim, not even if I'd like to. I'm doing this because I've been thinking about this for, what, fourteen years? And… you scare me. I feel like you're going to ride away on that damn motorcycle at the end of the weekend, delete the email address I finally found for you, and never…" She cupped my cunt with her palm, making me jump. I would never have expected her to be so bold. "I'm afraid I might never do this."

I had questions for her. These things she was saying… Her fingers, though, were sliding into me, and I was wet for her, and she wasn't shy about fucking me with her hand. Something about me had been locked away since the divorce, but here was the key, somewhere in Callie's mouth. I arched up, trying to find it there.

She grunted from the effort she was making, tearing away from my lips. "Is this right? Am I doing it right?"

I wanted to say *yes, it's perfect*, but in truth she was overwhelming me. "Slow down, baby. There's no rush."

"Yes, damn it. There is." She obviously had to fuck me hard before she could fuck me slow. So I pulled her all the way onto me and kissed her as I took what she had to give me. When her desperation ebbed a bit, I guided her fingers into helping me find a little pleasure. She was sweating and half-sobbing, and she wouldn't let me unbutton those ridiculous pink shorts.

"I can't. I can't."

I stroked her hair from her face. It made me tremble to do a thing I'd only been imagining earlier that afternoon. "What's wrong?"

"If you touch me and then you leave… I can't."

"Callie. You haven't really been in love with me all this time." The thought was too sad to contemplate. Back in college, any feelings I'd had for her had been so hidden even I hadn't been aware of them. And I didn't like the idea of her staying with Andy for all those years in some kind of spirit of suffering. It bothered me to imagine her thinking of me when I hadn't been thinking of her.

She shrugged. "Maybe not exactly. Sometimes, it was a way of thinking about… a lot of stuff I couldn't think about any other way."

"But you kept dating Andy."

She shrugged, and I tried another approach.

"Why did you finally break up?"

She took a deep breath. "Because I didn't want to cheat on him. And like I said, I kept imagining you disappearing again."

I held her tight, rocking her. "Oh, sweetie. Maybe

this is too much, too fast."

She laughed bitterly. "How can you say it's fast? How many hours did we spend at the dock while I danced around the things I was trying to say?"

"While you danced around…?" Letting her go, I lifted myself onto an elbow. In my head, facts rearranged themselves. Callie's probing about how I knew I wanted to marry Jordan. Her doubts about Andy. Her jokes that she'd like ballroom dance lessons more if they didn't involve dancing with men. "I didn't know what was going on at the time," I told her honestly.

"Oh," she said. I could feel her drawing away from me, her embarrassment sharp enough to cut. I couldn't bear it. I reached for her, pulling her close again.

"Let me touch you," I whispered, my fingers on her waistband.

She caught them, squeezing hard. "Only if you promise…"

Since the divorce, I'd been wary of promising anyone anything—I barely felt capable of making dinner plans for next week Saturday—and yet the words slipped out easily now. "I'm not going to disappear, Callie. I promise." They rang with truth.

Callie shifted her hand to undo her top button. I worried for a second about getting involved with this nervous girl. But she was sweet, and she'd always been that way. Whatever flaws she had—I had plenty, too. I'd been happy to let her talk about herself back then because I'd never liked to let anyone in. Funny that by listening so much, I'd managed to let her in anyway. At least, my ex would have thought that was funny.

Then I put my hand inside her underwear and thoughts of my ex dissolved as I pressed into her melting wetness. She gasped for me. She whimpered as if she were newly born. I didn't care how messy this would turn out to be. I kissed her. I might not be able to offer years of pent-up longing, but I could taste that there was something real here. I wanted to stroke away her tension from the inside out, to show her a sort of pleasure that could turn into ease.

Maybe I managed some of that, because after I made her come, I took her back to the Old Beast and the way she held onto me had changed. I still took the road carefully, but I could hear Callie laughing behind me. When we got back to the beach house, we walked in hand in hand, and for the first time in a long time, I wasn't afraid of the mess we might make of things.

FREE SUMMER

K.A. SMITH

"Okay, Leta. I'm off for the next four days." Bev slipped the master set of keys off the lanyard she wore around her neck and handed them to her young General Manager.

There was no doubt in Bev's mind that Leta would keep the bar running smoothly while she was gone. Leta was her right-hand woman and friend, always two steps ahead of any potential setbacks with the business and frequently available to lend an ear while slamming down tequila.

"I thought the festival was only *three* days?" Leta smiled nervously at her boss as she accepted the keys with both hands.

"I'll need a day to recover, if you know what I mean," Bev said with a wink.

"Grossss," Leta chided. "I can't believe how easy you make a relationship seem. Long distance too. I wish I had that kind of patience."

Bev grinned at Leta's words. She doubted she'd be able to do what she was doing if circumstances were different, or if she were still young and brash. But at thirty-eight, she'd found a perfect mix of passion and pleasure in both her personal and work life. She knew who she was, and she knew who she was with.

Bev caught herself before she started daydreaming. She had to get on the road soon.

Leta didn't let the look of whimsy slide by. "You

were thinking about her, weren't you?"

A big teeth-revealing smile lit up Bev's face and she nodded.

"Hey." Leta's features softened as she smiled back at Bev. "What's it like to be in love?"

Bev let out a deep, slow sigh, still holding the smile on her face. "It's fucking fantastic!" She turned to leave the tiny office they shared and swung her bag over her shoulder.

Bev let herself out through the back door and moved swiftly over to Rhoda, her blue-black Honda Rebel. Butterflies were creating a wave in her gut that she wouldn't be able to shake until she was on the open road, pushing Rhoda's 300-pound frame against the wind to the Free Summer festival.

For going on five years now, her nerves waged a storm within her until she was well over halfway to the festival, and a few miles closer to having Veronica in her arms again.

After a quick safety check—mirrors in place, bag secured, helmet on—Bev started Rhoda's engine and settled herself on the firm seat. *Free Summer here I come!*

She let out a tiny, excited "yelp!" and took off.

The first time Bev had gone to Free Summer was by mistake… sort of. A right turn out of Crestwood Park instead of a left had her two hundred miles off her planned course, and mad as hell. She'd known better than to follow directions from Chesney, her directionally-challenged friend from the motorcycle club, but the girl had sworn that she knew the way to their retreat in Corvali.

So much for getting my pick of the cabins, Bev had thought while easing Rhoda off to the side of the road to get her bearings. Hoping to reorient herself, she pulled out her map as a caravan of vehicles went whizzing by, the thump of music penetrating the air and a celebratory vibe trailing in its wake.

The next to last SUV pulled off onto the shoulder a few feet up from where Bev had parked her bike. Three, maybe four, passengers scrambled out of the berry-red Toyota Highlander and scurried beyond the trees for a quick piss. She tried to considerately ignore the mingled sounds of giggling and the trickling of urine falling onto the lush forest floor by continuing to stare down at her map.

"You lost, suga'?"

Bev's spine tightened as a shiver of lust fanned around her. *Whoa.* The way that word *suga'* rolled out towards her, unfurling its Southern implications and innuendo, triggered an unexpected weakness in her bones.

The woman's smooth, husky voice came from the front of the bike. Bev pivoted on her shiny, black boot heels, map still in hand, ready to warn the sultry, soulful voice not to lean on Rhoda the way strangers often did out of nervousness. Her mouth fell open when she looked up, unexpectedly meeting eyes with Veronica Santis. The award winning singer-songwriter stood mere feet away from Bev and her bike in a flowy, sunset orange tunic and skin-tight jeans.

Damn! She was more beautiful in person than in all of her promo photos and music videos combined. Her brownish-green eyes shone with a cool light that drew attention to the warmth in her flawless, cypress brown skin. Bev took in everything about the singer, noticing Veronica's hair was different from how she wore it while performing. Instead of a voluminous crown of black curls, her hair was loose and wavy around her shoulders. She was bare of all that glittery, shiny makeup she usually wore too. She was gorgeous. Stunning.

The irritation of being lost eased from Bev's limbs,

and she found herself mesmerized instead.

"Ah, um," Bev stammered, looking Veronica over and realizing she was staring like a starstruck fan. "I... erm... Yeah, a little."

Veronica laughed low in her throat, the sound a sexy growl registering in Bev's ears and igniting a second sensation through her body.

The singer tilted her head and grinned. "I thought so, darlin'. You were looking at that map awfully hard." She reached out her hand to Bev. "I'm Veronica—"

"Santis," they both said in unison. Bev offered her gloved hand for a shake, blushing and heating at the prospect of meeting someone so famous while lost by the side of the road.

"Aw, you recognized me." Veronica's cheeks shimmered with heat too. "I'm still not used to that, suga'." A hint of surprise and embarrassment colored her voice. A superstar who wasn't expecting to be recognized? *That has to be new*, Bev thought.

"Where you headed?" Veronica asked.

"I have a retreat. Down in Corvali."

"Oh, I love Corvali. It's beautiful there. Something about the air makes everything feel so fresh and new. But you're a long ways off, darlin'." The look on Veronica's face registered sympathy.

Bev said a silent *'thank you'* to Chesney and her poor directions. What luck to be standing beside Veronica Santis, chatting like it was nothing.

The gaggle of people who'd jaunted off into the woods returned, shooting glances at Veronica and Bev before climbing back into the SUV.

"We're ready when you are, Vern." The voice of a tall woman with blond braids falling down her back caught both ladies' attention. Bev recognized the woman as Veronica's drummer and, if the tabloids were right, her girlfriend of two years.

"Vern," she called again from the driver's side window, a twinge of impatience in her voice. But Veronica didn't budge, only looked over her shoulder and nodded.

Bev folded her arms over her chest and gave an upward nod to the tough-looking musician to signal she wasn't trying to encroach on their situation.

"Looks like your girlfriend is ready to get going."

Veronica's chuckle came out breathy and sarcastic. "Yeah, she's impatient. Protective too." Veronica cleared her throat, scooping her hair over the back of her neck to one side. "She's not my… We're just bandmates."

"So the tabloids are wrong? You're not queer?" Bev felt bold. Really bold. She'd just asked Grammy winner Veronica Santis if she was queer. *Shit.* Where were her manners? Bev tried to shake off the question, but she wanted to know. How often do you run into one of your favorite singers and get the chance to really learn a bit about them?

Veronica's mouth gaped open in surprise. "I didn't say that," was her response. She raised her eyebrows and smiled wide enough for Bev to get a glimpse of her teeth. "We tried it. But the music suffered. And neither of us wanted to sacrifice that."

"Wow." Bev relaxed her shoulders even though she could still feel Veronica's bandmate eyeing them. "I feel like I got the inside scoop or something. Can I quote you?"

They both giggled and Veronica shifted her weight from foot to foot, occasionally looking over her shoulder at the SUV. Bev grew confused as she clutched the map, now folded, between her hands and fingered its edges. *Why is she still here?* They both obviously had better places to be than on the side of the road, but they held each other's gaze for a moment longer, both noticing the easy flow of their conversation. "Well," Veronica was first to break free of their silent ogling. "I hope you get where you're goin', hon." She gave Bev one last, long look, then backed away from the motorcycle. She took a few steps toward the SUV before turning back. Bev hadn't moved.

"We're going to the Free Summer festival," Veronica said with a nod toward her fellow travelers. "It's only a few more miles up the road. You oughta come."

Bev had never heard of Free Summer. Sounded like some hippie thing. *No thanks.* "Thank you. But I got somewhere to be."

"It's getting dark." Veronica tossed a look up at the sky as if Bev hadn't thought about that. "Might be better if you try for Corvali in fresh light."

Bev thought on that for a moment. It was getting dark and she probably needed to start thinking about getting gas for Rhoda and a snack for herself. She didn't like the idea of being stranded on the side of the road with a hungry belly. Plus, there was something in the way Santis had called her *hon* that made her want to stick around. Bev immediately shook the notion from her head before she could make more out of the slight connection she'd felt stirring between them. It was probably nothing more than excitement over meeting Veronica Santis, Songstress of the South.

"I'll be all right," she said coolly. If she pressed on through the evening, she'd at least be able to get a good night's sleep in one of the nicely outfitted cabins reserved for the retreat.

Veronica looked disappointed with Bev's answer, then shrugged. "If you change your mind, we'll be there."

Beverly watched them pull away. Only once she was on her bike and headed in the right direction to Corvali did she realize her mistake. She'd been invited to Free Summer—whatever that was—by Veronica Santis. *The* Veronica Santis.

"Stupid!" Bev shouted into her helmet and revved

the gears after having driven several miles. Always overthinking and playing things cool made her seem aloof and removed, like she didn't care. Her last girlfriend, and the one before that, had said as much.

Bev chewed the inside of her cheek, thinking. She hadn't even let Veronica know she was a fan of her music, that she had all of her albums and even a few bootleg copies she'd purchased when she'd visited New York last. *I didn't even tell her my name, Jeez.* On the other hand, the singer had volunteered oodles of information and invited her to a festival.

What was I thinking, turning down an offer like that?

Bev knew what she had to do. She made a swift U-turn and put her foot down on the gas.

Catching up to the SUV might be a problem, since there were still quite a few cars on the road. Bev didn't care. Something told her to go. As the asphalt blurred by, she made a mental note to check in with Chesney and the others she was supposed to meet. She'd been to a lot of biker retreats. This one wouldn't be that much different, would it? People she'd seen before, with stories she'd heard a hundred times. The first day was routine anyway, right? Yeah. She'd maybe pick up a new keychain with some motorcycle club's logo on it from the gift shop while waiting for dinner. Big whoop!

What was that, compared to a summer festival with Veronica Santis as her guide? The thought of hanging out with Veronica made Bev grin wide inside her helmet as she dipped with the curve of the road. She changed gears and turned Rhoda loose on the blacktop, the bike's engine buzzing in the same way her blood hummed beneath her skin. She felt alive, chasing after the singer and the unknown that awaited her at the festival.

Bev was grinning now, thinking about seeing Veronica's face again. She and her band had been touring for the last nine months, traveling from Europe to South America. They talked on the phone and chatted online when Veronica could, but with rehearsals and shows, her schedule was tight.

Bev had obligations too. Being a business owner wasn't all sunshine all the time. There was managing the place, keeping it staffed, keeping the lights on—just about everything you could imagine went into running a business. That was why they did Free Summer every year. Three full, guaranteed days of uninterrupted quality time. Besides, Bev would never want to take Veronica away from her music. It was her livelihood, her passion, her life's dream. Who was Bev—some stranger Veronica had met on the side of the road one day—to ask her to completely change her life, to halt a dream come true because they'd fallen in love? They'd talked about it after their third year together, but it didn't sit right with Bev to ask for such a huge sacrifice.

"I'd give it up, ya know. All of it. The money, the traveling, the fans. All to be by your side every day and night. To see your smile and hear your voice whenever I wanted. Oh, suga', say the word and I'll give it up." Veronica was always so sure of herself.

"You'd give up the fans?" Bev asked jokingly. She watched as Veronica's nose wrinkled up, throwing lines across her forehead.

"Okay, maybe I'd keep a few fans," she said reaching up to kiss Bev on the nose. "I'd keep you for sure, darlin'."

Without being asked, Veronica had offered to give it all up. That was more of a declaration of love than Bev could have ever asked for. And at that moment, she had known she didn't need anything more.

"I'd never ask you to do any of that. Let's do our thing, our way, when we can. I have a feeling your love is strong, even from a distance."

That was when they had committed to making the festival theirs. Their dedicated time together. Of course, sometimes Veronica snuck away for a long visit or overnighted a ticket to wherever she was in the world so Bev could be with her. It worked for them, made them appreciate the love they shared all the more.

Bev's bike sped down the highway. The crisp air smelled like bonfire and pure joy, telling her she'd be there soon. She wondered if Veronica was already there waiting for her, or if she'd be the first to arrive. She remembered that uncertain feeling fluttering through her years ago, when she had turned her bike around moments after they'd met and kept her eyes peeled for that red SUV.

This is crazy. She'd chanted the words over and over while moving forward in the cool evening air. But something about taking Veronica up on her offer to check out Free Summer made Bev giddy. She'd never done anything like that before. Change plans on a whim? No way. Not Beverly Neiman. But she kept hearing Veronica's voice in her ears, the way it almost broke out into song while they lightly conversed, the way she'd called her *suga'* and *darlin'*. It did more than create a tight ball of desire within her. Bev didn't have a choice but to turn around and see what it was all about.

After driving what felt like a hundred miles or so that night, Bev started seeing the bright signs for the festival, with arrows guiding her way.

This is the right direction, she acknowledged, pushing Rhoda forward. The signs came closer and closer together, telling her to turn right, turn left, or keep straight. With each sign her nerves grew more and more jittery. She was on an impromptu adventure into the woods for a chance to have another conversation with the famous and fabulous Veronica Santis.

The last few miles seemed to zoom by. Bev had been lost in her thoughts, thinking of what she'd say when she caught up to Veronica and her group, and all the while wondering if the singer was just being nice when she asked her to come. Doubt swirled back and forth between Bev's stomach and head as she pulled into a huge parking lot full of cars, SUVs, and buses.

Holy crap! Bev's eyes widened at all of the people already there. What she had expected from something called "Free Summer" wasn't matching what spanned out before her. The venue stretched out over what had to be at least ten acres of lush, green land with minimal concessions. Different musical beats thumped and throbbed harmoniously in the air.

She eased her bike down one of the aisles looking for parking and wondered how she was ever going to find Veronica. *This is most definitely crazy*, she reasoned, shaking her head and looking this way and that.

It was dark by then, but Bev was relieved to find the arena was well lit and well staffed. The different areas were marked with bright signage, just as the roads leading to it had been. Overwhelmed and discouraged at the thought of wandering aimlessly in hopes of bumping into Veronica, Bev secured her bike and set out in the direction most people were heading. She scanned the crowd, looking for Veronica's orange tunic and trying to remember what some of the other people in the SUV looked like. But no one stood out to her, and no orange shirt crossed her path.

Several moments passed where Bev found herself just standing in the middle of hundreds of people carrying tents and chairs, setting off to find a good spot to bed down for the night. A shrill whistle pulled her out of her trance. Off to the right, away from the crowd, she saw someone she recognized. It was the tall drummer from Veronica's SUV.

"Aay! Lost girl!" Veronica's bandmate nodded in Bev's direction signaling her to come over to where she stood.

Relief flooded Bev's veins as she zigzagged between bunches of people to make her way over to the buff musician.

"We thought you'd be long gone to Corvali by now," the woman scoffed, her lips turned crooked at the corners. "I'm Jayz," she said with a protective tone, as if her name alone was supposed to mean something more to Bev.

"Beverly."

Jayz stared at Bev's outstretched hand for a long moment before taking it and giving it a firm shake. "She's down by the lake giving a little show for a few festival-goers who recognized her when we pulled up."

"Thanks, Jayz." Bev eased by the drummer's wide stance, making her way down a well-manicured path until she heard the soft lapping of the lake. She leaned against a tree and listened as Veronica serenaded a small group of women who sat enthralled before her. They all seemed to be coupled up, arms wrapped around one another, leaning into each other and swaying to the sweet melodic sound of Veronica's voice. She sang Sade's "No Ordinary Love," putting her own twist on it. It was already an emotionally telling song, made much deeper by Veronica's husky tone.

Bev felt the lyrics slicing through to her core, wrapping her in a tender sensuality, suggesting that fate—or something—had brought her here.

Bev swayed and hummed along with the song, watching Veronica the entire time. She was ethereal in a flowing, white caftan with tiny shimmering beads embroidered around the edges, her hair pulled back in a bun that showed off her slender neck and perfect shoulders.

Veronica took in each woman as she sang, the love in her voice infectious. Bev felt it deeply, the tune reaching out and hooking into her flesh. When the singer scanned the area and her gaze landed on her she felt it even more, a heat that spread up from her lower limbs.

Veronica finished her song with a soft expression on her face. It was clear that she absolutely loved to sing. It was part of her. She chatted a while with the ladies who came up to give her hugs and say "thank you," showing genuine gratitude to them all.

Bev watched from her place against the tree, taking in how easy-going Veronica was with people. She knew just what to say, all while being herself. When the last person walked up the path, Veronica held out her hand without a word, beckoning Bev to join her by the lake.

The evening was lovely and serene. A sliver of moon glimmered on the rippling water as the current eased by. The breeze gently combed through the trees as the first stars twinkled above.

"That was beautiful." Bev spoke first, trying not to focus so much on the smooth, delicate feel of Veronica's hand in hers. But admittedly, the connection was everything she needed to cast off any lingering doubts she had about showing up.

"Thank you. I'm glad you got to hear it." Veronica glanced at Bev, her lips parting to show off her shiny teeth. *She has a beautiful mouth*, Bev thought, tracing the outline of those lips with attentive eyes.

"I thought you'd be at your Corvali retreat by now."

That reminded Bev she needed to check in with Chesney to let her know she wouldn't be coming until the morning. But the thought quickly left her mind as she let Veronica guide them down to a spot by the water.

Veronica sat down first. "This is one of my favorite spots in the world. So quiet, but alive with energy and possibilities. I have a cabin just over there." Veronica pointed over Bev's shoulder. She took a deep breath, then leaned back on her hands. Bev mimicked her position on the ground, surprised that the grass was still somewhat warm beneath her.

"So, what made you come over to me on the side of the road?" Bev hoped she already knew the answer.

Veronica burst into a fit of giggles. She tried to stifle her glee behind long fingers, but the giggles overtook her. She looked like a carefree water sprite, mischievous and alluring at the same time. "You'll never believe me if I tell you." Laughter danced in her eyes as she turned to look at Bev.

"Try me."

"Do you read horoscopes? What's your sign?" Veronica was grinning so wide her cheeks looked like they would detach at any moment.

"Uh, no, not really. But I think I'm a Cancer."

Veronica nodded. "I can see that." She paused, pursing her lips together. "My horoscope said I'd meet the love of my life today when I least expected it." Another set of giggles erupted in her throat and she shook her head. "Silly, right?"

Bev didn't know what to say. She didn't believe in all that astrology, numerology stuff. But who was she to say what was worth believing in or not? She'd turned her bike around after all. "No, not silly, if you believe that. It had to be one hell of a horoscope for you to just start talking to a complete stranger though."

"Well, that and I couldn't resist how good you looked in those leathers. Hmm."

They both laughed until they collapsed through their elbows and fell back on the ground.

"I'm Beverly, by the way."

"Beverly," whispered Veronica into the air. "Beverly." Her eyes were closed when she started humming a song, something soft. "Beverly, it's nice to meet you, darlin'.""

They had spent that first night talking and laughing. She never made it to Corvali. Veronica's energy kept her there well into the festival's third day. Being in Veronica's favorite place made *her* feel special, as if she'd already become part of it. Because she had. Even Jayz warmed up to her, making her feel welcome among the members of the band and showing her around the grounds. After the three days were over, Bev and Veronica made plans to see each other again.

Reminiscing made Bev's heart ache to see her sweet Veronica now. They'd somehow made it five years together despite Veronica's busy schedule, the distance, and their differences. Bev pulled Rhoda up to the festival's main lot. Music was already going, and people arrived in a steady flow of cars and SUVs. Bev veered off to Special Parking, a secluded area Veronica had shared with her the third time they met at Free Summer—the summer they became committed to each other.

"If you're going to suffer through being my tabloid lover, you might as well get primo parking," she'd said. The paved road curved deep down the lane and wrapped around a thick grove of trees with parking all along the side. At the end of the road were two cabins, one on the left and one on the right. The one on the left belonged to Veronica. The space was small, but full of energy and life. Just like Veronica.

Bev was the first one there. She secured her bike and, with a key to the cabin, let herself in. Veronica and whoever was accompanying her this year would probably arrive soon. Bev stowed her bag in the back bedroom and turned on the shower for a quick rinse. As she was undressing, she heard the door opening.

"It's just me, suga'!"

"Vern?" Bev called out from the bathroom, peering

from behind the door with a towel draped around her neck and the leather pants she'd worn on the ride up.

"Yeah—" Veronica dropped her bag where she stood, ogling Bev's state of half dress. Her chest rose and fell quickly as she crossed the floor. In three strides she was directly in front of Bev, tugging on the ends of her towel, pulling her in close for a kiss.

"Well, hello to you too, Ms. Santis," Bev said between kisses. She held Veronica around the waist and nuzzled her neck.

"I've missed you so much," Veronica sang, pressing her face into Bev's bare shoulder. Plum-colored kisses instantly appeared on the side of Bev's neck.

"I missed you too, baby," Bev whispered, trying to angle as close as possible. "I thought about the first time we met the whole ride up here."

"You did?" Veronica pulled back to look in Bev's eyes. "I thought about you too. Not the first time we met, but that second summer…" Veronica raised her eyebrows.

Bev knew what Veronica was hinting at, but she played ignorant. "I'm not sure I recall, Ms. Santis. What happened the second summer we met up here?"

"If you don't remember, you're gonna have a hard time finding me for the reenactment." Veronica wiggled free from Bev's arms and took off out the side door. Laughter and the sound of feet slapping across the floor echoed in the small space. From where Bev stood, she could see the articles of Veronica's clothing falling through the air as she ran towards the lake near the cabin. Bev laughed, then darted into the bathroom for two towels before she slipped out the door behind Veronica.

By the time Bev got to the lake, Veronica was already splashing across the water. She dropped the towels on the dock and began sliding out of her pants.

"I thought you'd remember." Veronica swam over

and grinned up at Bev. "Hurry up! I want to kiss you some more."

"Is that all you want to do?" Bev followed Veronica and jumped in the cool, refreshing water.

Veronica squealed and swam to Bev, wrapping her arms around her neck and kissing the water droplets down the bridge of her nose. Their lips met in a luscious connection of warmth and wetness.

"Mmm, I think I recall that second summer now," Bev moaned against Veronica's lips as she felt the singer's legs wrap around her waist. Being close in her lover's arms felt exactly the same as when Veronica sang to her, the melody of her words wrapping around her heart, warming her from the inside out.

"Let's make some new memories for year five, okay?" Veronica kissed Bev full on the lips. She then licked at the sparkling beads of water dotting Bev's collarbone. Beneath the surface of the rocking water, Veronica's fingers plucked at Bev's hard nipple, making her sigh and whimper in her throat. "Tell me something, suga'."

"Mmm. Anything." Bev tried to concentrate, but the way Veronica's fingers glided over her skin made her buzz all over and she felt herself becoming wetter and wetter, even in the water.

"What made you blow off your plans that day? What made you turn around and come find me?"

"It was your horoscope, remember?" Bev murmured in Veronica's ear, out of breath, carelessly nipping her earlobe in the process.

"Come on, Bev. You don't believe in that." Veronica continued to squeeze and pinch Bev's nipples until she was breathing harder and harder, moaning at regular intervals.

"I do now. I felt something. When I saw you again, singing to those women I felt it so strongly. I couldn't explain it. I think it was fate, V. That day the stars brought you to me." Bev rested her forehead against Veronica's, softly kissing at her lips. "I love you, Veronica."

"I love you, Beverly. Oh, how I do!" Veronica trailed her fingers down over Bev's taut belly, circling around her bellybutton before delving lower. Veronica sang sweetly in Bev's ear, soft words about the summer being all theirs as she tickled and teased her in time with the water's rhythm.

Bev trembled as Veronica finally nudged her slick lips apart. She was about to break out into a song of her own. One of passion and desire, a song of summer love.

A MATTER OF INCLINATION

HARPER BLISS

I look out for her on the twenty-fourth of December every year. It has become our unspoken, informally agreed upon annual appointment. When we first met fifteen years ago, Amelia O'Brien's hair came to her shoulders, and she walked along the shoreline with two toddlers at her feet. So much has changed since then.

This year, she's late. For the first time in my life, I spend Christmas day alone. I had to stop Charles from flying down, what with it being only my second holiday season since Bill passed away so suddenly just after we returned from Seal Rocks at the beginning of last year. I had expected Amelia to be here—and I didn't want Charles to miss out on the busiest day of the year at the beach club he works at in Melbourne during his summer break.

Amelia and I exchange the occasional e-mail over the year, and that's how I know she has finally divorced Ralph. From what I've witnessed, it's been a long time coming. I never told her about that time he made a pass at me when we were alone on the beach one night, and about how I would surely have reciprocated if it had been her propositioning me. I've never told anyone any of that.

I guess we are seasonal friends more than anything, but over the course of fifteen summers by the beach, I have told Amelia much more about myself than I've told my 'everyday' friends back home. There's one thing she doesn't know, though. The thing I had hoped to perhaps address this summer.

Her eldest daughter Phoebe is spending the summer—winter there—in Barcelona, I know that much. I have no idea if Katy will be joining Amelia this year. In fact, it's beginning to look as though no one will show up at all. But I have it in writing. At the bottom of Amelia's last e-mail, sent a few weeks ago: 'See you on the beach this summer.' The stretch of beach connecting our houses has been mightily empty so far. I've had too much time to envision worst-case scenarios and I've concluded that the most disappointing outcome for me personally would be if Amelia showed up with a rebound lover.

"Is it too soon to set you up with someone new, Mom?" Charles asked me a few months ago. "You're obviously way too young to spend the rest of your life alone. I think Dad would have wanted you to be happy more than anything."

It was a very unsettling question. One I waved off immediately. As far as I'm concerned, Bill is and was the only man for me. We had a happy marriage. One that didn't leave a lot of room for questioning certain things, like that giddiness that descended on me every summer when we undertook the long drive over here. For fifteen years, I was able to just categorize it as a mere enjoyable sensation. It's not as though Amelia and I ever engaged in any flirtatious behavior, or that even the slightest of hints has ever passed between us. I've just always found her fiercely attractive, but more in an admiring way than in a sexual one.

Until after Bill's heart attack.

On Boxing Day, I venture out of the house early for a walk along the beach—and past Amelia's empty house. But the windows have been thrown open and the breeze rolling off the ocean is playing with the curtains. My heart is in my throat instantly. First, I fear she may have rented out the place to strangers, but—as though she's been waiting for me to walk past—the next instant she appears outside the house, her hand shielding her eyes from the sun that is rising in deep, hopeful oranges behind me.

"Merry Christmas," she shouts as I head over to her.

When our bodies meet in a quick but sturdy hug, my heart picks up even more speed. I try to mask my excitement by drawing a few discreet, shallow breaths.

"Katy decided rather last-minute to go horseback riding with Max instead of joining her old Mom at the beach, but I insisted we spend Christmas together, what with Phoebe gallivanting off in Europe. It's all so complicated when they grow up." Amelia is her usual waterfall of words. "I thought it was only supposed to become simpler." She sends me a smile that hits me straight in the gut. Perhaps it's the semi-unexpectedness of seeing her this early in the morning, or all the thoughts about her I've indulged in since I last saw her.

Last summer, everything was still different. It was my first time at the beach house without Bill, and Ralph was still in the picture. This summer—this day to be exact—is the first time I feel free to even have these feelings. To luxuriate in the wave of happiness that washes over me now that I've finally come face-to-face with my friend again.

"How's Charles?" she asks, and I inform her of his academic progress and his job at the St Kilda Beach Club.

"Have you had breakfast?" I ask, guessing that her pantry is probably empty. "I made fresh bread overnight."

She shoots me a seductive smile, of which I know it's not supposed to be seductive, but my brain interprets it that way nevertheless. "You're a lifesaver. I arrived late last night and just fell into bed."

I don't regret not seeing or hearing her arrive. We have weeks here together. At least, I think we do. "How long are you staying?"

"As long as nobody needs me in Sydney. You?"

"Three weeks, until school starts again."

"I would say we should drink to that, but it might be a bit early. Even for a fresh divorcee like myself."

If the divorce from Ralph was painful at all, it hasn't left her with any visible marks of distress. If anything, Amelia has a freed look about herself. As though she's turned over a new leaf—one that had been stuck for a very long time.

"I know he cheats," she said to me a few summers ago. "And I don't sleep with a man who fucks other women." The shortest of probing questions has always been enough to instigate a monologue in Amelia. She's the sort who likes to talk—and uses ten words when one will do. "If it weren't for the girls, he'd have been out years ago, but I just… can't do it to them. Not yet. I feel as though I need to protect them just a little while longer."

"That's why mimosas were invented," I say now, and, arm in arm, we walk back to my house.

"I like the way you think, Rachel," she says. "Always have."

* * *

"If you haven't had a proper Christmas, we'll have one this afternoon," Amelia says. "I'll drive down to the shops later and prepare us a turkey." She's on her third mimosa—perhaps the divorce has left some scars—so I don't really see that happening.

"Let's just relax. Catch up. I haven't seen you in a year." I don't care about turkey. It's too hot for roasted meat. And sitting on the front porch of my house with Amelia, my gaze flitting from the ocean to her, is all the Christmas celebration I need.

"And what a year it has been." Amelia stretches her arms above her head. "But—silver lining—with the way

Ralph carried on, I truly managed to squeeze every last cent out of the divorce settlement. I thought it was time he paid up for the shit he put me through." She shakes her head. "Men." She spits out the word as though it's a foul piece of meat. "How about you, Rachel? Or is it too soon to inquire?"

Again with the 'too soon'. I don't know when 'too soon' or 'appropriate' would be for me to start being interested in another man. "I don't find myself particularly enthralled by men my age."

Amelia lets the back of her head rest on her intertwined fingers. I don't think she's wearing a bra underneath that t-shirt. I have plenty of pictures of her in a bikini and I've seen her with her top off many a time. She can never keep it on when we swim to the small wooden jetty a few hundred feet into the water. "The sun on your nipples, Rachel," she would say. "What is better than that?" After I worked up the courage to lose my bikini top—and making doubly sure no one was around—I quickly learned to agree.

Amelia quirks up her eyebrows. "Oh really? Looking for a toy boy, are we?" Her hair is short in the back these days, with a fringe that falls over her eyes at times.

I blush. I can't help it. I can see how my comment might have been misinterpreted. "That's not what—" I start, but she cuts me off.

"I've considered it myself." She sits up and lets her hands drop onto the armrests. "A good fuck by a young, ultra-virile man who still has enough testosterone flowing in his veins… if you know what I mean? Not that Ralph ever had a problem with that, I assume. I just didn't want him near me for that." She peers into the ocean. "But really, who needs that sort of hassle at our age?"

I know better than to reply this time. This is an Amelia monologue moment.

"All I'm saying is that it's been a very long time since I've been touched by anyone but myself." She locks her gaze on me. "Have you?" She makes a sideways gesture with her head. "Since Bill?"

I refill our glasses. Little did I know that our first conversation this summer would take a turn like this.

"No," I say, after having taken a good sip.

"Do you want to?" Something glitters in her eyes.

My earlier blush hasn't properly receded yet before I'm hit with another heatwave on my checks. "W—what, erm, do you…"

"There are websites for that, you know? We could get some studs out here. It's probably not cheap, but Ralph's money has to be good for something."

My stomach drops. There's no viable reason why Amelia would have the same thoughts as I.

"I'm just kidding, Rachel. I know you're not the type." She slaps the table with her fingertips. "And I would never stoop to Ralph's level and pay someone to have sex with me."

"He did, erm, that?" I still haven't recovered. The images in my head are too vivid. It doesn't help that Amelia is sitting across from me with no bra, her breasts bouncing a little when she laughs.

"I don't really know. But it wouldn't surprise me." She shrugs. "Anyway, new rule!" She takes her refilled glass off the table. "Let's not speak the bastard's name anymore." She holds her glass out for a toast and we clink rims. "At first, I wasn't sure I wanted the beach house. For starters, God knows who he brought? But I have so many good memories here. Witnessing the change in the girls every summer. And if I let go of the house I wouldn't see you anymore, Rachel."

I think my neck is blushing now too, as well as my forehead and my ears. Amelia pins her gray-blue gaze on me.

"Are you okay? You look a bit flushed. Is it the alcohol?"

"Must be," I mumble. I know at that moment I will never be able to tell her. Some secrets are better kept. Doesn't mean I can't enjoy her company. The meals we will share. The wine we'll drink as the sun sets on the horizon. The tales we will tell about our children and what happened in our lives over the past eleven months. How is it even possible to have a crush on someone I only see for three weeks every year? A woman, no less. It's madness. I could never get those words over my lips.

"Here." Amelia hands me a glass of water. Our fingertips brush against each other briefly and I feel as though my ears may catch fire, burn to ashes and fall off my head. "I'll make us some coffee, shall I?"

She ventures inside my house. She probably knows it as well as I do. It's strange to be so well-acquainted with someone I don't see very often. I'm glad for the moment's respite of her presence. I steady my gaze on the ocean and draw air between my lips in rapid gusts. I hope it's not going to be like this for the next three weeks: me unable to control myself.

* * *

The next day we meet on the beach after breakfast. It's silly to each keep a house, I think, as I wander over to our meeting spot. But perhaps our children would disagree.

"I can't contain myself any longer." Amelia is wearing an earth-colored bikini. "I need to swim to the jetty."

In the fantasy I visited before falling asleep last night, it was the first thing we did as well. I nod.

We drop our towels on the beach, slip out of our flip-flops and tip-toe to the edge of the ocean. At least in the water my cheeks won't turn as red, and if they do, I can blame the strain of swimming the few hundred feet into the sea.

Amelia is a few years older than me, but her limbs are longer, and she has more purchase on the waves. Still, when you've swum in the ocean all your life, you don't forget how to move in it, and I reach the jetty only a few minutes after her. Her hands are already crossed behind her back. I can't keep my eyes off her when she drops her bikini top and stretches it out to dry next to her. She leans back and lies down, her breasts exposed to the sun—and me.

"Aaah. I've only waited all year for this moment." Amelia has closed her eyes, leaving me with ample opportunity to stare, but I avert my gaze. The view is too much. Like being offered something on a silver platter only to have it taken away again just as I'm reaching for it—over and over again.

I sit down next to her. Spin my head from left to right a few times to see if no one is around, but if this place is known for one thing, it's privacy. I live thirty miles from Melbourne. If Bill and I had just wanted the ocean, we could have bought a summer house on that coast. But Seal Rocks is different. It's drenched in the most beautiful solitude I've ever encountered. Blue skies, strong surf, white beaches, and no one around.

Assured that we're alone, I bring my hands behind my back and unclasp my top. The sensation of the hot sun on my wet nipples hits me much harder than previous summers. A throbbing ignites between my legs—I'll need some private time later. I stretch out next to Amelia and look up into the blue sky. I wish I had one of those drones so that I could take a picture of us lying side by side, chests bare. It's easy enough to imagine, however. I pretend I take flight and my gaze is trained on the jetty. Amelia's face is blissfully calm. Mine is also—that's how I know I'm just pretending.

I didn't get a lot of sleep last night, what with alternative versions of Amelia's arrival assaulting my mind, and then I do find a sense of calm. The sun dries my skin as my eyelids stop fluttering and I feel myself drift off into a light, sun-soaked, summer nap.

"Rachel." Amelia's voice reaches my ear, but I don't want to open my eyes because her fingertips brush against my arm and my skin seems to break out in goosebumps despite the increasing temperature. When her fingertips tap against my side a moment later my eyes fly open nonetheless. "If we stay here too long we'll be red as lobsters later."

I stare into Amelia's eyes. She's sitting up, watching me. I have to swallow a lump out of my throat. Instinctively—perhaps still drowsy from my nap—my fingers curl around her wrist. Her gaze flits from my face to her arm, then back. The sun may have dried my bikini bottoms, but I'm sure they're wetter now than when I pulled myself out of the sea onto the deck of the jetty.

"I'm sorry." I chicken out and let go of her wrist. "I'm just glad we're here together."

It's as though I can feel Amelia's stare on my breasts. My nipples stiffen under her gaze.

"I can tell," she says, then just smiles and pushes herself up. I take in her long shapely legs as she bends over to pick up her top. She throws me mine in the process. She has no idea—and I have no idea what to do with myself.

"Yours or mine?" Amelia asks after we've made it back to shore.

"I, uh, just need a little time. A bit of an upset tummy, I think," I stammer and start in the direction of my house.

"Do you need anything? I have tablets for that," she shouts after me, because I had to take a few long strides away from her.

"I'm fine." I briefly turn my head. "I'll see you later."

When I reach my house I stand under the ceiling fan for a long moment. It must be menopause, I decide there and then. These hot flashes. These inappropriate feelings for my friend. After all, I've never felt anything of the sort for any other woman. Or perhaps it's sunstroke. I can't believe I grabbed her wrist, can't believe I lost control like that. I'll need a better excuse than just being happy to see her. Or maybe Amelia will just forget about it. She's the type who would.

I resist the urge to go into my bedroom, peel off my bikini and pleasure myself. It seems too crass. As if I were reducing Amelia to someone I fantasize about during masturbation. Not that I'm not guilty of that already. But the moment isn't right. I need to find the strength to see her later, and every day after that.

Besides, this irrational crush—but aren't most silly infatuations devoid of logic?—isn't just a physical thing. It's something that's been building inside of me for years, and suddenly I think that in my life I've only had eyes for one man and one woman. I'm *that* type of person, I guess.

* * *

"I was worried about you, Rach," Amelia says when I finally dare to venture to her house a few hours later. She's preparing lunch. "Want some?" She points at the avocados she's slicing. "Or will your stomach not agree?"

I'm actually starving, but I'm not sure I should admit to that. "Maybe I'll try a little."

"I'll fix us both a plate. Why don't you take a seat in the shade."

As if she was expecting me, the table is set with two sets of cutlery and two wine glasses. A bottle of rosé chills in an ice bucket on a stand next to the table. I pour us both a generous portion.

"You've found the wine," Amelia says with a smile as she comes out of the kitchen. "Good."

We eat in silence, which is strange. Not for me, but for Amelia, who is never at a loss for words.

"We've known each other for a long time, Rachel." Amelia deposits her knife and fork on her plate, indicating she's done with her meal. "But in all that time, I've never known you to be so... I guess skittish is the right word." She leans back in her chair.

I haven't finished my salad yet, but my stomach is instantly closed for business.

"It's as if you can no longer fully relax around me." Her bikini top shines through the flimsy t-shirt she's wearing. It only reminds me of what lies beneath. Of what I've seen. "Tell me honestly... is it because Ralph hit on you and you don't know how to tell me, but you feel like you should now that we're divorced?"

"You know about that?" For a minute, I consider this a viable excuse for my erratic behavior around her. Although it won't pardon future occurrences of it.

"Does everyone just assume I was blind when it came to my husband? I have eyes in my head and two ears"—she taps her fingers against her earlobes—"right here."

"I'm sorry." I drink from the chilled wine to counter the flush I already feel creeping up my neck.

"Don't apologize for him, Rachel."

"I didn't give him even the slightest of leeway. Perhaps I should have told—"

"Stop!" She holds up her hands, palms out. "I know I brought it up, but I meant what I said. Let's not waste another word on that bastard. He'll always be the father of my children, but that's where it ends for me for the rest of my life. No more talk of bloody Ralph O'Brien."

"Okay." I hold the belly of my glass against my cheeks. "Gosh, it's hot today."

"It's not that, though, is it, Rachel? That had you speeding to your house earlier?" Amelia doesn't let up.

"What do you mean?" My cheeks must be the same color as the discarded tomato on my plate.

"You keep on blushing for no reason. Stammering your words. It's… strange. That's not the Rachel I know and love." She grabs her glass. "And before you even contemplate it, you can't run away this time. Just tell me, Rach. It's me."

How can she have me cornered like this? Not that I believed I was doing a stellar job of hiding my feelings. I don't have a lot of experience when it comes to that.

"It's nothing, really. Just having a bit of difficulty adjusting to the new, erm, situation."

"What new situation?" Amelia narrows her eyes to slits. "You mean just the two of us here together?"

"I guess." I really can't say any more. I'm not doing the best job of defending myself, but why do I need to?

"We've spent hours together just the two of us. Walking on the beach. Sunbathing on the jetty. Drinking wine after we put the children to bed. What's so different now?"

"Only everything." I take another sip. My fingers are curled dangerously tight around the stem of my glass. "Bill died. Ralph is out of the picture. Our children are all grown up."

"Well, yes. But I don't see what that has to do with you acting all silly around me. Like we've only just met and you—" She pauses. Her eyes narrow further. I take a few quick sips. My heart is in my throat.

"Do you, huh…" It seems as though I've rendered Amelia O'Brien speechless by not saying much at all.

I put my glass down. I can't stay quiet now. I have to say something. Or at least make clear that this is not a situation that requires anything from her.

"I'm sorry—" I start.

"Stop apologizing, Rachel. For crying out loud." Amelia sighs. She pushes herself up a bit in her chair, erasing the relaxed position she was in earlier.

"I seem to have developed… feelings for you. I don't know where they come from or why or how it happened, but they're there, and they're driving me slightly insane."

There, I said it.

Amelia doesn't speak for a long time. All my hopes are stretched out in those seconds of silence. I don't dare look at her anymore. Instead, I cast my gaze to the bench on the edge of the patio. It was Bill's favorite spot in the shade. Is this happening because of him? Because I miss him too much and I need someone else to dump my affections on and Amelia is the only viable candidate?

"Shit, Rach. I wish I knew what to say to that."

I steal a glance at her. "You don't have to say anything."

"My brain is working very hard to process this information." Her words are starting to come quickly again. "How long have you felt this way?"

"Oh God, I don't know." I'm not the most expressive person, but this is too much for me to hold in. "It doesn't matter. I mean, it's fine. I have no expectations. It's just a silly feeling." Fear tightens my stomach. I really shouldn't have eaten any lunch. I wouldn't have if I had known this conversation was going to be our dessert.

"How can you say that when it's obviously much more than that?" Is she scolding me now? For sitting here with my heart on my sleeve?

"I didn't say anything because I don't want anything to change between us." Words as hollow as how I feel inside.

"How could things between us not change when every time I merely glance at you, you freeze like a deer in headlights?"

"Let's just… ignore it," I blurt out. "Now that I've

gotten it off my chest, we can just go back to normal."

"No, we can't. Well, *I* surely can't. You can pretend all you like, but I can't un-hear what you just said."

"I'm sorry, Amelia." I push myself out of my chair. "I'm not running, but I need a break from this conversation right now."

"Hey…" She holds out her hand. "If anything, I'm flattered that a woman like you would fall for someone like me."

Am I supposed to grab her hand? And is that supposed to make me feel better? She's *flattered*? Although, I guess, it's better than offended.

"Come here." She beckons me with her fingers. I touch my thumb against the heel of her hand. The wine seems to have gone to my head, that's how dizzy I suddenly am. "There are not a lot of things a fifteen-year-old friendship can't withstand, Rach. We'll figure it out."

"Yeah." I want to cry. A wall of unshed tears is ready to crumble behind my eyes, as though they've been waiting until I admitted it out loud.

"Go have a lie-down, or whatever it is you want to do, and we'll talk tonight. Okay?"

I want to run away from her but want to stay near her at the same time.

"I need some time to think about this." She gives my fingers a quick squeeze before dropping them from her hand.

"Yeah," I say, again, and make my way back to my house along the shoreline without looking back.

* * *

"Knock, knock." Amelia mimics a knocking motion with her fist in the air. "Care for a G&T?" She holds a bottle of gin in her other hand.

It's after nine. I haven't had dinner. A G&T now could give me the confidence to continue the conversation we aborted earlier. "Sure."

"At your service." Before I can get up, she heads into the kitchen adjoining the deck where I've been sitting since I came back from hers after lunch.

Ten minutes later, she's back with two glasses and a packet of crisps. She hands me a glass, tears open the crisps bag and starts munching on a few straight away. "I missed my supper, but this will do."

I drink from the G&T and flinch. She made it a double, then. Perhaps it's the only way for us to talk about this further. I don't even know where to begin, nor how to explain the turmoil in my heart. I try, anyway. Silence is no longer an option. "I guess I first noticed something that time we walked all the way up to the lighthouse seven years ago. The wind was blasting in our faces all the way up there, and I didn't feel a thing, was light on my legs even, because it was just the two of us that evening, and your company lifted me up somehow."

"Seven years ago?" She knits her brows together.

"It wasn't so much a conscious feeling. Just flashes. And the desire to want to spend as much time with you as possible during the time we were here together." To give my hands something to do, I grab a crisp but don't eat it. "After Bill died, I started seeing those feelings in a different light. As if him no longer being around gave me free rein to properly think about it for the first time."

Amelia pops another crisp into her mouth. She even looks good doing that. The sky is a stunning shade of purple-pink above the ocean behind her. The picture is almost perfect.

"I didn't come here so you could explain, Rach. I don't need you to explain yourself to me. You probably even can't explain it properly…" This is more babbling than I'm used to from Amelia. These are strenuous circumstances for both of us, of course.

"And I just want to make it perfectly clear that I don't expect anything from you."

Amelia scrunches her lips together before speaking, as if she's ordering the words in her head first. "I did some research this afternoon. It's not as uncommon as I first believed."

"What is?" I need more gin in me pronto.

"*Latebians.*" She says it with an almost shrug. "You know, women who prefer the company of other women later in life. Like you said yesterday. Men our age are so unappealing."

I chuckle, and it feels so good to just have a little laugh. To release some of the tension from my strained muscles.

Amelia goes into monologue mode. As if she's teaching one of my sociology classes in school. "More like a preference that develops after a certain age. And I have to say, the articles I read made some damn good arguments." She makes a tempering motion with her hands. "But, before I get too carried away, let me just say that I'm not sitting here and proclaiming it would be for me. I don't know that. Unless I try, I guess."

My eyes widen. My mouth follows.

"Maybe we should go on a date." She sips from her G&T without taking her eyes off me.

"A d-date?" I stutter.

"Well, it would basically just be a meal together, the way we would otherwise also have done, just with an added… bonus. And perhaps a different outcome."

"Are you serious?" I don't know what to do with myself. This pragmatic approach is not what I had expected at all, but here sits Amelia O'Brien telling me that she's not dismissing my feelings for her.

"Yes. Why not?" She straightens her spine. "It doesn't only have to be a matter of inclination."

Inclination? I never really questioned that. Mostly because I never truly allowed myself to question my feelings for Amelia. I was happily married to my husband for twenty-five years. The matter of inclination never really presented itself.

"Okay." I have to keep myself from nodding vigorously.

"Can breakfast be a date?" she asks, a smile so sexy on her face, I wish the sun would set and rise already.

"Our lives, our rules," I say. "So yes."

"Breakfast it is then. I'll make pancakes. Say nine?"

As though she has a pressing other engagement, Amelia finishes the last of her G&T and makes to leave. "Keep the bottle," she says, spins on her heels and heads for her house.

* * *

When I reach Amelia's porch the next morning, I'm fairly certain my stomach is not up for pancakes—it's too much aflutter for any solid food. I also realize why breakfast isn't deemed the perfect time for dates: the absence of booze.

"Good morning," she says. She's freshly showered, her hair still wet, her fringe tucked behind her ear. "Sleep well?"

"No." I follow my reply with a nervous giggle.

"Neither did I, really. I did some more research… of the more physical variety." She cocks her head to the side. "Men really *can* be obsolete, I guess."

It feels to me as if Amelia skipped the date part and moved straight into foreplay. My skin tingles underneath my sundress. She pours me some coffee while I deposit the bowl of fruit salad I was cutting at four AM this morning on the table.

"Sit. Eat." Amelia prances around some more, bringing condiments to the table. "You know I make a mean pancake. Charles can eat at least five of them, if I recall correctly."

Then, we find ourselves sitting across from each other, a stack of pancakes between us. Silence descends.

Even Amelia can't keep up that sort of nervous chatter for too long.

"I've been thinking, though, Rach. I mean, technically we've gone on so many dates already." She cuts up a pancake into a dozen small pieces but doesn't eat it. "I think it's the 'want-to-come-in-for-a-coffee?' part that really needs exploring in our case. I already know that I like you. All I need to find out now is how it feels when I kiss you."

A sudden bolt of audacity hits me. Uncharacteristically, perhaps, but not really, because I've wanted to kiss Amelia for years. I've wanted to test what that feels like in real life for a very long time. "Then kiss me," I say.

"I will." She eyes me for a second, and I feel lust pool between my legs. She pushes her chair back. I do the same with mine. We stand up at the same time and meet halfway.

"I always knew there were hidden depths behind those eyes of yours, Rach." She sends me a half-smile before putting her hands on my neck and pulling me close. When our lips touch, in that fraction of a second, I know. I'm definitely a *latebian*.

I wrap my arms around her neck. My tongue slips inside her mouth and she leans into me a little. This is not the kiss of someone who doesn't want another, I conclude, as our lips and tongue meet again and again. When we finally break, her fringe has come loose from behind her ear and covers half of her face. I tuck it back and ask, "And?"

"So much better than pancakes," she says and tugs me close again.

ABOUT THE AUTHORS

ERZABET BISHOP is thrilled to learn writing naughty books is a whole lot of fun. She is a contributing author to *A Christmas to Remember*, *Sweat*, *When the Clock Strikes Thirteen*, *Can't Get Enough*, *Slave Girls*, *The Big Book of Submission*, *Gratis II*, *Anything She Wants*, *Coming Together: Girl on Girl* and more. She is the author of *Tethered*, *Sigil Fire*, *The Erotic Pagans Series: Beltane Fires*, *Samhain Shadows* and *Yuletide Temptation*. She lives in Texas with her husband, furry children and can often be found lurking in local bookstores. Follow her reviews and posts on Twitter at @erzabetbishop

HARPER BLISS (harperbliss.com) is the author of the novel *At the Water's Edge*, the *High Rise* series, the *French Kissing* serial and several other lesbian erotica and romance titles. She is the co-founder of Ladylit, an independent press focusing on lesbian fiction. Harper lives on an outlying island in Hong Kong with her wife and, regrettably, zero pets.

CHEYENNE BLUE's erotica has appeared in around 100 erotic anthologies since 2000. Her best lesbian stories are now available in the *Blue Woman Stories* collections published by Ladylit. She is the editor of Forbidden Fruit: stories of unwise lesbian desire also from Ladylit, and has edited short stories through to novels. Under her own name she has written travel books and articles, and curated anthologies of local writing in Ireland. She has lived in Europe and North America, but now lives and writes near the beach in Queensland, Australia. Visit her website at cheyenneblue.com

A.L. BROOKS lives in London where she is a systems consultant by day, and a Latin dancer by night. She writes the kinds of stories she herself would want to read, and lets her imagination have full rein while her fingers fly across the keyboard, which is a wonderful feeling. You can follow her at facebook.com/albrookswriter

EMILY L. BYRNE lives in lovely Minneapolis with her wife and the two cats that own them. She toils in corporate IT when not writing or reveling in geeky things. Her stories have or will appear in *Bossier*, *Spy Games*, *Forbidden Fruit: stories of unwise lesbian desire*, *The Princess's Bride* and *The Mammoth Book of Uniform Erotica*. She blogs at writeremilylbyrne.blogspot.com and can be found on Twitter at @EmilyLByrne

UK based CAMILLE DUVALL's careers in journalism and as a BBC drama script editor and storyliner—what she calls the wonderful world of 'makey-uppy'—inspired her to create her own worlds and inhabit them with a liberal sprinkling of lesbians. She initially penned stories as gifts for her partner, who has since encouraged her to seek a wider audience. Having produced a Bafta Award-winning film under her real name, Camille continues to develop drama projects for her own production company, including a feature film with a host of fabulous lesbian characters.

LUCY FELTHOUSE (lucyfelthouse.co.uk) is a very busy woman! She writes erotica and erotic romance in a variety of sub-genres, lengths and pairings, and has over 100 publications to her name, with many more in the pipeline.

These include several 'Best' anthologies from Cleis Press.

TAMSIN FLOWERS has been writing erotica for a few years. She has featured in more than 20 anthologies curated by some of today's most celebrated editors, including Violet Blue (*Best Women's Erotica 2014* and *2015*), Rachel Kramer Bussel (*The Big Book of Submission: 69 Kinky Tales*), Alison Tyler (*Twisted: Bondage with an Edge*, *Bound for Trouble: BDSM for Women*) and Kristina Wright (*Best Erotic Romance 2014* and *2015*, *Passionate Kisses: Erotic Romance Fantasies for Couples*).

KATYA HARRIS lives in the UK with her family and spends most of her free time writing stories of lust and love. She has had stories published in *The Sexy Librarian's Big Book of Erotica*, *The Big Book of Domination* and *She Who Must Be Obeyed*. You can find her on Twitter @Katya_Harris

RJ LAYER resides in the Midwest with her partner of twenty-five years. She loves to work at writing lesbian stories that capture the heart of the romantic. In addition to traveling to new places, RJ can be found relaxing in rolling hills on the water dreaming up engaging characters and stories.

ANNABETH LEONG wears high heels and frequents the former haunts of H.P. Lovecraft. Her work appears in more than 50 anthologies, including D.L. King's *She Who Must Be Obeyed*, Sacchi Green's *Women with Handcuffs*, and R. Gay's *Girl Crush*. She is the author of *Heated Leather Lover*, a butch-femme BDSM novella, and many other erotic novels and novellas. Find Annabeth online at annabetherotica.com, and on Twitter @AnnabethLeong

K.A. SMITH is a writer of poetry and fiction. Writing is

her first love and women are her passion. She seamlessly merges the two to bring you sensual scenarios and titillating tales of women's love, sex, and desire. She's the author of *Get At Me*, *Gina's Do-Over*, and *The Players*. Her blog is at authorka.wordpress.com and you can find her on Twitter @authorkasmith

BROOKE WINTERS is a 30-year-old British woman living in London. She runs an active meet-up group for bisexual and lesbian women, spends far too much time drinking red wine with her writers group and likes to escape to writers retreats around the world as often as her job will allow. She enjoys walking, history, feminist debate and bad reality television. You can find her online at brookewinters.wordpress.com and on twitter @3brooke33

ALLISON WONDERLAND devotes her summers to carnivals, concerts, and literary events. She has contributed to over thirty anthologies, including Ladylit's *Forbidden Fruit: stories of unwise lesbian desire*. Besides being a Sapphic storyteller, Allison is a reader of stories Sapphics tell and enjoys everything from pulp fiction to historical fiction. Find out what else she's into and up to at aisforallison.blogspot.com.

Printed in Great Britain
by Amazon